Princess of Grim

A NecroSeam Chronicles Prequel

NECROSEAM CHRONICLES

Prequel 1: Princess of Shadow and Dream
Prequel 2: Princess of Grim

Book I: Willow of Ashes
Book II: Orbs of Azure
Book III: Pearl of Emerald
Book IV: Phoenix of Scarlet
Book V: Blossom of Gold

Other Books by Ellie Raine
Nightingale

Princess of Grim

A NecroSeam Chronicles Prequel

ELLIE RAINE

Author's Note

Welcome Adventurers!

Thank you so much for picking up this second prequel to the NecroSeam Chronicles series! This is an alternative starting point for your journey through the world of Nirus. While this novel is a small glimpse of Willow's and Xavier's pasts before *Willow of Ashes* begins in earnest, it is by no means required that you read this prequel before, after, or during *Willow of Ashes* and onward. Similar to *Princess of Shadow and Dream*, (which features the histories of Willow's parents, a young Serdin and Myra), *Princess of Grim* can be read whenever it pleases you.

However, it is interesting to note that the experience of reading *the NecroSeam Chronicles* as a whole will be different depending upon which book you decide to begin with. If you would like my opinion on what sort of experiences you'll undertake with each starting point, I will list them as such:

"The Tiny Sample/ I Don't Mind Spoilers"
Princess of Shadow and Dream

"The Origin Story/ I Don't Mind Spoilers"
Princess of Grim

"The Original Canon Opener/ How Dare You
Suggest Spoilers, You Soggy Wart"
Willow of Ashes

And for those who prefer technicalities:

"The Numerically Chronological Order
According to The Story's Timeline"
Princess of Shadow and Dream
Princess of Grim
Willow of Ashes

Wherever you decide to begin, always remember to have fun! Happy
Adventuring!

~ Ellie Raine

PROLOGUE

KAEL

Blisters moaned under my fingers.

My knuckles shrieked with fatigue, arms aching to collapse as I tightened my grip on the sword's hilt. The leather wrapping had grown rough from abuse and bit into my raw flesh. I'd never held heavy steel for this long, but I hadn't time to rest. I had a beast to fell.

I raised my sword, the blade saturated in a veil of blackened sludge. Its tendrils lapped over the steel like floundering tongues as I held the sharpened edge over the golden-haired king I once called my liege.

"Where," I snarled, "is my son?"

The king's reply came as a gurgle of sputters, drool seeping from his slacked jaw. Black veins crept from the puncture wound I'd gifted his shoulder moments before. They pulsated and slithered from the gash like a swarm of maggots, his flesh eating itself alive. He began to spasm, his breaths strained and miserable.

The infectious veins spread to his throat as the corner of his lips bubbled with foam. His face began to deteriorate, flesh blackening and revealing cheekbones. The poison simmered into his temples. His gaze grew distant. Death would soon greet him, and he looked desperate to succumb.

Yet, he glanced past me. Something seemed to catch his attention.

"Ana…belle…?" King Adam whispered, yielding to a violent spasm.

I turned, my sword ready for any fools daring to deny me my rightful game. But none appeared save the corpses around us in the blood-spattered ballroom.

A hallucination? I scowled down at the dying king. *His end draws closer.*

My voice hissed like scalding oil. "If you've so much as touched a hair on his head—"

A crooked, glowing blade swung from my right, nearly slicing my neck. I lurched back to evade and staggered to regain my footing, glaring at the new man who dared to interrupt my deserved wrath.

Wielding a radiant scythe, a grey skinned man with ash-white hair and milky eyes stood before me. Perched on his shoulder was a large crow. The black bird hunched threateningly, flaring its neck feathers.

I growled, lowering my poisoned blade. "The King of Death dares to interfere with my justice?"

The man's ears began to grow fur, sprouting white wolf ears that curled back. His teeth sharpened to thick points. "As someone from my realm, one would think you'd recognize when my family's most sacred law was violated." He took an offensive stance before the fallen king while his crow flew off his shoulder to alight on a chandelier above. "Yield now, butcher," he warned, "the King of Land is under my protection."

My cat ears folded back. "You dare call me the butcher when you defend that *monster?*"

I barreled toward him, thrusting my blackened sword forward, poison licking over the steel. "Those who defend the guilty are guilty themselves…!"

My blade *clashed* against his scythe, my poison crawling onto his weapon and sinking into his hands with a satisfying squelch.

Yet, the black veins didn't root under his ghoulishly grey flesh. My poison dissolved on contact, hissing away like vapor and leaving the man unmarred.

He pushed his scythe against my straining blade with a grinding scrape, shoving me off him. He twirled his scythe, the crooked blade arching over his ashen head.

"What's wrong, poison-spewer?" the bastard mocked. "Unfamiliar with dueling against a fellow Infeciovoker?" He lowered his scythe, readying another assault. "We're immune to each other's infections. Now why don't we see how you fair without your precious Hallows?"

He charged at me, and I staggered back, hurrying to deflect.

Clang!

A fragment of my blade snapped off.

Clang! Clash! Clang!

Over and over he struck, wearing down my blade to a jagged stump above the hilt.

I ground my sharpened teeth, my gaze locking onto one spot along his neck: the carotid artery. My years as a surgeon helped me locate every weak point of a shifter's body. Right now, that artery was the most exposed… and the only chance I had at killing this sympathizer.

I waited for him to strike, sidestepped away, then hurtled toward him to jam my shortened blade into the exact spot—

A blinding glare obscured my vision. A white gleam was radiating… from *me*. It was as if my very flesh were made of light, the glow brightening and stinging my retinas.

I screamed and fell to my knees, dropping my blade. A burning pain seared across my forehead like a knife carving into my brow.

My vision shivered, and I glanced up.

Through the glaring shroud, I found one other man shining with this ethereal light outside the snow-covered balcony. I couldn't see past his brilliance to recognize him. But I *could* see who was casting this enchantment.

Through the brightness, an azure-haired man was huddled over the marble floor, his arms crossed over his face as his hands glittered with a haze of blue light. He squinted through the blinding lights he had created, and his icy eyes caught my murderous glower.

"Dream…!" I sneered. "Seamstress help me, I will pry your limbs from every one of your sockets…! I will destroy the souls of your family—*I will see that the Seamstress Cleanses you all…!*"

The light blazed out of me, the world drowned in whiteness.

Until nothing remained.

Part One
Half-Blooded

1

QUEEN MYRA

I jolted awake.

The royal bedchambers in the Death Palace were still dressed in darkness. I looked to the windows. The underground caverns of Grim were still under the Dim Light hours of the night. My azure locks bounced over my shoulders in frazzled curls, my breaths still strained as I gazed round the chamber.

My ashen-haired husband, Serdin, dozed beside me, perfectly at peace as his soul visited the Dream realm of Aspirre—the subconscious kingdom I once called home.

And where Kael still waited.

I shivered, the cavern's freezing air burrowing under my flesh. I drew up the velvet comforter. Contrary to its name, it didn't bring much comfort.

It had been centuries since my father imprisoned that lunatic. Yet father's recent prediction foretold we had less than a decade before the seal would expire.

I turned to a tall, gothic portrait along the wall. The painting depicted Serdin, myself, and our young daughter. The girl's ashen hair tumbled down her shoulders and curled over the floor past her feet. In the portrait, my daughter's azure eyes matched mine, bright and full of cheer and mischievous laughter as her tiny crow nuzzled her grey cheek.

Willow...

I clutched the comforter, the fabric quietly ripping under my growing claws. Perhaps I should check on Willow's dreams? It may have been paranoia, but I wouldn't rest well until I made sure my barriers were secure around my family's dreams.

I evoked my Dream Hallows, my hand glittering with sparkling azure light, and tapped my forehead. I let my soul slip into the subconscious plane of Aspirre as my body drifted to sleep.

2
WILLOW

Xavier knew nothing but pain.

I watched the angry children kick him again and again, feeling each blow as if I were their target instead. Xavier's skull throbbed as they threw stones at him. His gut lurched under their cruel boots, his ribs splintering, his back aching, his arm fracturing... But none of it mattered.

His brother lay limp before him, so bruised and beaten Xavier barely recognized him. His face was splotched with scrapes and dripping with blood from his broken nose.

"What's going on down here?" A woman barked down the alley. Xavier turned to look, his neck screaming. An armored guard was running toward them.

"That's enough!" The woman clipped, scaring off the boys who were beating the twins.

They'd vanished by the time she reached the bleeding pair, panting and cursing under her breath.

"Alex..." Xavier wheezed and crawled to his brother. He reached out a trembling hand, one with a birthmark of three, black diamonds, and shook his slumped brother in a panic.

"Alex...?" Xavier's voice was coarse and gritty. "Alex, please... wake up..."

For the slightest, relieving moment, Alex blearily cracked open his mismatched, blue-and-clear eyes.

My vision of the odd-eyed twins faded.

I was surrounded by flowery gardens in my dreams. My feet touched the soft grass as silver butterflies flitted around my head. Three landed on my long, ashen hair that draped past my feet and trailed behind me.

Realizing the disturbing vision had ended, I looked up at the see-through ceiling that resembled Grim's overcasting cavern mists.

"Mother?" I called, cupping my hands around my mouth. "Mother!"

"—yes, darling?" my mother answered behind me.

I whirled. My mother's wavy, azure hair tumbled over her shoulders in playful curls, and her matching, icy eyes gave me a concerned look.

"I had another vision," I announced. "Of those same twins, like before. With the strange eyes."

"Oh… is that so, dear?" Her tensed features seemed to relax, and she kneeled to match my eye level. "Well, I'm glad to hear you're practicing."

"They were… being beaten," I said softly. "Xavier thought his brother was dead." I found myself dabbing at tears. Visions were strange things. As a Seer, I often find myself linked to the narrator's emotions. Xavier's fear had been so strong, it still clung even now. "It was nothing like the last one."

Mother tapped a finger to her chin. "Remind me what the last one was?"

"They were on a ship," I recalled, "In Grim's straits. And I was looking through a woman's eyes… I think I knew the voice. It almost sounded like Mother Alice."

My mother gave a knowing grin. "Did it, now? How interesting…"

I quirked a suspicious eyebrow at her. "Do you know who those twins are, Mother?"

She pushed a finger over her lips. "I may, I may not… perhaps you should borrow my crystal ball when you wake and practice with your visions to discover more?"

My fox ears grew in annoyance. I crossed my arms. "Oh, fine. Always making me work for answers, just like Grandfather Dream…"

"I learned from the best." She smiled and kissed my crown.
—Then the flowery garden disappeared as her kiss woke me.

GRIM—THE REALM OF DEATH

My eyes flew open.

The realm of Dreams was gone. I was back in the physical world, in the underground realm of Death in my bed within the royal palace of Grim.

I hurriedly threw off the comforter and hopped out of bed.

The servants hadn't arrived yet to help me dress, so I rushed to my closets to find something suitable to wear. I chose a black gown with long, lacey sleeves like silky dark cobwebs that I pulled over my arms, tying the sash at my waist into a hectic bow off to the side. I inspected my attire in the mirror, adjusting the silver butterfly brooch from the gown's high collar. Everything seemed in order, but I was still missing two essential pieces—pieces I wasn't *allowed* to miss.

I went to my jewelry drawer and peeled it open with a soft *shhhk*. Inside was an array of necklaces and hairpins, various bracelets and other accessories I was often required to wear for special occasions... but the only items I sought today were the silver tiara decorated with diamond raven skulls, and the circular amulet dangling from a hook by a silver chain.

The amulet resembled a delicate, wired pocket watch, large and round with pointed sides encrusted with diamonds that glittered in the lamplight. It was attached to a sleek silver chain that hushed as I picked it up and hung it around my neck, letting the amulet dangle at my chest.

This was my music watch. It was a gift from my parents when I was born, to commemorate the birth of the first *mixed* princess of two Relic Bloodlines.

The music-watch had a knob at the top. I wound it back with soft *tick-tick-tick-tick-ticks*, then pressed the button to unlatch the amulet's glittering case. The diamond-coated casing popped open and swung on its hinge, revealing the inner framework that showcased a stylized fox and wolf between a revolving, ebony disk. The disk was speckled with ash-white crystals, so soft that it looked as though it would rub off at the slightest touch.

Twinkling music played from the watch. It was a slow, gentle song, lovely and melancholy… the sound of it had me smiling.

I clicked the amulet closed, stopping the music, and placed my tiara over my hair before hurrying out of my closets. Throwing open my chamber doors, I ran down to the corridor with my long hair dragging over the floor behind me, passing several wispy ghosts who floated by.

"*Chanerr*, your highness!" one ghost greeted me as I passed him. It was one of my father's vassals—a spectral helper that carried out various tasks in exchange for being resurrected on occasion. This vassal had antlers and an angular face. He was the Head Vassal of the palace: Conrad.

I curtsied politely. "*Chanerr*, Conrad."

"Where are we off to today, young miss?" asked Conrad, floating above the marble floor as he put his wispy hands on his sides. "You're up earlier than usual."

"I had another vision this morning," I said. "Mother is helping me channel it through her crystal ball, as part of my training."

Conrad chuckled. "Ah, very good, young miss! Then I'll leave you to it, shall I?" He bowed and floated through the wall, perhaps to continue with his duties for the day.

I skipped onward through the palace corridors, nodding and greeting the other ghosts who floated by just like Conrad had. Some of them were servants, some visitors, and others were my ancestors who smiled at me kindly. Aside from the many ghosts, *living* servants bustled here and there, and the halls echoed with clatters of armored Reaper knights who patrolled the palace diligently, saluting me with gauntleted fists to their chests when I gave them all polite greetings.

When I finally reached my parents' bedchamber, I pulled open the blackwood doors.

My mother was already awake and out of bed. My ashen-haired father, on the other hand, was still in bed and pulling his goose-down pillow over his head.

I gave a mischievous giggle and climbed onto their tall mattress. Then jumped onto the bed, disturbing the sheets and causing father to grumble from under his pillow as he clutched it harder over his face.

"Willow!" Father's muffled voice warned groggily. "Go outside with your mother, for Death's sake!"

"You mean for *my* sake?" I grinned and hopped off the bed, landing in front of Mother.

Mother inspected me with a hum. "Well, I see you chose quite a lovely gown today, didn't you? But you missed a button on the collar, dear. Come, turn about."

I twirled and swept my long hair away from my collared neck, letting Mother fasten the top button. When she was done, Mother gave me a final examination and cocked her head. "Are you sure this is warm enough for the cold weather?"

"Yes," I huffed and put a fist at my side. I raised my other hand, violet light radiating from my palm as I evoked my fire Hallows.

A small red flame puffed into existence over my palm.

"I'm a Pyrovoker, just like Father," I said. "Our souls' fire keeps us warm wherever we are."

Mother laughed. "I see you've been training *that* half of your Hallows with your father. But it's my turn today, dear… cold aside, I suppose it's presentable enough, isn't it?" She clapped her hands. "The Devouhs are returning from their trip overseas, and we'll be visiting them today. Try to keep your gown clean, will you? I'd like you to look your best."

"Why?" I asked, confused. "It's only the Devouhs."

"Because I said so," Mother sang as she strode to her black-varnished vanity, where her crystal ball was mounted on a silver, three-footed dais. The seeing-stone was as large as a dragon skull. I could see my faint reflection in its polished surface when I lifted to my toes to look past Mother.

She plucked the crystal ball off its dais and hefted it with an arm before ushering me out to the corridor.

"Come along, darling," Mother chimed as she led me down the hall. "We have a busy day ahead of us. We'd best get started, hadn't we—?"

"Willow!" a girl's shrill voice cried behind us.

A bat-winged girl with silky black hair was running toward me.

The girl was my age, dressed in a fetching rose-pink gown that had buttoned slits on the back to make room for her large, leathery wings. When the girl came panting up to us, her sharp, chartreuse eyes snapped to me angrily.

"There you are!" the bat girl shouted. "I was knocking and knocking at your door, but you weren't there!"

"Sorry, Lilli." I smiled weakly. "I was with my parents. Mother says we're to visit the Devouhs today."

"Yes, I know!" Lilli's bat wings flapped in a huff. "My father said the same for me! He suggested I come and help you find something suitable to wear—but now I find out you're already dressed, so that was a useless suggestion." She rolled her eyes. "Though, I'm not sure what the fuss is about, anyway. It's only the Devouhs."

"That's what *I* said." I flicked a suspicious glance at my mother. She only gave me a wry grin in return.

Lilli stuck up her nose at my mother. "Well, I for one want to know what's so special about this visit, exactly?"

Mother led Lilli and me through the hall and down the staircase to the first floor, humming as she hefted her crystal ball in her arms. "It's a surprise, girls. And I'd like to see you both on your best behaviors. First impressions can be most important."

Lilli snorted. "Then, we're meeting someone *other* than our Spirit Parents?"

I crossed my arms and gave my mother an expectant look. "I wonder who it could possibly be?" It must have been the twins I saw in my visions. She'd been acting strange about those two, who else could it be?

Mother gave a puckish smile, as if admitting it.

Lilli huffed, "Well, since you're already dressed, you've no need of me right now. I'm going to House Devouh early."

"I'll meet you there shortly," I said. "Mother and I are going to train first."

Lilli nodded. Then she went to an open window in the hall, spread her leathery wings, and hopped off the stone sill before flying off outside.

"Come along, Willow," Mother called as she strolled through the palace.

"We're meeting those boys, aren't we?" I asked as I skipped alongside her. "That *was* Mother Alice in my vision! Who are those twins? How do they know the Devouhs?"

"Patience, dear," Mother assured. "Training first. Answers after."

I glared at her. Why must I always earn such simple answers? Not *everything* was a riddle to solve, for Bloods' sakes.

We turned the corner and walked outside to follow under an arched breezeway until we reached the palace gardens. Like my dreamscape, the garden was filled with lovely flowers and vines, butterflies fluttering about. Though, to my dismay, none of the winged beauties landed on my hair as they'd done in my dream.

A twitter suddenly caught my ear. From the sky, a tiny, canary-sized crow flew down and perched on my shoulder.

"Good morning, Jewel," I giggled as the little crow's beak nuzzled my jaw. "Come to watch me train, have you?"

Jewel gave a flighty twitter in response. She was a Songcrow, a subspecies of black bird that sang in delightful chimes rather than atonal croaks and caws. Jewel has been with me since before I could remember. She was my messenger—a companion that all Reapers shared a special soul-bond with. She felt my emotions as strongly as I felt hers, our spirits bound together by the Seamstress of Souls.

Jewel stayed perched on my shoulder as Mother and I settled under an autumn-leaved tree. I copied mother's cross-legged position as she sat across from me and placed her crystal ball in the grass between us.

"Now," Mother said, "as we've practiced."

I placed my hands on the crystal ball, drew in a deep breath, and focused my gaze on the orb. I was sure to look *into* the crystal using my mind's Third Eye, instead of the two I physically had.

"Think of the vision you'd Seen," Mother instructed, "and try to project it into the crystal."

I puffed up my cheeks, my stare hardening at the ball. I felt a tingle in my soul, inflating like a balloon of mist. The soft pinpricks trailed from my chest down to my arms, pouring out of my fingers in the form of shining, azure lights. The lights sank into the crystal, billowing into a clouded fog within the clear globe.

Then the fog shifted into a wafting, wavering face of a boy. His eyes were unveiled next: a pair of odd, sapphire and white orbs that stared at me from the crystal.

"Wonderful!" Mother praised. "Now, push further. Try and See where they'll be next, in the future."

I grunted, straining. My throat scratched from exertion as the Hallows poured from my soul, sweat beading my face. Evoking Hallows was like exercising your spirit. The longer you used it, the more taxing it became. For most Evocators, their Hallows stamina was fairly decent.

But I was *not* most Evocators.

My vision spun, and the moment I blinked—*poof!*

The fog in the crystal ball snuffed out. The tingle in my soul was gone. I now stared at an empty crystal ball, panting for breath.

Death, I cursed to myself as a wave of tears stung. I hurried to rub them dry as my fox ears grew and draped to the sides of my neck.

Mother sighed and laid a hand on my shoulder. "Don't be discouraged. You'll get it… in time."

"When?" My stomach twisted. "When will I get the hang of it? I'll be nine in three days, and I can barely make a single *face* appear. You said you were three when you could project your visions in a crystal ball."

Mother hesitated, her own, azure fox ears growing.

"Well…" she began, clearing her throat. "I was the daughter of *one* Relic Bloodline. I only needed to focus on three elements of Hallows.

You have six, since you're of two Bloodlines, and…" She pressed a finger to her chin broodingly. "And I suppose… hmm. Even those of the royal Bloodlines have more difficulty than other Evocators, since we must balance three elements… the non-royals with one or two elements tend to catch on faster than us to begin with. I suppose adding an *additional* set from your Dream Bloodline severely depleted your natural stamina…"

"Then…" My fox ears folded down. "I'll never be as strong as everyone else?"

Mother winced, her smile crooked as she assured, "No, no…! You'll get there, darling. It simply means it will take you… a bit longer." She cleared her throat. "Why don't you practice your Somniovoking? You were able to make one phantom copy of yourself, weren't you?"

I nodded, closing my eyes. That same tingle trickled down my soul as I evoked the new element, and I clutched my chest… then slowly peeled it outward to the side. My figure split into two, the copy of myself coloring the air, and it sat beside me.

Mother gave a praising applause. "Oh, wonderful! Very well done, Will—"

Poof!

The copy disappeared in a puff of blue smoke. I slumped and sighed miserably. "It only lasts for three seconds…"

Mother tried to disguise her grimace with a painfully awkward smile. "Ah… w-well, it's a start, I suppose…" She tugged on her ear in thought. But when her fingers touched a silver earcuff hooked to her lobe, she blinked. "Ah! How about your Decepiovoking? At our last session, you were able to change the color of your hair and eyes with an illusion."

I propped my chin up with a fist and grumbled. "Which only lasted for, once again, three seconds."

"Well, why don't we try something new?" She plucked off her earcuff and pushed it into my palm. "Today's lesson shall be how to seal your illusion Hallows into an item. I think it's time you learned enchantments."

I stared at the earcuff in my hand with a furrowed brow. "What do I do?"

"First you'll need to etch a sealing rune into the metal," Mother instructed. "Since we don't have a needle on hand, use your claws. You'll need to scratch two rings on the cuff, one large, and the other slightly smaller *within* the first. Like a ripple, or a target. As you etch the rune, evoke your illusion Hallows, thinking of the changes you wish to make."

I had one of my claws grow. They weren't delicate and thin like Mother's. I was only half a fox-shifter, having inherited my coned ears from her, but the other half of my shift was wolf thanks to my father. I'd gotten his thicker claws and teeth, so it made scratching on this tiny surface difficult. But I managed to make the rune Mother described after some time, all the while pouring my illusion Hallows into the scratches in the form of glittering, azure light.

"I'm done," I said. "I think."

Mother opened her hands encouragingly. "Why don't you test it out and see if it worked?"

I hummed and slipped the cuff on my ear.

A strand of my long, white hair suddenly bled to a charcoal grey color, making me gasp. I quickly gathered the rest of my hair and marveled. It was *all* grey. Right down to the curling ends.

"It's staying!" I squealed. "It's actually staying!"

Mother chuckled. "And your eyes have changed to a lovely onyx. Well done, darling." Mother paused, then picked up her crystal ball from the grass and rose to her feet, handing me the orb. "I'll tell you what. Why don't I lend you my crystal ball for you to practice on your own, for extra training? If you can master a sealing rune on your first try, I'm confident you can improve your visions with more study."

I pushed to my feet and took the globe from her, having to use both hands to carry it. "Of… of course. I'll do what I can."

"Wonderful!" Mother patted my newly grey hair. "Now, you keep training. It's my turn to prepare for our visit with the Devouhs."

I watched her leave, sighing while glancing at Jewel on my shoulder. "Who exactly *are* those boys we're meeting?"

Jewel twittered and shrugged her tiny wings.

I glared at the large crystal ball, straining to focus my thoughts as Mother had instructed before she left. "Maybe if I focus hard enough, I can..."

—Jewel suddenly perked from my shoulder. She snapped her gaze down a cobbled path through the gardens. Then she flew off.

"Jewel?" I called, following after my messenger. "Where are you going?"

3

XAVIER

Thunk! Thunk! Thunk! Thunk! Thunk! Thunk! Thunk…!

My feet vibrated the ship's hardwood floors, rushing straight ahead with grown wolf ears curled back in determination.

My sights were locked on my grey-haired mother sitting on a crate while she read a book, her back facing me. Her wolf ears were lowered and calm. Her tail swished idly behind her.

Perfect! She didn't suspect a thing.

I kept a firm grip of the short-handled, wooden scythes I clutched in either hand, cocking them back.

My throat ripped a thrilled holler as I charged for my unsuspecting target at full speed, swiping my wooden blades at her—

Thwak!

Mother swatted her book over my head without even turning my way. The hit was so powerful I yelped and stumbled to the floorboards. My wooden scythes clunked to the ground. I winced and rubbed a tender hand to my throbbing head.

"I thought I asked for stealth, Xavier," Mother sighed, turning to peer down at me with an expectant hand on her hip. Her storm-blue eyes were not impressed, one wolf ear flicking up. "Lighter steps next time. I could feel you coming the second you moved. And *no yelling*." She lightly tapped the book's spine over my nose. "One cannot celebrate their victory until they've *seized* that victory. And speaking of which."

She held up three fingers. "Wait for it." She lowered each finger one by one. "Three. Two. One…"

"—*Rrrraaaagh!*" My brother dropped down from the overhanging netting, cackling with triumph as he swiped his own wooden scythes over her head and—

She stepped aside, letting him fall straight down.

He landed right on top of me.

His head *thunked* against mine, making us both cry out, his shoulder digging into my gut so hard, I thought I would vomit.

Mother pinched the rim of her nose in disappointment. "Too obvious, Alexander. I saw you climb up there ten minutes ago. Find a better vantage next time… preferably, a less *reckless* one." She spun on her heels, her wolf tail swishing as she walked toward the ship's cabin. "Now, come along, boys. We've almost arrived, and I want you both presentable."

Alex pushed off me, and we collected our fallen blades. "Y-yes, my lady!" We said in unison.

"We're meeting very important guests this evening," Mother said. "They have children your age. I expect you to be polite… *Alexander.*" She flicked Alex a testy glare with that. Then she cast a sharp look at me. "And Xavier, for the love of Death, remember the traditional protocols this time. What does one do when meeting a new lord?"

I tucked my wooden blades under an arm. "We… bow?"

She nodded. "And when meeting a new lady?"

"Bow again?"

"And?"

"And…" I scratched behind a wolf ear, making them recede back to human ears. Unlike Mother, Alexander's and my shifts were hidden unless we were under stress, like most shifters.

Mother's throat rumbled. "You take her *hand*, Xavier. Delicately."

"Oh—yes, my lady." I blushed.

Alex grumbled, "As if they'll come close enough to let us *do* these protocols…"

"Alexander," Mother clipped. "The shifters on this continent are different. You won't be met with… unpleasantries here. Not like your last home."

Alex snorted. "We'll believe that when we see it."

Mother flicked us a saddened look. Then she sighed, "Come along. Be ready to dock within the hour."

Once we docked and climbed into the luxurious coach hovering above the street, the horses clopped forward, tugging our floating vehicle through the city of Low Rastiria.

Mother and Father sat on the coach's inner bench across from us, both dressed in their finest, silken-black attire. Mother's gown flared down to her ankles, her wolf tail curled delicately around her waist as she sat in the cushioned bench with pristine posture. Clipped to Mother's hair were silver marriage-vines: two glassy chains pinned to the sides of her head and connected at the center of her forehead with a diamond centerpiece.

In Mother's lap were two scythe blades attached to a long, clattering chain. They gleamed with a soft, blue light, their reflective surface crystalline and ghostly. Mother alternated sharpening them with a whet stone, the grating *scriiit, scriiiit, scriiit,* filling the silence alongside Father's fervent chatter on his personal communicator.

To match Mother's vines, Father wore a diamond marriage-stud that was pierced through his left ear, and a silver wedding band hugged his left, fourth finger. His thick beard was groomed and trimmed along his face, his raven-black hair slicked back and lustrous.

Father's communicator was a disk-shaped device with many gears and whirring springs. Projecting out from a green gem in the center of the communicator was a screen of light. On the screen was a man's face I didn't recognize with bat wings and black hair. A dark goatee wrapped around the man's mouth and grew into a wide forest at his chin.

Father had been speaking to this man for the past two hours, before our ship even docked at the harbor of Grim's capital city, Low Rastiria. He kept to his conversation with the man as the horses pulled our hovering coach through the gothic city toward the palace grounds far in the distance.

Alexander and I were bursting with energy as our gazes soaked up the city life outside the coach's windows. We passed through the markets, the bustling roads filled with vendor booths and open shops of Grimish goods and services.

On my side of the coach, there was one shop with many vision-screens at their window. The Evocator Games were playing. I watched as magic users blasted their colorful lights all over a dirt-filled arena, skidding and sliding and leaping all around the screen of light in a kaleidoscopic haze.

After a time, the coach hovered through the city and into the palace grounds, following a cobbled path that echoed with the horses' clapping hooves. Mother kept sharpening her scythes with a quiet intensity until we arrived at our destination.

Our new home.

This manor was smaller than our last one. I thanked Death for that. Maybe now it wouldn't feel so empty with all the extra rooms. Our parents had left a year before Alexander and I to conduct business while the two of us stayed behind to finish our primary schooling. An entire year without them. It had become so commonplace, Alex and I hardly noticed their absence after long. It wasn't as if we'd seen much of them before they left, anyway. With Father always off on diplomatic conferences, and Mother busy commanding the Reaper military, we'd grown accustomed to the solitude.

After we graduated to the next level of schooling, Mother and Father had come to retrieve us so we could join them in this new home. It had been some time since we lived under the same roof. The whole idea felt unnatural. As if we'd lost our thumbs and now they'd suddenly grown back. Bending the knuckles were achy and foreign. Though, I couldn't complain. The month-long voyage provided a rare opportunity to... well, to spend *time* with our parents.

When the coach stopped before the front doors, Alex and I craned our gazes up at the new estate from the window. The new blackstone manor had wolves for gargoyles and arching buttresses, the spired rooftops curling at their cornices and dressed in grey shingles.

Father was the first to leave the coach, still deep in conversation with the bat-winged stranger.

I hurried outside after him, Alex at my heels, ready to explore the new manor right at Father's side and…

Father veered left, still talking on his communicator, and left the grounds without noticing either of us.

I suppressed a sigh. Of course Father would leave to do business the minute we arrived. I supposed I could cross that off the list of changes we could expect.

Creeeeeak.

The tall, front doors of the manor peeled open. Under the door-frame was a ram-horned butler. It was our Father's Head Vassal, Thateus.

"Ah, here at last, Young Sirs," the Head Vassal greeted kindly with a bow. He swept a gesturing hand inside. "Come, we've been waiting quite some time for you both. It's been far too long, hasn't it?"

"It certainly has, Thateus," Alex and I said in unison, stepping under the frame to take our first steps into our new life.

The grand foyer was dressed in black-and-silver wallpaper, portraits and obsidian busts of past generals decorating nearly every wall and pedestal. A crystal chandelier hung over our heads and twinkled with bright lights that refracted off the prismatic bobbles shimmering under the high-arched ceiling.

Mother stepped inside behind us, tossing her braid over a shoulder. "*Chanerr*, Thateus. I hope all is ready for our guests tonight?"

Thateus closed the door behind him and affirmed, "Indeed, my lady. I hope your trip with the Young Sirs went undeterred—"

"The Young Sirs are here!" a choir of giggling voices cut in.

From the walls, several misty, disembodied heads popped out of the wallpaper, nearly surrounding us entirely in the foyer. They were the heads of familiar ghosts, each face a sight we hadn't seen in a whole year ever since they left with Mother and Father. There were too many to count. Our parents had an unprecedented amount of spectral vassals, far more than the average Necrovoker usually had.

Before Alex and I could greet them, the ghosts flew out of the walls all at once and danced around us with such dizzying speed, my head nearly spun right off my neck. I tried like Death to give the proper respect and attention to each one. It was a losing battle. But Bloods, was it good to see them all again.

"It's about Bloody time ye lads came round!" a burly ghost with a thick beard and misty bear ears guffawed, shoving his way to the front of the wispy crowd. It was Nathaniel, our Father's closest vassal. "I was beginnin' ta think yer primary schoolin' would ne'er end!"

"So did we, Nathaniel," Alex and I laughed—until I was crushed in his spectral figure as he grappled us into a hug.

I chuckled, returning the hug as wide as my arms would allow. Nathaniel was quite big, I barely reached his sides, his watery skin rippling under my touch.

Though, while my skin had made contact with the ghost, Alex was drowned in the mist, standing within Nathaniel and loosening a deep, depressive sigh. My brother shoved his hands in his pockets as he waited for Nathaniel to release me and step away so Alex could be free of his wispy form. Not that Alex could feel the difference either way. I was the only one of us who could touch souls.

A second, winged ghost—my mother's closest vassal, Aiden—shoved Nathaniel aside. "*Excuse* me, you can't hog the Young Sirs all to yourself!"

Aiden tried to take us both by the necks with a wide grin. But he winced when his ghostly arm fizzled through Alexander's neck without contact. Aiden motioned to pat my brother's shoulder with a small laugh. "Ah, sorry, Young Sir… It's been so long, I nearly forgot your, er… condition."

Alex let out a breath, his mood souring again. But he shook it off. "It's all right… Bloods, it's good to see you, Aiden. How has the city life been around here?"

Aiden fluttered his translucent wings. "Oh, it's to die for!" Aiden elbowed me in the ribs and chuckled at his own jest. It didn't hurt, it was more of a cold tickle. "Why don't Nathaniel and I take you both on a tour of the city soon, hm? It'll give us plenty of time to catch up!"

"Aye," Nathaniel agreed heartily. "Look at that, feather-brains, ye actually had a good idea fer once—"

Mother clapped her hands. "Yes, yes, that's quite enough, everyone! Give the boys some space. I need them presentable for dinner… Ah, Aiden and Nathaniel, stay a moment. I've need of you both."

While Aiden and Nathaniel stayed, the other ghosts gave a collective sigh and dispersed through the walls.

Once all but Aiden and Nathaniel had gone, Mother turned to us and huffed, "Now, you two may gain your bearings if you wish, but you must come to greet our guests when I send for you. Understand?"

"Yes, my lady," Alex and I replied in unison.

"Good. Aiden and Nathaniel, please come with me if you would. I've much to prepare and I'd like you to patrol the premises for any threats—"

"Can't they give us a tour of the estate first?" I blurted, then winced. I'd interrupted her. Mother's glare was on me like a dragon to cattle. I quickly amended, "I… I meant… could you perhaps grant them leave… to give us a tour, my lady…?"

Mother sniffed, her tone still rough. "I'm sorry, Xavier, but I need them for scouting tonight."

Aiden leaned into my ear and whispered, "Don't worry Young Sir. Tomorrow night, Nathaniel and I can give you an even better tour… in the city." He winked, and I nodded excitedly.

Mother, who hadn't heard, wafted her hand absently. "Why don't you and Alexander give yourselves a tour of the yard out back, hmm?" Mother gave a wry grin. "Let's make a game of it. Find something intriguing and report back to me when I return. Whoever finds the most interesting item will be awarded extra dessert after dinner… we're having pumpkin galling."

"Galling?" we shouted in a thrill. "Yes, my lady!"

Alex and I raced through the manor's multiple rooms to find the backyard, shoving each other to try and be the first outside.

Mother's voice called behind us, "But don't you dare dirty those suits…!"

4

LILLI

I gave a delicate yawn as I kept my wings steady and flew through the caverns, gliding under the misty ceiling and weaving between the sparkling balls of light floating around me.

My, the Floating Lights were lovely this morning. They cast the underground caverns in a beautiful, bluish light down below. The dazzling sight was almost enough to keep my mind off this morning's stressful events.

Almost.

"I swear, that girl *must* keep me informed about schedule changes," I muttered, tugging my long, pink gloves over my arms. There was an unsightly thread dangling from the hem's seam-line, and I tucked it in to hide the unacceptable blemish. Perhaps I could ask Mother Alice for a thread snip when I arrived at their manor.

"What is the point of being the Aide of the Death Princess if that very princess refuses to clue me in on her plans?" I huffed. "Honestly, could she make my job any harder?"

I felt my black hair tangling in the wind and tried to hold it in place with a hair pin. I would certainly have to give it a long brushing after my flight. The only downside to flying was the awful affliction of *untidy hair*.

I curved around a rocky pillar shooting up from the cavern floor all the way to the veiled ceiling, the crisp winds cool against my leathery wings. It was warmer than usual, for the middle of autumn.

Well, warm by the Death realm's standards. Grim was known to be cold all year round thanks to these glowing orbs of light in the ceiling mists.

When the Devouh's manor came into view below, I adjusted my wings and descended toward its sharp rooftops.

But I halted mid-dive, spotting a boy I didn't recognize skulking around the Devouh's backyard. His grey-haired head ducked under a large boulder, as if searching for something with a tight scowl.

A thief? My teeth sharpened, bat ears growing. *In MY Spirit Parents' home?*

I tucked my wings and dove downward at a furious speed.

ALEXANDER

I crouched behind the large boulder, my stare focused on the black and white lizard laying on the grass, its tail curled around itself in a quiet snooze.

Almost... I crept closer, hunching down with my hands reached out. *Almost... and...*

I pounced for the lizard, trying to grab it. The thing woke in a start and scuttled away before my fingers could catch it. It disappeared behind a patch of tall grass.

"Blast it..." I growled, my wolf ears growing as I rose to my feet. "That would have surely won—"

"Stay where you are, thief!"

I whirled. There was no one there. Frowning, I looked up, squinting at a small, winged figure flying above our manor's rooftop. It was a bat-winged girl with silken, black hair. Her chartreuse eyes glinted with the deadliest glare that rivaled my mother's as she dove straight for me.

Thump!

She slammed into me. I was thrown on my back in a hard yell, and she dug her knee into my gut. The crazed girl pulled off her gloves with her sharpened teeth, spit them out, and grew her claws to raise them over my face threateningly.

"You will return what you've pilfered at once!" She demanded. "I will not tolerate a burglary at my Spirit Parents' residence! Surrender your stolen goods, or I will make sure the guards throw you in prison—!"

"Get off me, you lunatic!" I tried to shove her off. She only dug her knee deeper into my gut, making me gag. "I'm not a thief! I live here!"

Her chartreuse gaze narrowed at me. "You expect me to fall for such a pitiful lie? I happen to be personally familiar with the Devouhs, and I'm well informed on their staff members—"

"I'm not a servant!" I snapped. "I'm their Bloody son!"

That made her stiffen. "Their son…?"

Good, I thought bitterly. *Maybe now she'll run, like everyone else did at our old home.* This time, I'd welcome it.

Annoyingly, she didn't follow the usual script. Her lids turned into thin slits. She gave a suspicious hum and examined my face. I reared my head back into the grass. What in Death was that look about?

She snatched a tuft of my grey hair between two prim fingers.

"Shadowy hair, like Mother Alice…" She glared at my eyes, making me rigid. "*One* sapphire eye, at least, like Father Lucas…" Her wings lifted curiously. "Are you blind in your left eye?"

I groaned. "No! The color is just gone! Will you get off me already?"

She gave a haughty *hmph* and finally lifted off my stomach, letting me shove to my feet and rub my sore gut tenderly. I had to dust the crumbled soil out of my hair, hoping Mother wouldn't notice and see fit to disqualify me from the contest.

I patted the dirt from my silken sleeves. "Bloods, look what you did… If I take the fall because some psychotic girl attacked me—"

"My name is Lilliana Tessinger." She rose taller and folded her bat wings delicately behind her. There was a long pause, as if she was waiting for applause. She frowned when she didn't get any. "High Howless? Daughter of the Death King's Hand?"

I snorted. "My father is the king's Hand, last I checked."

She circled a flighty hand in the air. "The king has two Hands. My father is the other. If you really are the Devouhs' son, I suppose that makes you a High Howllord as well? What shall I call you, then?"

"Alexander." I plucked a furry caterpillar out of my hair. Would this be interesting enough? I supposed it had a curious black-and-orange diamond pattern… and it was quite intriguing, inching along my finger with its tickling legs.

Something scuttled to my right, and my eyes snapped to that same lizard that escaped earlier.

"Ah! There you are." I gently placed the caterpillar on a blade of grass, then leapt for the lizard.

It scampered away. I leapt for it again, hopping from place to place. I finally snatched it, grinning with a triumphant laugh… until the lizard slipped between my gloved fingers and zoomed off into a dirt hole.

I kicked a rock. "Death! I was *this* close…!"

The girl, Lilliana, cocked a disgusted eyebrow at me. "You were looking for a… feral lizard?" Her thin brow scrunched. "Why on Nirus would you want one? They're disgusting things."

"Then you're more than welcome to leave," I muttered. "Seamstress hang me, I'll never win at this rate…" I paused. Then spun on my heels, looking at Lilliana. I tapped a considering knuckle to my chin. "Then again… *you're* somewhat interesting. More than a lizard, at least."

She bristled. "I beg your pardon?"

I snatched her wrist and tugged her toward the other side of the yard, where Xavier was exploring.

"Come on." A smug grin tugged my face. "There's no way Xavier can top you."

"Who can do what now?" she questioned, sounding as if she were battling between outrage and curiosity. Then another thought seemed to hit her, and she cupped her face with a blushing smile. "Hang on. You think I'm interesting?"

"It isn't every day I meet a real-life madwoman—*ow!*"

She punched my shoulder. "You rude little…!"

5

WILLOW

My little crow fluttered down the path through the flower gardens, leading me all the way to the edge of the gardens where it ended at a tall, stone wall. That wall was the Devouhs' fence that separated their yard from the royal gardens.

Jewel zipped over the wall in a determined whistle, disappearing.

"Jewel!" I glanced left and right to look for a way over the wall.

When I found a tree with many climbable branches, I set down Mother's crystal ball and climbed up. I scooted over the last branch that was almost level with the wall, looking down.

I stopped cold.

This was far higher than. expected, leaving me dangling halfway between the royal gardens and the Devouhs' yard. A small pond was now visible beyond their stone fence. My limbs locked up, and the ground started wavering. I was getting queasy, fox ears growing in fright.

What am I doing? My arms shook. *I-I need to get down before—*
CRACK!

The branch snapped under me, and I screamed as I fell on the wall's wide ledge. My raven-skull tiara slid out of my hair and tumbled to the grass on the other side of the wall far below me. My claws grew on instinct and scratched over the stone, keeping me stuck there so I wouldn't fall. But now that I was here, and the closest branch was now broken and floating in the Devouhs' pond, I couldn't climb down.

In a scared whimper, I flattened on the wall. "J… Jewel!"

XAVIER

I searched our new yard for anything interesting.

There was a small grove of trees that looked strangely twisted, and I examined their bark with an appraising eye. Maybe I could find some sort of curious insect. Or a peculiar rock that would catch the eye. Or a—

A high-pitched twitter sounded from the sky. My head snapped up.

There was a tiny, canary-sized crow above me. When it caught my stare, it chirped happily and fluttered before my face.

I stared at it, baffled. "What in Death…?"

The bird chirped again and zipped away.

"H-hey!" I called after it and sped off. "Wait!"

I wasn't sure where this crow came from, but a tiny thing like that was sure to win our contest. Extra pumpkin galling, here I come—!

The crow suddenly stopped at the end of the yard where a tall, stone fence waited. I ran over and panted. "What are you… doing all… the way out…?"

I paused, looking up the fence.

There was a girl there.

She had incredibly long hair that tumbled over the wall in curly, charcoal-grey strands. Her fox ears were grown and flattened to the stone wall in fright, just like the rest of her. Judging from her glittering butterfly brooch and diamond-encrusted amulet round her neck, I assumed she was a young Howless—a noblewoman from Grim. And with the way her arms shook, I also assumed she didn't want to be there.

"What are you doing up there?" I called.

She flinched and hurriedly pulled her charcoal strands away from her face, finding me below her. She looked stunned when she saw me.

She's staring at my eyes, I realized. Not surprising. Alex and I knew from experience that our heterochromia was hard to ignore.

"Before you ask." I put fists at my sides. "I'm *not* blind on my right eye. The color is just gone."

She blushed. "I didn't mean…"

"It's all right, I'm used to it." I gave her an assuring smile. "Now, what are you doing on my fence?"

Confusion puckered her brow. "Your fence?"

"Yes, well, I only arrived a few hours ago, but it's still my house."

I eyed the small pond by my feet. White-and-grey koi swam in the clear water, a slight breeze rippling the surface in glassy ringlets. Floating in the pond was a broken tree branch. The tree it once belonged to loomed over the wall from the other side.

I inched away from the water, careful not to fall in. "Given the branch in the pond," I began, "I take it you climbed that tree and fell on the wall after it broke?"

She nodded, looking embarrassed. "I didn't mean to intrude. I wanted to see where Jewel was going."

I frowned. "Jewel?"

She pointed at the little crow fluttering by my head.

I snapped my fingers. "Ah! Is this your messenger?"

"No," the girl muttered sarcastically, "she's a little house pet I'd taken a fancy to. Are you sure you're not blind in that eye?"

I chewed, "Yes… I only thought it was curious… most Reapers don't get their messengers until they're older. You're far too young to have a messenger."

"I'll be nine in three days, I'm not a lost little kit."

The crow, Jewel, buzzed up to her Reaper, chirping in scolding tunes. The girl bit her lip and glanced down at me. "Uhm, I'm a bit… stuck."

I smirked. "You don't say?"

"Could you fetch a ladder?"

"It's not that high a fall, is it? Can't you jump?"

Her onyx eyes splintered in horror. "I can't *jump!* Do you want me to die?!"

"You won't die." I stifled a laugh. It really wasn't that high, was it? "Look, it's only what, fifteen feet? You won't even get a scrape."

"I am *not* jumping."

I shrugged and stalked off. "All right. I guess I'll see you tomorrow—"

"NO!" she wailed. "Wait, all right! I'll… I'll jump. But you have to catch me."

"Honestly, it's not that…" Her sharp glare froze my tongue. I cleared my throat. "All right… fine." I held out my arms in a sigh.

Her gaze narrowed. "You won't drop me, will you?"

"Hmm." I tapped a finger to my chin. "You know, now that you mention it, I *am* a terrible catch—"

"Swear you won't miss!" she clipped. "I'll die if you drop me! And-and you'll be responsible! Everyone will know!"

"You won't die," I laughed. "And I won't miss. I was only joking—"

"Swear it!"

I rolled my eyes, but raised a fist to my chest and gave an ostentatious bow, muttering, "I *swear* with the Mother Goddess as my witness that I won't drop you, miss… um…" I stopped, realizing I hadn't asked this. "Sorry, but what was your name?"

She looked suspicious, but answered, "Willow."

"Very well, Howless Willow." I held out my arms again, waiting for her to jump. "Ready when you—*Oof!*"

She dropped like a stone, her chin nicking my brow and her knee sinking into my stomach. I lost my footing and sent both of us splashing into the pond with a cold *ka-plunk!*

The fish rushed away from us, a bubbled curse escaping my lips before Willow and I gasped up for air. We'd hit the algae-covered floor, our clothes stained with green and brown sludge as we coughed up water.

"Th-th-there…!" I stuttered, the chilled water making my teeth chatter. I cringed when hearing she was still coughing. "At least I c-c-caught you, didn't I…?" My mouth shut. "What happened to your hair?"

Instead of grey, her long strands had changed white, and her onyx eyes were now a very pretty azure.

She blinked at me, reaching a hand to her ear. "Oh! M-my ear-cuff must have f-f-fallen off…"

I caught a glint in the water and bent to pick up a silver piece of jewelry.

"Ear-c-cuff?" I turned the jewelry over in a shiver, guessing she meant this. I handed it back to her. "What does that have to do with your hair ch-ch-changing?"

"I was practicing Decepiovoking with my mother," she explained. We waded back to land, and she circled a hand in the air. "The earcuff has an illusion in it that changes my hair and eyes when I wear it."

I pulled myself onto solid ground and helped her up, both of us dripping and covered in mud. "You're a… a Decepiovoker?" I asked.

"A *soaked* Decepiovoker." She wrung out her hair, the strands dragging on the grass past her feet. She'd stopped shivering, somehow. Did she warm that quickly?

"Right." I coughed behind a fist. *That's a lot of Bloody hair…* I spied a few twigs and globs of gunk tangled in there. Her dress was in even worse shape.

"Sorry," I offered awkwardly. "I'll, er, ask the servants to wash your dress?"

She let out a fogged breath. "Thank you. And, I suppose, thank you for helping me down as well. I… may have a fear of heights."

"Do you, now?" I drawled in fake surprise. "I wouldn't have guessed."

She rolled her eyes, choosing to ignore that. Instead, she squinted at me. "You're Xavier, yes?"

"Oh, yes, that's…" I paused. "Wait. I never told you my name."

"I'm a Seer." She tossed her hand back. "I've had a few visions of you and your brother this past week. I even managed to project *your* face in my mother's crystal…" Her eyes flew open in horror. "Mother's crystal ball! I left it in the gardens on the other side of the wall…!"

A crystal ball? I'd never seen one up close before.

"I can get it," I offered, toning down my excitement. "I mean… Since you probably don't want to climb back up the wall, yes?"

She glowered, but didn't argue.

I couldn't help the enthused smile from splitting my face. "Thought so. I'll be right back."

I waded back into the pond, gritting my teeth against the chilly water as I made my way to the patch of vines along the wall. I didn't like going back in the water, but I also didn't see a faster way up. I was beyond dirty and cold anyway, a little more mud wouldn't matter. Mother would kill me either way at this point.

Besides, I was too excited to care now that I knew she was a Dual-Evocator. Those were so rare! It was rare enough to find another Evocator with one element of Hallows, but to find one who possessed *two?* I'd never met one of those!

I reached the patch of vines and grabbed the thickest strands that could hold me before climbing up the wall, then hopped over the other side. I touched down in a flowery garden, seeing the tree she must have climbed up, and scanned the ground around it.

Sure enough, a crystal ball the size of a dragon skull sat in the grass by the tree's trunk. I grabbed it, staring at it in wonder. It was perfectly smooth and polished, not a scratch to be seen. Inside were rivers of jutting crystals like shards of ice, some shooting in geometric angles and others swirling like works of abstract art.

I was getting dizzy looking into its mesmerizing depths. Then I blinked back to reality and remembered why I was here.

"Right," I breathed, refocusing. "Now to get back."

I carefully secured the orb in one arm and climbed the tree to get over the wall, as the Howless had done. But unlike her, *I* wasn't afraid to jump down.

I leapt off the wall and landed in front of her, holding out the crystal ball with a smug grin.

She took it with a flat expression. "Thank you…" She flushed when a clump of mud slid from her chin and dripped onto the crystal ball.

I stifled a chuckle and helped her wipe the algae off the crystal. "You're welcome."

Her little crow twittered at me, hopping from Willow's shoulder. I hummed at the bird. If she had a messenger, that meant she'd be a Reaper one day. I'd bet a Decepiovoker could use illusion tricks to confuse opponents. And a Seer would predict their moves before they made them. Bloods, if Alex and I could do that, we could sneak up on Mother without her *always* knowing when…

I noticed Willow was giving me a narrow look, as if mulling over a thought.

"What?" I asked.

She took a moment, then said, "You're a Devouh, aren't you?"

The freezing air sank another ten degrees. "W-why do you say that?" I choked. Blast it, I'd hoped I wouldn't have to tell her my family name at all. The last thing I wanted was for the first girl I met at our new home to run away screaming for her life.

"Because you've moved into their estate," she said casually. "Are you the High Howllord's nephew?"

I kept a guarded tone. "Why does it matter?"

She shrugged. "I suppose it doesn't. I was only curious. Ah! I bet you and your brother are his sons, aren't you?"

I stared at her, confused. "You aren't afraid of us?"

"Afraid?" She sniffed. "The only thing I'm afraid of is heights. Don't go around telling people otherwise. If I find out you've been spreading rumors, I won't come visit."

"All… all right—?"

"Xavier!" My brother called.

I whipped round, having forgotten about Alex.

When he trotted over, we exclaimed in unison, "I win. I found the most interesting…"

We both paused. Neither of us were alone.

Alex found Willow beside me, and I noticed a second girl behind him. This girl had jet black hair and leathery wings, wearing a silken, pink dress with numerous bows and frills.

"Who's this?" Alex and I asked together.

"Lilli?" Willow sounded surprised, looking at the bat. "What are you doing out here?"

The bat girl crossed her arms. "I should ask you the same. And what in the five realms happened to your gown? It's filthy!"

The bat, Lilli, took off her cloak to wrap it around Willow's shoulders.

Alex eyed my equally muddy state with a smirk. "Went for a swim, did you?"

I shrugged.

He gave a sly laugh. "Mother will be furious. I suppose this means I'll get the extra galling *and* your single serving—*huah?!*"

I shoved him into the pond with a loud splash. He surfaced just as muddy and wet, coughing water.

"That was n-n-*not* f-fair…!" he chattered, trudging back to land.

I gave a vindictive smile, matching his glare. "I thought we agreed to share everything?" I asked. "That includes punishment."

"Remind me to revise that agreement!" He stormed toward the manor, knocking water out of his grown wolf ear. "Blast it, now we have to change before Mother sees us…!"

Lilli's wings gave an expectant flap. "What about us? Aren't you going to invite us in?"

Alex scowled back at her. "After you accused me of thieving and attacked me?" He snorted, head shaking. "You know what? I don't care. You all can do what you wish. But you'd better decide quickly before I have the servants shut the door in your faces." He stomped off toward the manor.

So much for Mother's order of being polite, I thought in a sigh.

I turned to the girls and gave a nervous laugh. "Er, that's his way of saying 'welcome'." I coughed into a muddy fist. "Er, come, we have a fire ready inside. Shall I ask the servants to make tea?"

Lilli *hmphed* and stuck up her nose. "Well, I'm glad one of you knows his manners. What was your name again?"

"Xavier," I said.

She held out her hand, as if expecting me to take it.

Oh, right. Mother's reminder from earlier flashed to memory. *Protocols.*

I awkwardly took her fingers, bowing as instructed. Wait, should I have done this with Willow?

I flicked a nervous glance at Willow. She didn't seem to care, from what I could tell. The white-haired Howless was still wringing out her muddy strands and murmuring to her tiny crow.

Seeming satisfied with my belated bowing, Lilli cleared her throat and stretched taller. "I am High Howless Lilliana Tessinger. The daughter of the Death King's Hand." She had an afterthought and wafted a hand in the air. "Though, I suppose if you and your brother are the Devouhs' sons, I'll allow you to call me Lilli."

She nodded as if this was a great honor, then turned round to strut after Alexander.

"Well, then." I peeled off my soaked gloves and turned to Willow. "You're welcome to stay as long as you like, but I should warn that we're having guests soon. Bloods, Mother is going to kill us if we aren't 'presentable'…"

Willow hummed. "No, she won't."

I flicked her a skeptical glance. "You sound oddly sure of this."

"Because your guests are already here." She held out an algae covered glove. "And I don't exactly look presentable myself, do I?"

I halted. "You're our guest?"

"And Lilli. Our parents told us we were visiting the Devouhs today, to meet someone. I already knew it would be you and your brother, though, since I Saw it in my vision."

"Ah…" I shivered, the chill getting to me. "I suppose that explains mother's insistence with protocols…" A freezing gale cut past us, making my skin ice over. "Bloods, let's get inside. I could use a fire."

"I can fix that." Willow said cheerfully, then shoved the crystal ball into my arms. "Hold this."

She peeled off her gloves before taking a deep breath. A white gleam shone from her chest under her gown—and her hands burst with red fire.

The heat wavered from the new ball of flames rippling over her palms, smoke curling around her fingers.

"This should hold us until we get inside," she said. "I can't make orange fire yet, but red is better than nothing."

I gaped at her. "You're a… a Pyrovoker?"

"Yes."

"And a Decepiovoker?"

"Yes."

My voice dimmed. "*And* a Seer...?"

She rolled her eyes. "Among other things, yes."

"But... but that's three..." I pointed a limp finger at her. "Evocators can't have more than two elements. Not unless you're a..."

"A Relicblood," she finished for me. Then she bent to pluck something from the grass at her feet. It was a silver tiara engraved with raven-skull that glittered with polished diamonds. She placed the tiara on her head and curtsied while one hand still gleamed with red fire. "Perhaps I should have given a more formal introduction. My name is Princess Willow Ashleya Ember. I am the daughter of Serdin Ember, the King of Death, and am heiress to Grim's throne."

My throat went dry. "H... heiress?"

"Yes." She smiled. "Lovely to meet you in person, Howllord Xavier. Now, if you don't mind, I'd like to take you up on that offer of having my gown cleaned. And you mentioned tea? Do you have spiced cider? It's my favorite."

She strode toward the manor, leaving me petrified in the yard.

6

XAVIER

The hearth crackled from the center of our manor's greatroom as I leaned back in a wide leather chair and let out a hard sigh.

It seemed I was first to finish bathing. Only the servants haunted the chamber with me, some resurrected and carrying out various household tasks and others floating through the walls as misty specters.

One of those specters was Aiden, who hovered beside me with a hum. "Well, snap my string, Young Sir. You had a busy day, didn't you? Sinking royalty on your first day. Impressive initiative."

"I didn't know she was the Bloody Death Princess." I knocked the water from my grown wolf ear and adjusted the raven-skull cufflinks at my wrists, checking my alabaster suit for signs of its former marring. The servants had done an excellent job cleaning it. Mother and Father hadn't returned yet, thank Death, so there was still time to pretend the evening had passed without incident.

Aiden gave a ghostly smirk. "Oh, of course, Young Sir. She only has six feet of hair and wears a tiara. Anyone would have been fooled."

"Yes, thank you, Aiden…" I smeared a hand over my face. "You can take pride knowing I'm thoroughly mortified now. Aren't you supposed to be scouting for assassins or something?"

"Oh, but I am!" His feathery wings fanned upward as he patted my shoulder with a misty hand. "I'm scouting the greatroom, Young Sir! And besides, Nathaniel's on his rounds outside."

"I'm doin' what now, feather-brains?" Nathaniel's raspy voice sounded behind us. I turned to see the bear-eared ghost had popped his head through the wall in a watery ripple. "I thought ye were suppos'ta be out there while *I* be in here?"

Aiden's wings flattened with feigned shock. "Well, now I'm as befuddled as a flying penguin."

Nathaniel pushed the rest of his wispy self through the wall to join us inside. "Aw, it don't matter now. The royal guards'a come to take over anyhow."

"The royal guard?" I asked.

Nathaniel floated to the other side of my armchair. "O' course, lad. Ye didn't think ye'd be dining with royalty without their personal protection unit, did ye?"

"I suppose not…"

"—You have soul-sight?"

I nearly jumped out of my chair. The ashen-haired princess had entered the greatroom alongside her little crow, Jewel. Her long hair was still damp from her bath, newly cleaned and free of mud and twigs. Her black-lace gown had been washed as well, and she was now fastening the final button on her high collar as she strode toward us with her messenger buzzing by her head.

I hurried to my feet and bowed. "Your-Your Highness! I've asked the servants to bring the cider you requested… er, your grace…"

Her nose crinkled, and she glanced at Jewel who perched on her shoulder. "Hm. No. I don't like how that sounds, from you. Keep calling me Willow. It sounded much better." She curtsied to the ghosts floating by the armchair. "*Chanerr*, Aiden. *Chanerr* Nathaniel. I suppose if he can see you, he must be a Necrovoker?"

Aiden chuckled. "Indeed he is, your grace!"

Nathaniel thumped my back with a watery squish. "One o' the best! The young lads both be, to be sure."

I coughed into a fist. "They're being kind, Your High… W-Willow." I rubbed my neck. "I barely count as a Necrovoker."

"Oh, not to worry," she sang dimly, "I'll make any Evocator more confident with my dismal Hallows."

My brow knitted. "What do you mean? You're a Relicblood."

"Which makes it all the more unacceptable." She went to the hearth and sat on the rug before the fire. Her little crow buzzed off her shoulder to alight on the mantle instead, twittering a melancholy tune above us.

Willow reached her bare hands into the licking flames and pulled out a small wisp of red fire, embers bursting from her uninjured fingers. "At my age," she hushed, "most Pyrovokers can produce orange and blue fire… Even with aided tutoring, I can barely do this much. And my Necrovoking is even more disappointing."

I sputtered. "But… you can do illusions. And you're a Seer. And a… wait." A thought hit me. "Those aren't elements from the Death realm."

Aiden nudged Nathaniel in the spectral ribs. "Took him long enough to notice, eh?"

Nathaniel gave a bearded grin. "Me thinks the lad's a bit distracted, ain't he?"

Willow cast the ghosts a chiding glance. "He *is* new here. Show him some leniency." She turned back to me, the ball of fire over her palms casting her face in a rubied glow. "But yes, Xavier. Those are not elements from the Death realm."

I knuckled my brow. "But… you're a Relicblood of Death, aren't you?"

"Yes again." She tossed her fireball back into the hearth. "But you see, I also happen to be a Relicblood of Dreams."

I went to watch the fire beside her. "I don't understand… how could you be two Relicbloods?"

She shrugged. "My father is from the Death Bloodline. My mother is from the Dream Bloodline."

I was struggling to wrap my head around that. "Two Relicbloods married…? From different realms?"

Her icy eyes flicked to me, seeming irked. "Yes. Is there a problem?"

"N-no." I held up pacifying hands. "I just didn't know Relicbloods *could*… Well…"

She sighed, tucking her legs to the side as she shifted her weight over the rug. "My parents are the first to do so. There's never been a hybrid Relicblood until now. There are some who find it… disturbing." She returned her frosted gaze to the crackling fire, ashen fox ears growing. "Who find *me* disturbing."

Her expression sagged, sitting in silence for a time. I lowered to the rug beside her. "Alex and I know a thing or two about that… We have a bit of the… opposite problem, I suppose."

One of her fox ears flicked to me. "Opposite?"

"It's hard to explain." I scratched my head. "Your Hallows are two halves in one person. Alexander's and my Hallows are more of… the reverse? Where we come from, we were called freaks."

Willow looked puzzled. "For being Necrovokers?"

"Not quite, it's…" I stared at the embers in a sigh. "It's hard to explain."

A small silence grew. One of the logs in the hearth snapped and crumbled to ash, causing the logs above it to shift in a puff of embers. Some of those embers spit out from the hearth and landed on a lock of Willow's long hair.

—The strands caught fire.

I jolted. "Death!"

"Yes?" Willow looked at me curiously, oblivious to her burning hair despite the pungent scent swelling in the fire's wake.

"Y-your hair…!"

She lowered her gaze to the burning strands. "Oh. How embarrassing." She combed her fingers through her hair and snuffed out the fire with a gentle fist.

The ends were singed off at her shoulder. The strands had been burned to ash.

Ash that hung in the air around us like floating specks of grey-white dust. They flittered and fluttered around my head as if waltzing to a silent melody, the flakes caught in a trance as they wafted back toward Willow. Piece by piece, the flakes reattached to the singed ends of her burnt hair until the lock had returned to its full length over the rug. Strangely, the hair was still damp from her bath, as if nothing had happened at all.

My mind blanked. "What in Death… What just happened?"

She twirled the newly "grown" lock of hair between her fingers. "A Pyrovoker's skin may be impervious to burning, but that doesn't mean our hair is."

"But why did it *grow back*?" I threw a bewildered hand at her. "It turned to ash!"

She snorted a laugh. "It didn't *turn* to ash. It *is* ash. If anything happens to it, it just comes back to me."

"But how?" I crouched over the rug and examined a curling lock of her strange hair. "I thought only Death was known for…" I paused. Craned my gaze to her face. "Oh, Death. You *are* Death. Aren't you? Her next incarnation?"

She grinned. "Up to speed, are we?"

Aiden and Nathaniel were roaring with laughter behind me now.

"Holy Bloods." I squeezed my face in a groan. "Seamstress Cleanse me, I sank the soul of Death." I peeked an eye between my fingers. "Is she really your Soul-Mother? The Seamstress?"

Willow shrugged. "That's what I'm told."

"Does She speak to you?"

"No more than the rest of us."

I snapped my fingers in a laugh. "Is that why you're afraid of heights? I suppose the legend is true: all of Death's incarnations hold that fear!"

She buried her face in her hands. "Could we skip over that bit? There are plenty of other things about my incarnations that aren't mortifying."

I lowered to my stomach with an eager smile. "But your eyes—Death is said to have eyes as white as polished bones. Why are yours blue?"

"As I said." She cocked an eyebrow. "I'm a hybrid Relicblood. I get my eyes from my mother. I'm sorry to disappoint the expectations of your holy legends."

"Hah! Forget the legends. Your eyes are far more beautiful than the tales—" I clicked my teeth shut.

The ghosts behind me ceased their laughter. They were now staring at me. The hearth's fire blew hot air at my face, the new silence suffocating.

Willow's grey cheeks reddened, and she turned toward the fire. "Oh… Thank you."

I sat up with a rigid spine, gluing my gaze to the hearth in a swallow.

Behind me, I heard Aiden hum. "I think we lost him."

Nathaniel agreed under his breath, "Aye. Let's have a moment o' silence for the fallen."

I twisted back to see the ghosts were hanging their heads in mock mourning. Aiden wiped at a fake tear.

I rolled my eyes.

"—pardon, Your Grace," Thateus suddenly piped from above us. He'd been so quiet I hadn't noticed the ram-horned butler approach with a silver tray of steaming cider. He glanced at Willow. "Your refreshments."

Thateus offered us both a saucer and cup, which we accepted.

Willow took a delighted sip. "Thank you, Thateus. How have you been? Busy as ever?"

"Always, my lady," Thateus said with a bow. "And alas, I still have much to do to prepare for dinner. Please excuse me. Call if you need anything more, either of you."

I nodded to him and blew on my own steaming cup to cool the drink. "Thank you, Thateus. See you tonight."

He bowed again and took his leave.

Willow sipped from her cider in a calm sigh.

"—*AHHHH!*" a yell split from upstairs. It sounded like Alex. I could hear him through the metal vent in the ceiling. "*What in Bloods are you doing in here?! Get out!*"

"*I was just looking for a hairbrush—ahh!*" A feminine shriek vibrated the vent. This voice sounded like Lilli. "*Did you just throw a sponge at me?! How rude!*"

"*Rude?! You're the one barging into random washrooms while others are bathing! Now get out!*"

Splashing ensued, followed by thumping feet and various objects clattering against the floor above us.

Willow, Aiden, Nathaniel and I all watched the ceiling with tilted gazes. Our eyes followed the rumbling of what sounded like footfalls storming across the floor. More yelling. More splashing.

Willow and I sipped our cider with interest.

"Well," Willow hummed and *clinked* her cup on the saucer. "They're certainly getting along… swimmingly."

I spit out my cider in a snorting laugh.

When it came time for dinner, Willow's little crow eyed me from the lip of the heiress's obsidian goblet atop our family's blackwood dining table, directly across from my assigned seat.

I sank into my chair and sipped from my own goblet with nervous fingers, trying to ignore the black bird's incessant staring.

Willow herself ate her meal heartily with regal delicacy fit for a princess indeed, idly chatting with Lilli and remarking on the skill of our undead chef, as if nothing were amiss.

Mother sat at the foot of the table while Father sat across from her at the head. Lilli was seated across from Alexander, and to her right were her bat-winged parents. Her father was enjoying his seasoned soup, spiced with Jarrach peppers and cumin, while her mother politely patted her lips with a napkin.

Beside Willow were her own mother and father. The Bloody king and queen of Grim.

It was terrifying to have monarchs sitting right across from me— yet it was also bizarre to see them relaxed and mingling with my parents like old friends. The royal couple was such an interesting pair. The Death King shared Willow's ashen-colored hair, but his locks were short and cropped at his temples. His eyes weren't blue like hers, either. They were like Alex and my white eyes, clear and empty of color with faint, grey rings around the irises to make them visible at all. They matched the holy legends verbatim.

The queen, on the other hand, shared Willow's icy, azure eyes, just as Willow said. But the queen's wavy hair was also a cool, mesmerizing blue. It was so strange. Yet so fascinating…

My mother cleared her throat and began introductions, waving a hand around the table. "Boys, I know you likely have questions about our guests. We've wanted to introduce you earlier, but we hadn't had the opportunity while you were away. These are your Spirit Parents, the Tessingers and the Embers." She gestured to Lilli's winged parents first. "High Howless Maria was my Lieutenant when I was still captain of the royal guard. After my promotion, she took the job instead. And High Howllord Daniel is the First Hand of the king, counterpart to your father."

Lilli's mother, a narrow-faced beauty with long, silky black hair, chuckled. "You can call me Mother Maria."

Lilli's father, a goateed gentleman, tucked his wings to his back with a bright smile. "And you can call me Father Daniel, as Willow does."

My mother gestured to the king and queen next. "And, of course, their Majesties: Death Queen Myra and Death King Serdin Ember. The rulers of Grim, obviously. Well," Mother amended with a light wave to the blue-haired queen. "Perhaps it's not so obvious with you, Myra."

A round of laughter rippled through the table, but Alex and I were awkwardly silent.

"Er, if I may ask…" I began carefully, "how long have we had Spirit Parents, exactly?"

"Since you were born," Mother said as she sipped her wine. "They're very good friends of ours. They have granted us the honor of serving as your Spirit Parents, as we've done for the young ladies Willow and Lilli."

Beside me, Alex grumbled, "So, if you had a job to do as our Spirit Parents, why in Bloods didn't any of you come visit us in that Void-hole back home—*ow!*"

I kicked his leg under the table, and he shot me an angry glare.

"It's a pleasure to meet you," I said hurriedly, hoping to erase my brother's thoughtless comment in front of the Bloody king and queen.

The ashen-haired king chuckled. "Oh, we've already met. But you were both quite small when you left overseas, so I imagine you wouldn't remember."

Alexander snorted. "Obviously—*ow!*"

"*Ow!*" I winced when Alex kicked me back.

We glared at each other for a long minute before our father cleared his throat. "Yes, well… Thateus tells us you've already met the girls. I hope you both have been courteous hosts while we were gone?" There was a warning look with that question.

Alex and I went rigid.

"Oh, yes," Willow chimed. "They were quite accommodating."

We loosened our lungs.

The king turned to his long-haired daughter and cocked his head. "Willow?" His Majesty lifted one of her damp locks. "Why is your hair wet?"

"Oh, it's silly, really." Willow twirled a wet lock of her long hair. "It was caught in a thorn bush. It had all sorts of leaves and twigs in it. So, I asked to borrow their bath when I arrived."

The queen chuckled—then flicked me a knowing glance across the table.

"Caught on a thorn bush?" The king shook his head. "Again? Willow, what have I told you about leaving your hair down while out in the gardens? You must keep it tied up. It would help keep everyone from stepping on it, as well."

"I lost my last ribbon." Willow picked at her food. "It was too small. It fell out after two steps and was blown away in the wind. I need a longer ribbon if I'm going to hold all of it together."

"Well," Mother hummed. "I don't know about any ribbons, but do you know what else you'd like for your *Rae'u Shelic?* Your Day of Birth is only in three days' time, and I hear your father is throwing a ball to celebrate."

The reminder made Willow smile. "I haven't thought much on it. Father already gave me my own scythe, now that he thinks I'm ready. I should think that's enough."

Mother tapped a nail against the lacquered table. "A scythe will be difficult to surpass indeed… Well, perhaps I'll surprise you with something small, then."

Willow smiled again. But it fell when she looked back at Alex and me, and she asked, "Mother Alice? I've been wondering, if you and Father Lucas have been living here for a while…" She hesitated, nodding to us. "Why are *they* only here now?"

Father answered gruffly, "The boys still had another year to finish in their old academy. We didn't want them falling behind in their studies, so we waited until they'd finished the year."

"They will join you in your own tutoring, girls," Mother added, "Along with the other young children on the palace grounds. So please see that they're well integrated, if you'd be so kind."

Lilli and Willow spoke at once, "Yes, Mother Alice."

We all went back to our meals as the adults chatted amongst themselves.

I sighed and looked up—froze. Willow's blue-haired mother, Queen Myra, was staring at me. Her gaze was unnervingly chilling. My ears started to grow fur, my pulse shivering under that look.

But whatever fear had gripped the queen, it evaporated in a moment's notice. Now Her Majesty's eyes unfocused and her Dream mark gleamed with an azure light.

"Ah," the queen breathed cheerfully, turning to my mother. "Alice, I do believe the boys are owed their rewards for their little contest you conducted?"

Mother was mid-sip into her wine, blinking. "Hm? Oh, yes. That. I'd nearly forgotten."

I perked in my seat, as did Alex beside me. I'd almost forgotten, too. The queen gave me a sly wink.

Mother flicked her stormy eyes at us with an inspecting gaze. "Well, boys? Present your findings and I will measure their intrigue."

We both pointed to the girls and announced, "Them."

Mother scowled at us. "The girls?"

We nodded. I explained, "We met them in the yard, within the qualifying boundaries you set."

Mother's teeth sharpened, her wolf ears folding down as she growled, "That hardly counts as interesting—"

The girls gasped and cast our mother hurt gazes.

Mother's scowl blanched. "Er… I meant… That wasn't…"

Alex and I discreetly knocked triumphant elbows together, trying to stifle our snickers.

"Well, my lady?" I encouraged.

Alex's chuckle was smug. "Which of them is more interesting?"

"Oh, all right, all right!" Mother rubbed her temples, deflating in defeat. "It's a tie…"

I hit knuckles with Alex, both of us cackling. "Two whole pumpkin gallings!"

"—But," Mother added. There was a devious twinkle in her eye. "Your findings are so interesting, in fact, that I should think your rewards ought to be split *with* them. Wouldn't you agree, girls?"

It was the girl's turn to laugh.

7

WILLOW

After dinner, Thateus pulled the heavy doors open to allow us outside to the cobbled courtyard.

The Floating Lights dancing in the cavern's ceiling mists had dimmed to deep indigo hues for the evening.

Mother Alice and Father Lucas followed us out, their twin sons at either of their sides.

A coach was already waiting for Lilli and her parents, and they said their goodbyes to the Devouhs and set off to their own manor.

As for my parents and I, one of the Devouh's servants had fetched my father's large Flamedragon from the family's stables.

The dragon, Raavith, was my father's oldest steed. His marbled black-and-red scales hissed with steam in the cool night air, the creature warm to the touch from his barbed tail to his long, serrated snout. His leathery wings were tucked to his back as the servant adjusted the saddle and tightened the girth.

My father climbed onto Raavith first, and Mother lifted me onto the saddle before taking her place behind me herself. I was wedged between them, clinging to Father.

Father waved to the Devouhs, smiling down at the twins last. "Grand to officially meet you. I suppose we'll see more of you around the grounds from now on."

The twins flushed and bowed together, stammering, "Y-yes, Your Majesty."

I caught Xavier's mismatched eyes, and his grey face reddened. I waved. "It was a pleasure meeting you in person, Xavier."

His gaze dropped to his feet. "Er, yes… and a pleasure meeting you, Your Highness."

I wafted a hand at him. "Again, do call me Willow. I've Seen too many visions of you for any of that formality nonsense."

He swallowed visibly. "Ah… very well… Willow. *Chanerr nohkosch.*"

"*Chanerr nohkosch*," I returned with a smile, then secured my grip around Father and drew in a preparing breath.

Father snapped the reins. The Flamedragon spread its wings and took a running start, then launched into the air with a burst of speed.

The wind rushed through my hair as we soared through the cavern mists high aboveground, the lurching beast beneath me pulling at my stomach and nearly making me lose my dinner. The Floating Lights swirled and coiled around us in their evening indigo hue as we passed them at a sickening pace.

I clung to Father in fright, Mother holding me in her arms from behind.

Raavith's leathery wings glided along the cavern winds like sails, giving the occasional flap and making us lurch along with him.

Bloods, I hated flying. We were so high up, I felt like I was slipping off the saddle. If not for Mother and Father securing me, I would never fly on one of these. But today, I agreed to tolerate the flight. We didn't have much time left of the night, and we wouldn't have time to visit this sacred site in the coming weeks. I wanted this trip. I thought heights and I could form a truce for now… I was wrong.

"I-I-I changed my mind," I shivered behind Father. "G-g-get me down! Get me down! Please…!"

Father sighed and finally steered Raavith downward. We landed in the farther side of the Weeping Woods, near the foot of a mountainside.

Raavith tucked his wings closed as Father slid off the saddle first. He helped me down, and I puffed over the grass in rattled relief, letting the nausea settle. Next he helped down Mother, who fetched a lantern from the saddlebag at Raavith's side. Two gleaming white bubbles of Floating Lights misted from inside, fogging the glass with their chilled aura. Mother held her lantern high to light the way, nodding to Father.

Father returned the nod and reached for the blue-glowing sphere that dangled from the chain around his neck. He plucked the metal sphere off its magnetic link and pressed a sealing rune etched on the surface. The sphere glittered with a golden light, melting in his palm like liquid silver and stretching into a long-staved scythe. The crooked blade radiated with a beautiful glow, its mirror-like surface reflecting his face as he gripped the Crystal weapon dutifully.

"Stay close, both of you," Father reminded. "I'll handle any stray Fera, should they surprise us."

I huffed, regaining my wits, and reached into the Storagesphere clipped to the delicate chain at my hip. My fingers sank into the gummy surface of the sphere with quiet ripples, and I plucked out the shrunken hair-stick encrusted with diamonds and azure gemstones. While it was inside the sphere, it was the measly size of a toothpick. But once it touched the outside air, the small thing grew to the length of two hands. I pressed the sealing rune etched in the middle of the ornament's staff, and just like Father's weapon, it melted in my fingers and stretched into my own long-staved scythe, the Crystal blade curving above my head in a brilliant blue light.

I twirled my scythe round and dug the butt into the grass at my boots. "*We'll* handle them," I corrected.

Father's lips split into a smile, chuckling. "Ah, my mistake. I suppose now that a certain princess has passed her final test in the art of the scythe, she's eager to put it to practice?"

I gave a toothy grin. "Of course. I haven't been on a proper hunt with you, yet. I'm ready to kill my first demon."

Father laughed. "Well, don't be disappointed if we don't find any tonight. They've been absent around this area for the past month. I'm merely taking precaution."

"Then I'll take precaution with you. Mother will be better protected with two Reapers guarding her."

Mother pressed swooning hands over her heart. "What chivalry! I feel safer already."

I kept my scythe at the ready and took my place on Mother's side, keeping her between Father and me for safety. She wasn't equipped to fight demons out here in the physical plane. Her battles were fought in Aspirre's subconscious realm in our dreams. She protected us in sleep, and now it was our turn to protect her in the waking world.

Jewel fluttered by my head while my father's messenger crow, Locke, soared above us to keep watch. Should any beasts be nearby, the black birds would sense them and alert us.

Raavith lumbered behind us as we made our way through the veiling branches of the surrounding willow trees. The Weeping Woods were quiet tonight, the thousands of draping branches rustling in the breeze and sending the leaves in a roaring whisper for miles.

The temperature dropped the nearer we came to the mountainside. The cold was refreshing for me, since my Pyrovoker's heat kept me warm, but Mother began trembling from under her cloak. Her rattling fingers couldn't keep the lantern steady.

"Come, Myra," Father hushed and reeled her in by the waist, keeping her wrapped in his warmer hold. "You should know by now this is no place for fireless souls."

She chuckled between shivers. "I s-suppose I sh-should-d have fetched an ext-t-tra cloak."

I frowned at Father, keeping pace with them as we strode through another wall of long branches. "Is that why I'm never allowed to bring Lilli here?" I asked. "Because of the cold?"

Father shook his head. "No, Willow. It's simply not allowed."

"Why?"

"It is forbidden to speak of the Relics to those outside the Bloodlines." His tone hardened. "And it is *especially* forbidden to bring outsiders to them."

"But Lilli is practically my sister—"

"She isn't a Relicblood," Father emphasized. "Now, I love Lilli, as my Spirit Daughter, but the rule has been in place for over a thousand years. Even spouses are forbidden from knowing the Relics exist outside of legends."

My nose scrunched. "But you bring Mother here all the time."

"Because your mother is also a Relicblood," Father explained. "You could say it's uncharted territory."

"A loophole, if you will," Mother added whimsically. She giggled behind a hand. "You should have seen your father's face when we first came here together. He'd forgotten I'd come to this Relic for the last five hundred years and thought he'd destroyed a thousand years of royal code."

He tightened his grip around her and let out a sordid laugh. "Forgive me for being a tad *distracted* back then."

They shared a reminiscent chuckle.

I gritted my teeth, my fox ears growing. "But… *why* is it forbidden?"

Their chuckles dimmed. Father's head wavered. "There is an… ancient legend that speaks of a great power tied to the Relics. *What* that power is precisely isn't written, but it warns that, should those with darkened hearts abuse it, the realms would face unspeakable destruction."

"Thus, it is vital you tell no one of their existence," Mother's tone was suddenly intense. "Not even Lilli. And especially not the twins."

My brow furrowed at her. "I never said I would bring the twins."

Mother paused, as if realizing she'd made a mistake. She cleared her throat and amended, "Yes, well… I thought it should be extra clear, is all. In case you had any unscrupulous inspiration."

There was something strange about her tone. There was more she wasn't saying, I was sure of it. I thought to press her, but as we continued our trek through the woods, I noticed flakes of ash began flitting through the air around us.

We're here.

The various sounds of wildlife dimmed into a swelling silence. The air dropped another few degrees, the ash swirling thicker as we walked. We crossed a trickling creek and finally reached the foot of the mountain. Father and Mother walked through the veil of leaves that hid a wide cavern, and Raavith stomped inside after them.

I peeled back the curtain of leaves last, stepping into the chilled cavern behind them.

In the cavern was a towering, white willow tree.

Its draping branches stretched to the grass in a delicate stream of leafy twirls, dipping into a small creek that ran through the mountain's cavern at the tree's thick roots. The Willow of Ashes radiated with a chilled aura, crystal leaves twinkling the delicate song of the Requiem like elegant wind chimes.

I put away my scythe, reverting it back to its hair-stick form. There was no need for it here. The Willow repelled rotten souls with its own magic.

I joined Father and Mother at the base of Death's Relic, kneeling alongside them and bowing my head in reverence.

"Nira," I whispered, feeling a creeping chill run down my spine as I inhaled a deep breath, "Seamstress of Souls, Mother of Death and Rebirth. Hear us, humbly, and bless these lands with your light. I have seen another year in the bosom of your love, and wish to show my gratitude as I enter into the next year a newly matured soul. May you guide my spirit toward a life of prosperity and honor. *Mu necros neschali yettek.*"

I touched my brow to the willow's ashen roots. Beside me, I saw my parents do the same. We lifted our gazes in unison, taking a long breath as we sang the ancient prayer of *Death's Requiem*—the Call of the Relic—in the Grimish tongue together.

Kris la vheh, weh shae'beahl hu'leigh
Neschalist p'laven ash kemn mea la schae
Heist e spell du'beahl hu'dohn
Yechet heme kraveshahe trist khon

A'speles speles la a'hoh hoh
Tatacha veben shelic'u nahohko
Nira veilla ke halaa pievf
Necrotha myel'u dohn la sheft

O myel heist timbriw lahla'beahl?
Murrderes craw hellacha lola'beahl?
Heist craw'u lole fret myel ena

Yechet wuw kemn droh la wuw kemn thal
Yechet wuw kemn droh la wuw kemn thal

QUEEN MYRA

"Did you enjoy yourself, Willow?" I asked, tucking my daughter in bed with her velvet comforter. Once we'd returned to the palace, it was well past her bedtime. But, I supposed, this had been a special occasion, so I was willing to allow the slip in routine this time. "It's been quite the busy day, hasn't it? The ritual, the new scythe… and I'm sure you're thrilled to have finally met those twins after so many visions?"

Willow sat up with a bright smile, her tiny crow twittering from the headboard. "I am. It was strange to see them in person, honestly. And to actually have them respond to what I say, for once." Her nose scrunched with a puzzled expression. "It wasn't something I was prepared for."

I hummed, sympathizing, and sat on the mattress beside her. "Yes, I've had a number of those moments. It's quite disconcerting."

Willow pulled up her knees and leaned closer with interest. "What were they?"

I tapped a nail to my lips, recalling. "Hmm… well, there was a time I had a vision of an entire conversation with your Grandfather."

"Grandfather Dream?" She asked in a giggle. "So, you knew what would be said when it finally happened?"

"Actually, it never *did* happen. I discovered *he* had a vision of the very same conversation, so neither of us had a need to hold it." I twirled a lock of my azure hair. "Perhaps that's why it was so faint when we'd Seen that vision. The less likely outcomes of the future will always be fainter than the more likely ones."

Willow hugged her knees, seeming hesitant suddenly. "Mother…? You've been around for five centuries, yes?"

I knitted my brow. "Yes. Why do you ask?"

She blushed, her long hair falling over half her face. "Well, did you… did you ever meet… *me*… before I was me?"

"Oh," I breathed, realizing what she meant. "You mean your last incarnation?"

She nodded. "The last Death, before me. Was she… was she stronger with her Hallows?"

I winced, painfully unprepared for that question. *Shepherd guide me, what should I say?* I cleared my throat, taking a careful tone. "Well… I suppose in a way… she, erm, had her own strengths…"

Willow's white fox ears grew and draped to her neck depressively, and I quickly added, "B-but! You—er, *she*—was always the best with a scythe, just like you are now."

"But her Hallows strength was better than mine," Willow sighed, burying her face in her knees. "I'm never going to reach what my last incarnation had… I'm history's worst Relicblood."

Oh, my heart. I reached a hesitant hand over her shoulder, but retracted it, clutching my fingers instead.

"Willow," I began gently, "not all Relicbloods are as powerful as the world thinks. There are many common Evocators with stronger Hallows than us. Bloods, even your Grandfather Dream met his match, and your grandfather was pushing 1,500 at the time. Macar was just a boy of fifteen and already bested him—"

I shut my mouth, realizing too late whose name I just spoke.

Bloods, it's been so long since I'd heard that name. And even longer since it came from my own tongue.

I grew sick.

Willow's brow creased with disbelief. "Someone bested Grandfather Dream?"

I shivered at the memory, shaking my head. "N… never you mind, dear. It isn't important."

Willow cocked an ashen eyebrow at me. "It certainly seems important. Are you feeling all right, Mother?"

"Of course, dear." I put on a tight smile, tucking her back in bed as she laid down over her silken pillows.

I reached for her music watch on her nightstand, intending to wind it back and start the Requiem her father and I usually sang to her—

"Wait," Willow blurted, stopping me. She looked away in a blush. "Could you sing *your* lullaby? The one Grandfather Dream used to sing to you?"

I blinked at her, not expecting this. "Are you sure? I thought *Death's Requiem* was your favorite?"

"It is, but…" She pulled up her knees under the comforter shyly. "You never tell me much about your side of… my… family…" She squirmed. "Every time you finally talk about *something*, you stop. Like just now. Are you ashamed of your Bloodline?"

"Shepherd's Crook, of course not," I said in a start. Then I sighed. "Dear, you must understand. There is much history my family has personally lived through. Thousands of years. Much of it is… well, they're not suitable tales for someone your age. I promise, we'll have a very lengthy discussion on everything when you're older."

Willow squinted an eye at me. "Everything?"

I shuddered, my voice dim. "Yes… everything. For now, though, I can grant you our family's Call. If you still wish?"

Willow nodded eagerly.

I set down her music watch and scooted closer to hold her, then drew in a breath to sing.

Sleep
Dreamest thou of me
Breathe
Mine ears beg thee to sing
May 'ere mares be
repelled from thee
Pray, sleep
And dreamest thou of me

I evoked my sleep Hallows, hands glittering with azure light as I stroked her long hair.

Drink
Ye faerie the river's mead
Sweet
And cherished thou shalt be
May daylight sleep
Till moonlight flees
Pray, Drink
Ye faerie the river's mead

It didn't take long for her to fall asleep under my Hallows, snoozing soundly in my arms. I gently laid her down and kissed her brow. "Sleep well, darling," I whispered. "I'll be sure your dreams are safe."

8

XAVIER

"You're going the wrong way," Alex snapped, flapping the map of the academy's graveyard in my face. He pointed to a faint-grey splotch on the parchment, then tossed his chin toward a granite statue of a wolf that loomed above us. "See? It's a right turn past this tombstone."

I snatched the map out of his fingers, flipping it over and comparing the surrounding gravestones to the wolf above us. "You're holding it wrong. It's a left, see?"

"Are you blind? It's a right!"

"Left!"

"Right!"

"—*Stu*-dents?" a raven croaked from the wolf's stone snout above us suddenly.

The bird was an old thing, its black feathers peppered with grey patches. It fluttered its wings at us, croaked again, and flicked its head back in a gesture, "Stu-*dents*? Lost?"

Alex and I hesitated, then nodded at the bird. I held up the map and murmured, "Erm, we're looking for… Introduction to Necrovoking?"

"Fo-*llow*," it croaked, "*Fo*-llow."

The raven launched into the air, flapping toward the northern gravel path.

We shuffled after the raven, lifting the long, draping hoods of our warm cloaks the school had provided as uniforms. After passing row upon row of gravestones, the bird perched over the crooked scythe of an elegant statue of the Seamstress of Souls that stood guard atop a beautiful mausoleum. The building was made of obsidian, the statue matching its glossy dark hue as its molding was lined with gilded raven skulls and tall columns curling like lily petals at their tops.

The raven cocked its head at us from the Seamstress's statue. Then it glided down and flew inside the mausoleum in silence. Alex and I followed, stepping through the elegant entrance.

It was Deathly quiet inside. Various statuettes and mosaic murals decorated the interior with polished white and grey marble. Not a speck of dust burdened the vision, and I couldn't spy a single cobweb in any corners. It was clear the mausoleum was routinely tidied with the utmost care.

The raven led us to a curling stairwell in the back corner. I climbed down first, Alex right behind me, keeping my grip on the iron railing as we descended down the long spiral steps.

It took longer than expected to reach the bottom. Once we touched down on the final step, I saw where we were.

Catacombs. It must have been the academy's private crypts under the schoolyard.

The air was unsettlingly warm and damp down here. Lanterns filled with Fallen Lights lined the walls of these underground tunnels and split through the darkness with cool, blue lights until the rows of crypts made the corridors look like glowing ribcages. Cutting through the center of the stone floor was a stream of gently flowing water. Within, I saw several dazzling Fallen Lights gleaming with various shades of blue and white. They cast wavering lights along the walls and ceiling of the catacombs, the mesmerizing patterns dancing along Alexander and my faces as we admired them.

The old raven croaked up ahead, sounding impatient. Alex and I hurried to keep up with the black bird, our footfalls echoing through the tunnels as we passed each crypt in wonder.

"... and of course, our small battalion held strong to the last breath," a woman's voice bounced around the walls up ahead. "Sadly, our fates had been sealed, and we all met our doom in the end, but hang me, it was worth every scrape!"

As the raven led us near, I could see the woman was a wispy ghost clad in spectral armor, floating by one of the waterways. She wasn't alone, either. There were many people, living *and* dead, clustered around the center of an intersection chamber. There were a handful of ghosts mingling with cloaked children our age as they all waited around a large statue of the Seamstress. The Goddess's divine sculpture was made of white marble this time. The waterway we'd followed along stopped at her feet and converged with four other streams that split through their own designated tunnels. Those Floating Lights shinned from the water and illuminated Her figure in those same entrancing designs we'd seen earlier. Instead of a scythe like the statue outside, this one held a sewing needle and thread that curled alongside her long stone locks toward the conjoined waterways. Her sculpted eyes were cast down at her feet with a look of sorrow.

As Alex and I approached the murmuring group, I counted six ghosts. The specters were translucent white, their feet misting beneath them without connecting to the floor. As for the living, three children present. I only recognized one girl: the bat-winged Lilli.

Lilli nodded to us as she patted her neatly tied-up hair and smoothed down a stray strand with prim fingers, keeping to her conversation with three of the floating souls in the group.

There was a boy chatting with another ghost behind Lilli. He had black hair and sharp, sienna eyes that lit like glowing embers against the wavering lights dancing from the waterways.

A second boy stood farther back, away from the crowd. This one had ashen hair that was tossed to the side in a spiky, peaked cut. He was leaned against a stone pillar far away from everyone else with a look of disinterest, electing not to interact with the ghosts at all.

He cast Alex and me the briefest milky-eyed sneer before focusing his gaze on the ceiling with a bored sigh.

"There we were," the armored ghost woman from earlier recounted by the waterways with excited gestures, "seven Reapers against two dozen Necrofera. They were led by a Sentient with Terravoking

Hallows. I managed to get close to the bloke and slit my scythe along his inky throat, but he cast an enchantment on the stones beneath me and skewered my head in a single blink. Poof! That was the end of me."

"You weren't eaten?" A shocked voice questioned from behind the Seamstress's statue.

I craned my gaze around the sculpture. Willow sat with her bare feet dipped in the stream across from the armored ghost, holding a glowing-blue Fallen Light that cast her grey face in a cool radiance. Her long ashen hair tumbled over her shoulder and playfully cascaded into the gently flowing water without a care. The Fallen Light in her hands lit her azure eyes like icy gemstones.

"Oh, you bet we were nearly those demons' next meals," the armored ghost continued, casting Willow a toothy grin. "And we would've been, if'n reinforcements didn't arrive to exterminate them and cut our Seams in time."

Willow sounded captivated. "It must have been terrifying? In the darkness?"

The ghost rubbed her misty nose. "Aye, that it was, Princess. I could still hear everything, too. My vessel's ears might've been deaf by then, but my soul's ears were still working loud and clear. I could hear the beasts tearing into my flesh before the other Reapers came to cut them down, and…" The ghost paused, noticing me. I flushed when she caught me staring, and her pale lips stretched into a wide smirk. "Ah, what's this? You have a new admirer, Highness?"

Willow followed the ghost's gaze, then spotted me. "Oh, Xavier."

I gave a half-hearted wave and stammered, "*Ch… chanerr*, Your Highness."

"Again, just Willow. The formal title sounds odd, from you." She gently tossed the Fallen Light back into the water and pulled her feet out of the stream to rise. Willow curtsied to the ghost before approaching me. She noticed Alex standing beside me and hummed, "I suppose I should have expected to see you both here. I nearly forgot you're both Necrovokers."

I rubbed my neck. "Of sorts."

She cocked her head. "You said that before, didn't you? What exactly did you mean—?"

"Who is this, Your Grace?" blurted a voice to my right, startling me.

The sienna-eyed boy I'd seen earlier was now standing beside me. His picture-perfect face was stretched ridiculously wide with a thrilled smile. "*Chanerr*, Howllords," he greeted, "It's nice to see new faces in these catacombs for once."

My brain died. No one ever smiled at us at our old Academy. Alex seemed tongue-tied next to me, also.

"A-ah…" I stammered, not sure how to respond. "*Ch… Chanerr…?*"

"It's about time we had other students enroll in this class," the boy went on, looking far more enthusiastic than I was prepared for. "Thank Death you both are here to fill up this depressingly empty chamber. This class is always such a wasteland."

"I-I see." Anxiety bubbled. It had been a long time since I held a conversation this long with a stranger. Granted, he was doing all the talking, but even that was outrageous in itself.

He snatched my hand and shook it so hard my vision tumbled.

"I'm Matthiel Inion," he said. "Son of Matth*ew* Inion. Perhaps you've heard of him?"

He was still shaking my hand like mad, and I fumbled to reply, "Er, n-n-no… s-sorry…"

"Oh, well that's quite all right. You *are* new here. My father is the Claws of Grim's military. That's the Grand Lieutenant of the entire Reaper forces. He's only outranked by the Grand General, First Fangs Alice Devouh."

I nearly flinched at the mention of my mother.

He finally released my hand and smiled. "Terribly sorry, I'm rambling, aren't I? Let's hear of you, then. What is your name?"

"I-I… I'm… X-Xavier…"

"Grand to make your acquaintance, Xavier." Matthiel released my hand and gave a courteous bow. "And your family name?"

I swallowed. Our family name had been the most feared of any name where we came from. But then… if his father was our mother's lieutenant…

Before my cowardice won over, I said, "D-Devouh…"

Matthiel paused. I braced for the inevitable squeal of his boots scuffing the floor to get away from us.

"Devouh?" Matthiel questioned, hushed. "You're the sons of the First Fangs…?"

I cringed, knowing his scream was coming—

He snatched my hand a second time and shook harder than before.

"I didn't know the Devouhs had children!" he gasped. "It's an honor to share a class with highlords of your stature!"

I twisted my head back to Alex, who shared my stunned expression. *Bloods,* I thought, *Mother was right. This continent is much better.*

Was this how normal shifters lived? Was everyone usually this kind and welcoming?

Craaaw!

The old raven we'd followed here gave a scratchy croak that echoed through the catacombs. It had alighted on an elderly man's arm. He was a bearded old elk with steel-grey hair and sharp antlers that bowed from his head. He looked at Alexander and me, then cast us a wrinkled smile as he strode toward the group.

"I see Gallahorn found you both swiftly," he said and gave the raven an appreciative pat on the head. "*Chanerr machet,* young Howllords. I was worried you may get lost in this new territory, so I sent him out to find you."

"*Find,*" the raven, Gallahorn, croaked with pride. "Did *find.* *Sa*-me face."

The man chuckled. "Yes, good work. I suppose telling you they were twins made them easier to spot, eh?"

I stared at the miserly raven, asking, "Is that your messenger?"

Alex questioned next, "Does that mean you're a Reaper?"

The man gave a scraggly guffaw, rubbing a knuckle over Gallahorn's beak. "Yes, and yes, Howllords. I am Sir Gale, your new Necrovoking instructor—as well as your combat trainer in tomorrow's elective. Though, my days as a Death Knight are long past me, I'm afraid. These old bones aren't what they used to be. I use my knowledge to teach the next generation. Best to let the youthful handle the demon-slaying, eh?" He winked in a jolly chuckle. "Now then, why don't you both introduce yourselves to everyone? It's a rare day indeed when we get a new Evocator in the palace grounds. Let alone two." He looked at me and tossed his chin curiously. "Which one are you, then?"

I swallowed nervously and stammered, "X-Xavier, Sir."

Sir Gale pointed his chin at Alex next. "And your name?"

"Alexander," my brother grumbled as he looked about the crypts lined along the walls. "What exactly do we do at these sort of classes?"

"Is this your first Necrovoking elective?" Sir Gale asked.

We nodded, and I explained, "Our old Academy didn't offer this course. There weren't enough Necrovokers our age to fill up a class."

"We've been self-studying at home," Alex finished.

Sir Gale folded his arms with interest. "Have you, now? Well, we'll see where you both place today, and you let me know if extra tutoring is needed later, hm?" Sir Gale clapped his hands. "Now! Everyone, before we continue with yesterday's practice of weaving NecroSeams, I'd like to see everyone's progress with your resurrection projects. Please bring out the bones I sent you home with and begin building your skeletons."

I watched Lilli and Matthiel reach into Storageboxes that were clipped to their belts. They each pulled out identical, velvet sacks that clattered with small bones hidden inside. They carefully poured the bones on the stone floor before their feet and began twiddling their fingers, violet lights shining from the tips.

The bones quivered and slowly began floating into place like puzzle pieces, engulfed in the same violet lights the two controlled.

I wasn't exactly sure what they were trying to build, but it looked like some sort of rodent.

I peered toward the ashen-haired boy against the column at the far corner of the chamber. He mimicked them with his own pile of bones over there. He yawned as his pieces drifted into place at a slightly faster pace than everyone else.

Willow was the only one with a different set of bones. She struggled to lift a single, tiny piece by her bare toe, managing to place four bones together before two of them collapsed in a wobbling clatter.

"Pathetic," I heard the boy in the corner mutter from the column. He was nearly finished building his skeletal rodent, scoffing at Willow's delayed progress.

Willow's fox ears twitched, straining to ignore him.

Sir Gale came up to Alex and me and handed us two separate sacks of bones. "Since I don't know what level you both are, I'm having you start with toad skeletons. If you can complete this task, you'll move onto rat skeletons."

Death. My stomach twisted. Of course we were starting with resurrections.

Alex and I poured our assigned bones onto the floor by our boots. Sir Gale loomed over us with his arms folded behind his back, watching patiently.

Alex glanced at his toad bones for a mere second, rolled his eyes, then gave a flourishing wave of his hand.

A white Death mark shined bright from under his right knuckles. The bones clacked and clattered in a cyclone of purple light, each piece falling perfectly into place. The skeleton was assembled so quickly, it was over in a blink. Then with the next blink, the bones had muscle, blood, nerves, and skin—

Rrrrbttt!

The soulless toad belched at Alexander's feet, the sound bouncing off the walls as a silence swept through the catacombs.

The chamber grew still.

The other students' mouths hung open. Willow had lost control of her last two pieces during her gaping.

Sir Gale stood in silence for a long, dazed moment. Then he found his wits again and reached into to his Storagebox to fetch another sack of bones.

"Er… right then," he said and placed the new sack of bones before Alex. "Rat skeleton it is—"

Another swirl of violet light from Alexander's fingers, and a living, breathing rat now sat on the ground.

Another moment of swelling silence.

"A-ah… All right…" Sir Gale bit his knuckle in thought. Then snapped his fingers as if an idea struck him. Sir Gale went to the smaller crypts along the walls, stacked on a higher row above the larger tombs. He found a small, stone casket the size of a house-pet and slid the lid open with a heave. After gathering the contents of the casket, he returned with an armful of slightly larger bones. "How about *cat* bones—?"

He didn't have a chance to set them down before my brother evoked his Hallows and snatched the bones out of Sir Gale's arms to assemble them in another whirlwind of light. In a matter of seconds, a furry orange cat now sat alongside the toad and the rat on the floor, all lined up along the edge of the waterway.

They went through this twice more with a large hound's skeleton and a horse skeleton. Just as before, Alexander sailed through the resurrections with little difficulty. Though, the horse took a moment longer to assemble than the smaller animals. It was quite large.

The waterway before Alexander had become a miniature zoo of resurrected animals. They were empty shells of course, there were no souls in those vessels since feral animals didn't keep their ghosts like us shifters. They didn't have NecroSeams tying their souls together.

Sir Gale glanced from animal to animal with a hand cupped to his mouth. Then he smeared the hand down his chin and rubbed his fingers ponderously. "Hm…"

Sir Gale glanced over at the armored ghost Willow had spoken to earlier, cocking an eyebrow at her. "Renna? I know this is unexpected, but would you be willing to lend us your bones today?"

The ghost, Renna, spread open her wispy hands in an encouraging motion. "I'd be honored, Sir Gale."

Sir Gale went to one of the larger crypts on the bottom row of the walls and strained to slide open the stone lid of the heavy sarcophagus with an echoing, grinding scrape.

Sir Gale used his Necrovoking to drag the awaiting skeleton out of the sarcophagus, and he piled the bones around Alexander's feet.

Alex cracked his knuckles. "Finally."

My brother scrutinized the ghost carefully, then altered his gaze from the soul to the bones as he began his assembly.

He used both hands this time, his fingers a beautiful stream of violet lights that wove and tangled around each femur and spinal disk. It took far longer than the animals had, but soon enough, after two careful minutes, the skeleton was complete.

Alex kept his hands raised to the fully assembled puppet, then closed his eyes. He drew in a slow, steady breath through his nose.

Sir Gale and the others watched with rapt intrigue.

Alex exhaled, and the bones grew muscles. Tendons slinked over the bones like oozing jellyfish and stretched taut, nerves and veins latticing like wild vines. Skin boiled to life, concealing the organs and blood. A plume of hair sprouted from the scalp, pore by pore in a flourishing rush of growth.

Finally, Alex gave a push to jumpstart the heart.

The room rippled with impressed gasps as the naked vessel stood in perfect reflection of her wide-eyed ghost.

Alex opened his eyes again and stepped back, folding his arms.

Sir Gale gave a hearty laugh and clapped his hands. "Well done! Very well done indeed!"

The instructor turned to me next. I wanted to vomit.

"Your turn, Xavier," Sir Gale said with misplaced enthusiasm. "Would you like to start with a shifter's skeleton as well?"

The nausea roiled hotter. "E… Erm…" I stared at the toad bones before my feet. A flood of terror shook my arms. "N-no… the toad is… f-f… fine…"

After an unmoving minute, Sir Gale urged, "That's quite all right. Go ahead, then."

I raised a trembling hand to the pile of tiny, unimpressive bones.

I sucked in a deep, deep breath… then *pushed* with all the strength my soul could muster.

Nothing happened.

Sir Gale nodded encouragingly. "When you're ready."

Bloods, he thinks I haven't even started yet. My face heated. Everyone was staring at me, their eyes like hungry vultures. I shook my hand harder, concentrating so intensely, I thought my eyes would pop.

"Any time," Sir Gale said, sounding uncertain.

"I'm… trying…" I gritted my sharpening teeth, my wolf ears growing.

There was no tingling in my soul. There was no rumble or vibration from my chest, no cottony well of warm power shaking my belly.

There was nothing. Nothing but pure, hollow coldness.

When Sir Gale saw that my fingers emitted no violet lights, his brow knitted. "Xavier? What's wrong?"

Tears stung, blurring my view of the bones. I hurriedly rubbed my eyes dry, my voice tight. "I can't do it."

Sir Gale lifted an eyebrow. "Not even one bone?"

I shook my head. "I'm sorry…"

"—Oh, Death, this is rich," the ashen-haired boy muttered from the back column. "His brother's a Bloody genius while he's worse than the hybrid princess. He got the short end of that stick, didn't he?"

Willow glared at him, but before she could retort, Sir Gale clipped, "That's enough, Felix. We're all here to learn. No one journeys along their path at the same pace."

Sir Gale's face softened in sympathy when he turned back to me. *Brilliant.* Now he was looking at me like a poor little puppy with three legs.

"It's all right." Sir Gale clasped an assuring hand on my shoulder. His patronizing tone was worse than if he'd scolded me. "We'll work on it. That's why we're here." He waved at the other five ghosts, signaling them to float over. "In any case, let's continue yesterday's lesson. Everyone, to your assigned ghosts. We'll practice weaving temporary NecroSeams again."

I breathed a sigh of relief. "Finally."

Alex, however, stiffened beside me. His smug expression vanished.

The other students rose from their seats and paired up with the ghosts along the waterway.

I approached my ghost with a much brighter mood now, smiling at the misty figure who nodded to me. This one was a young man looking about twenty, his ears webbed and translucent skin glistening with smooth scales. He looked to be a fish shifter of some sort, but I wasn't sure exactly what species.

I twisted back to Alex, seeing he hadn't moved. His ghost, the armored woman whose vessel he'd just resurrected, waited beside mine in confusion.

Sir Gale frowned. "Alexander? Come along. To your ghost."

Alex's wolf ears grew. He went to his assigned ghost with rigid steps.

"Very good," Sir Gale cleared his throat. "Now, as before, everyone shake hands with your specter and thank them for volunteering to help with your education."

A resounding 'thank you' rippled through the chamber, and the students shook hands with the wispy figures.

I clasped my ghost's hand and thanked him kindly, his watery skin cold in my grip.

Alex hesitated beside me. He lifted a trembling hand to his ghost and reached for her spectral fingers—

Her skin misted through Alex's hand without contact.

Everyone stared at him.

Alex shrank.

"What in Death…?" the kind boy, Matthiel, murmured.

"It…" Lilli began skeptically. "It just slipped right through?"

"Like air?" Willow's brow furrowed. "But every Necrovoker can touch ghosts—"

"Yes, well, apparently the Seamstress missed one of us, didn't She?" Alex snapped.

Willow hesitated. "What do you mean?"

His face turned scarlet, wolf ears curled tight. "I was… born without soul-touch."

Everyone quieted.

"Pfffft—!" The boy in the back, Felix, cupped his eyes as he broke into hysterical laughter. "Seamstress, they're *both* defective!"

"*Enough*, Felix," Sir Gale clipped. He turned to Alex with a pitying look. "Alexander, no Necrovoker is born without soul-touch. I'm sure it could feel that way if you find it difficult, but we can find ways to improve in that area. Sometimes it takes a tighter grip, you see. Perhaps if you focus on how the spectral mist feels around your skin—"

"You're not listening," Alex plunged his hand into his assigned ghost and waved it around like a madman. "I can't touch them *at all*." He stepped inside the ghost without a single, misty ripple. "I can feel the cavern air, I can feel the wind when I'm outside, but ghosts? No. Xavier tells me ghosts are supposed to feel cold to us. But I feel nothing. *They* feel nothing. Neither of us can feel a tiny breeze."

The ghost spun about with Alex still standing within her, stammering, "H… he's right. I don't feel a thing."

"Exactly," Alex huffed, stepping out from the specter. "In this area, I may as well be Hallowless. But that's not my job, anyway. *This* is my job."

Alex shot a furious hand toward the crypts beside the opened sarcophagus. My brother's hands shimmered with violet light. The many sarcophagi rattled wildly, then all of them open on their own, pushed by the boney skeletons that were trapped inside.

Five sets of clattering skeletons rose out of their tombs and clambered toward our group, causing the other students to yelp and shuffle behind Sir Gale.

Some of the puppets' bones were dressed in cobwebs as if modeling evening scarves, their joints clicking and clacking as each appendage was tethered in place by the light of Alexander's Hallows. My brother waved his hands like a writhing conductor to his orchestra, violet lights zipping and streaming all around the corpses until, after a mere five minutes, all six of them were fully resurrected bodies alongside the vessel he'd raised earlier.

Sir Gale's mouth hung open.

Alex folded his arms in a glower and tossed his head toward me. "Xavier?"

I nodded and evoked my violet Hallows—the half I actually wielded—and crossed my hands before my face. Then I flung them outward with a flourish. My fingers twisted and turned and braided the strings of light that flowed from my fingers as if pulled from a spindle, and all at once, each ghost's chest gleamed with shimmering violet threads. They were temporary NecroSeams, woven all at once in the six ghosts.

I held onto the strings of light and clenched my fists—*yanking* the ghosts by their Seams and thrust them into their awaiting bodies. I went through the circle of vessels one by one, acting swiftly as if trapped in a waltz, and stitched the souls' NecroSeams onto their beating hearts before tying each one securely.

I finished in a long, satisfied exhale.

Sir Gale stood as rigid as the marble sculpture of the Seamstress beside him. They all did.

Sir Gale ran a dazed hand through his hair between his elk antlers. It took him several moments longer before his wrinkled gaze hardened.

"You two." His tone grew dark suddenly. "Bring your parents to your combat elective tomorrow. I wish to speak with them… You are dismissed."

Alex and I paused.

"*Go*," he snapped, jabbing a sharp finger toward the tunnel we'd come from. He didn't look at us, his eyes stuck on the resurrected vessels who were all murmuring in confusion. "Out. Now."

We both stuttered, "R… right now—?"

"Immediately," he snarled. He shoved his hand into his Storagebox and ripped out a notepad, scribbling a message on it. When he was done, he tore out the lone parchment and shoved it into my hand. "Give this to your parents. Bring them to the training grounds outside tomorrow morning. Understand?"

We shivered. "Y-yes, Sir…"

"Good. You are *dismissed*." He shoved us toward the exit, still not looking away from the vessels as we rigidly shuffled out of the catacombs.

9

XAVIER

Alex and I waited in the drawing room of our manor, sinking into our individual seats while we waited for Mother and Father to return home.

The grandfather clock's methodical *tick, tick, ticks* made each second seem like ages until we finally heard Thateus open the front doors. Mother's clattering, armored footfalls echoed from the foyer.

With Sir Gale's note in my quaking hands, Alex and I melted out of our chairs to greet Mother.

She had slipped off her silver helm and tucked it under an arm, letting her grey braid fall over a shoulder as her wolf ears perked toward us.

"Boys?" Mother questioned. "What are you doing up so late? For Death's sake, I know Yulia stayed at the old estate with your grandfather, but you can't rely on a Dreamcatcher to remind you when it's time for bed forever."

"Y… yes, my lady…" we said shakily.

"If you're waiting for your father, there's no point." She yawned, her wolf tail swishing idly around her legs. "He's in an important conference with Daniel and the king. He'll likely be out well past midnight. There was a demon horde stalking the city today, so they had to be dealt with. Two of the beasts fled to the sewers, unfortunately, so the hunt will continue when…"

One of her pointed ears flicked when she saw the note in my trembling fingers.

"What is that?" she demanded.

The note rattled in my shivering hands as I held it up to her and explained, "S… S-Sir Gale wished for us to… t-t-to give you this…"

Alex added in a trembling voice, "He w-wants to speak with you and Father tomorrow…"

Mother snatched the note from me. She squinted as she read, disturbingly silent. Then she crushed the note in her fist.

"*What*," Mother roared, her wolf ears curling back, "*did you do?*"

Alex and I cowered under her glare. "N-nothing!"

"Nothing my tail! Her curling tail flicked for emphasis, and she shook the crumpled note in our faces. "Do you two have any idea how busy your father and I are? I have an entire country's military to manage! I have demons loose in the city's sewers that need exterminating! I don't have time for my sons to cause trouble in school and make me waste my time speaking with their *teacher!*"

She chucked the crumpled note at the wall and stormed off, dismissing us with a terse hand. "To your rooms! We will deal with this irritation tomorrow…"

Alex and I quickly bowed and fled upstairs, hiding in our separate chambers with our bones still rattling.

I thunked my elbows on my desk in my private chambers, giving a shiver. "Well, at least we're alive."

The nearby vent on the wall reverberated with Alexander's voice from the other side. "*For now. There's still tomorrow. And that's with Father.*"

I folded my arms over my desk and groaned. "Bloods, I wish we could ask Willow to use that crystal ball of hers to see what Sir Gale is so angry about."

"*How would that help?*" He snorted. "*We'd still have to live through it personally afterward.*"

I sighed. "Fair."

"And for Death's sake, are you ready yet? Aiden and Nathaniel have waited long enough."

"Oh—yes." I shot up and grabbed the textbook on the desk. Then I swiped my burgundy cloak off the wall-hook, strapped my Storagebox to my belt, and shoved my textbook into its gummy surface. The book shrank the moment it sank into the see-through, blue Storagebox and dropped to the bottom of the pile of items I had stored inside it.

I hurried to the balcony doors and slid them open. Alex had stepped out to his own balcony next door, and we exchanged a nod as we climbed over the rail and made our way down the vine-covered lattices that went all the way down to the backyard. We touched down at the same time and walked side by side toward the western side of the yard.

"Aiden said the new cemetery is over here?" I asked Alex.

"Yes," he confirmed and tugged his vermillion cowl over his face. We passed a large boulder, and he backpedaled, pointing at the boulder. "Oh, and this is where Lilli tackled me."

My brow furrowed. "She tackled you?"

"She saw me looking around for a feral lizard and thought I was a snooping thief." He grimaced, continuing forward. "I almost caught the little thing, then she came barreling down and knocked me to the dirt." He rubbed his gut tenderly. "Gave me a good Bloody bruise."

We crossed the iron fence that separated the backyard from our cemetery, and I followed Alex through the many well-kept plots and gravestones, rounding a dwarfed willow tree that leaned sideways by a trickling stream of fogging water.

"Aiden says if we follow this stream," Alex explained, "it goes straight through the iron fence *and* stone fences of our backyard as well as the royal gates. The stones open at the bottom of the fence into a canal. We should be able to fit through it and follow the stream. He says it leads directly into town."

"Brilliant." I scratched my neck, hesitant. "But before we go, I wanted to test out that new Evocation I read about in our

Necrovoking textbook. I need a ghost for it, so I was hoping Aiden or Nathaniel could help."

"The sensory-illusions?" Alex asked curiously. "Do you need a ghost for that? I thought it's supposed to work on living souls as well?"

"The book suggests to start with a ghost directly." I reached into my Storagebox and pulled out my Necrovoking book. I settled under the willow tree by the stream and flattened onto my stomach, flipping open the book. I leafed through the pages until I reached the chapter I had bookmarked with a crinkled leaf.

Chapter Twelve, the page read, *Sensory-Illusions of the Soul.*

I traced the passage with my finger and read aloud, "If this is your first time attempting this Evocation, it is suggested to begin with a deceased soul, *un*-resurrected, to ensure that flesh and bone do not interfere with your magic's effectiveness."

Alex crouched beside me. "Hm. Well, I guess we'll have to wait for them to show up—"

"Wait no more!" a new voice piped behind us.

The two misty ghosts of Aiden and Nathaniel floated above us. Aiden's wiry arms were crossed, his feathered hair tossed to one side and wings fluttering soundlessly behind him.

Nathaniel floated beside him with one meaty fist on his burly side, his rounded bear ears swiveling as he gave us a bearded grin.

"There you are," Alex and I greeted the ghosts. "We thought *we* were late."

The burly ghost, Nathaniel, shrugged his thick shoulders. "We be checkin' the premises fer assassins. Had ta be sure it was clear 'n all."

Alex grunted. "Makes sense. Maybe if we're lucky, one of the changes over here will be no more threats to our lives."

Aiden chuckled as his spectral wings gave a flutter. "Fewer, yes. But when both parents are in such high positions, one will never be rid of threats completely." He waved his wispy hands. "Oh, enough gloomy chatter! Shall we be off? We've a grand city to venture!"

"Oh, before that," I interrupted, raising my Necrovoking textbook to the ghost's faces, peeling open the pages to show them the current chapter. "Could you help me try this Evocation?"

The ghosts peered at the textbook curiously.

"Ah." Aiden's head cocked when he read the chapter title. "Sensory-illusion?"

Nathaniel whistled. "That's mighty advanced, Young Sir... That be fer older Necrovokers."

I shrugged. "I've already gotten through the previous chapters. This is the next one on the list."

Nathaniel lifted an eyebrow. "Ye mean the next one that ain't about raisin' corpses?"

I flushed. "If I can't *do* those Evocations, I may as well focus on the half I *can* do."

Nathaniel gave a bearded smile. "Aye, I s'ppose that be reasonable." He crouched down beside me and held out a ghostly arm. "How 'bout I be yer first practice partner?"

I smiled wide and eagerly sat up, Alex pushing to his feet to give us space. I looked around for some sort of texture I could use as a reference.

There was a patch of Candle Lilies by the trunk of the willow tree. Candle Lilies were waxy, white flowers with long anthers spilling from their curled petals. These anthers could be lit with fire, much like a candle wick, which is where it got its namesake.

I plucked a Candle Lily by its stem and kept it in one hand while tracing the passage of instructions with a finger from the other.

"Let's see..." I read from the page aloud, "Begin with a soft texture to drag down your bare arm... keep the sensation fresh in mind. Then, while placing your hand on the targeted soul, project the sensation onto them." I cleared my throat. "Very well."

I rolled up my left sleeve, then placed that hand on Nathaniel's extended, spectral arm—the hand that had my birthmark of three, black diamonds under my left knuckles.

Nathaniel's ghostly flesh rippled under my palm like watery mist, cold to the touch and so thin I could squeeze harder to sink my whole hand inside. But I kept my fingers lightly floating on the surface instead.

With my left hand touching Nathaniel's wispy skin, I dragged the Candle Lily's waxy petals over that arm with my right hand, trailing

down to my wrist, as the text instructed. I drew in a deep breath…
and evoked my Hallows.

My tri-leaf birthmark gleamed white under my knuckles. The
diamonds shifted and twirled off to the side, two new marks
appearing beside it in the shape of two scythes standing back
to back. This was my Death mark; the mark that shined when I
evoked my Hallows like this. All Evocators had a mark, all different depending on your Hallows element. Since mine was the
element of death, I naturally had a Death mark. Well, half the
time, anyway.

As the magic tingled through my soul, the sensation tunneled
through me like a storm and leaked out of my palm in the form of
licking, violet lights. The lights sank into Nathaniel's ghost, and I
focused on the waxy petals that I'd brushed over my arm gently.

Nathaniel's gaze widened. "Well, color me impressed," he praised
with a toothy grin. "I feel it as surely as if it be on me own resurrected skin."

I beamed and dismissed my Hallows. The violet lights faded, and
my Death mark dimmed black and returned to its original, tri-leaf
of diamonds under my knuckles.

Nathaniel nodded proudly. "Aye. Ye be a quick study, Young Sir.
Ye may not be a whole Necrovoker, but ye sure are strong with the
half ye got."

My smile faltered, and I thumped the book closed before putting
it back in my Storagebox, where it shrank and fell to the bottom.

"Thank you…" I mumbled, my heart sinking. "Perhaps… if I get
strong enough with *this* half, I might eventually get the other half,
or…" My wolf ears grew and folded to my neck.

Nathaniel shared a saddened look with Aiden. "Er, sure ye
will, lad," Nathaniel offered. He didn't sound any more convinced
than I was.

I sighed and pushed to my feet with a forced a smile. "Shall we
go see this city's nightlife?"

Aiden clapped his intangible hands soundlessly. "Ah, yes! You'll
love the markets this time of night! We'll start with the…"

Aiden chatted on as he and Nathaniel led the way down the stream. I lagged behind, a nauseating pit churning my stomach.

Alex came and bumped his shoulder into mine, flicking me an understanding look; a look that said I wasn't alone.

I twitched a grin, but it didn't last long. We walked side by side while following the ghosts out of the cemetery.

10

LILLI

"You should have seen it, Mother!" I squealed, bouncing alongside my mother through the palace corridors as she made her rounds of evening guard patrol. "They resurrected *six corpses!* And even sewed their ghosts to them! All at once! I've never seen anyone our age do that!"

My mother wore her usual silver plate today, the metal clinking as she carried on her patrol, her bat wings bowing to give the ghosts and servants room to pass. She didn't wear her helm, instead tucking it under an arm. Her silky black hair was tied in a pristine bun, just as mine was, though she wore a purple ribbon to tie it together while mine was rose-pink. Mother's beautiful features were entrancing under the cool lamplight in the corridors. She had a delicate nose, pencil-thin eyebrows, sculpted lips the color of amaranth blossoms, slender cheeks, a sharp chin…

I gave a swooning sigh. It was little wonder my father fell for her. Would I ever be as lovely as her?

"Ah, yes," Mother hummed, her pauldron clattering against her armor as she saluted her fellow Reaper guards passing by on patrol. She hefted her helm under an arm. "Alice mentioned her boys were a strange pair with their Hallows. Strange, but… powerful, in their own way." Mother's eyes grew distant. "Though, Alice worries for them. They're certainly capable of great things together, but separately… she says they're crippled. She worries what will happen when they've grown and must venture different paths."

"Will they have to?" I asked. "Can't they just stay together?"

Mother breathed a long sigh through her nose. "Growing up isn't that simple, dear… but I suppose that would be for the boys to decide. And for all of you."

I wasn't sure what she meant, but I bowed my wings, accepting this was the best explanation I was going to get.

A crow swooped down from behind us, alighting on Mother's pauldron and giving a prim caw.

"Ah," Mother greeted her messenger crow, scratching the bird's neck feathers lovingly. "There you are, Twilight. Has Sir Tanner arrived to take over my shift?"

Twilight cawed in affirmation, fluttering his feathers.

Mother stroked a delicate finger over his beak. "Thank you, Twilight. I suppose we should head home, shouldn't we? Lilli?" She turned to me. "Have you finished your duties for the night, here?"

I gave a proud nod, cupping my hands before my skirts. "Yes. I spoke to the royal tailor regarding Willow's gown for the ball. He should be finished by tomorrow evening. I also sharpened and polished her scythe and left it on her vanity in its peaceful form. I may need to go into town tomorrow after school to find something suitable for her hair, perhaps something that will hold it together this time."

Mother's gaze was concerned. "I'm afraid it isn't a grand time to go into town alone, Lilli. There is still a pair of Necrofera on the loose, according to Alice. Why don't I send one of my Reapers to escort you, just in case?"

I crossed my arms. "I wouldn't need escorting if I had my own scythes…"

"We've talked about this." Mother's tone was polite but peeved. She started down the corridor and led the way down a flight of stairs. "Only Reapers are allowed to wield scythes."

"And apprentices," I corrected as I followed her down the stairs. "I've been training with the wooden replicas for years—"

"You aren't officially an apprentice, Lilli," Mother chided, scratching at Twilight's chest feathers and prompting a soft coo from the crow. "You must be chosen by a messenger, first. When your messenger finds you, you can switch to Crystal scythes instead of the wooden replicas."

My bat ears grew, and I hunched over. "*If* one finds me, you mean."

Mother smiled. Then wrapped one of her leathery wings around me to scoot me closer to her as we walked.

"It will find you, Lilli," she assured. "Be patient. It needs time to find you."

"And if I'm not meant to be a Reaper at all? What then? I'll be stuck with useless toothpicks to guard Willow?"

Mother sighed. "Lilli… this isn't something to worry over. What comes to pass is up to the Shepherd of Time and the—"

"—Seamstress of Souls," I recited with a flap of my wings. "She's the one who threads our Bonds with the messengers. I know, Mother. I just…" My wings lowered. "I have a job to do. Willow chose *me* as her Aide, and part of that role is protecting her. But if I'm going to do that, I'll need better… tools."

Mother's brows arched as we stepped onto the main floor of the palace. She slowed to a stop in the corridor. "Lilli…"

"Oh, look who it is," a man drawled behind us suddenly. "The scullery maid and her bastard creature."

Mother and I turned with matching scowls.

The one who'd spoken was an ashen-haired man with milky white eyes that looked much like the Death King's. And of course he would. This was Death Prince Yvann: the King's younger brother. And Felix's father.

There were several lords and ladies surrounding him, all chuckling behind prim hands from Yvann's rude comment.

Mother's gaze was stale at the prince, her tone even. "*Chanerr,* Your Highness. It's good to see some of us are enjoying themselves while the rest of us have vital duties to see to."

"Ah, yes." Yvann tapped a gloved finger to his temple and gave a wry smile. "Those kitchen floors won't scrub themselves, will they?"

The lords and ladies burst with laughter around him.

"Apologize at once!" I demanded, my wings shooting straight up. I stormed toward the group. "My mother is a High Howless now.

She isn't Father's maid anymore. She is captain of the royal guard. You will show her respect—"

"Ew, ew, *ew!*" One of the ladies backed away from me in disgust, batting her hands. "The grimy girl almost touched me! Shoo! Go! Find some other hall to stain!"

My face blistered. "How dare you—?"

"Lilli," Mother clipped behind me. Her tone was sharp enough to halt me where I stood. "Our tasks are finished here. It's time to join your father back home."

I spun back to her with stiff wings. "But they…!"

"Now, Lilli." She turned to leave, striding down the corridor.

I gave a final glare at Yvann, then stuck up my nose and followed at Mother's side.

"Howllord Tessinger must have grody tiles these days," I heard Yvann mutter to the group nastily. "But, to each their own, I suppose. Who am I to judge if he wishes to sleep in filth?"

Their laughter bounced through the corridors as Mother and I left.

Later that night, I melted over my balcony's railing with a deep sigh, my bat wings draping low.

I knew Mother said I shouldn't be bothered by what everyone says about us, but… it was *so* infuriating.

I'll just have to prove them wrong, I decided, pushing up and gripping the rail determinedly. *I will be the very image of poise and nobility! So much so, they can't call us dirty—*

Something crawled over my fingers. I reeled back in a startled yelp.

Oh. It was that grotesque lizard Alexander had been chasing the other day. Or was it a different one?

I glowered at the reptile, its beady eyes blinking up at me.

"Hmph." I crossed my arms. "I don't know why Alexander was so keen on getting his hands on you. You probably *are* filthy."

The lizard cocked its head in reply.

I rolled my eyes. "Bloody ridiculous…"

Though, Alexander did look thrilled for that one second he'd caught it. And he looked anything *but* thrilled today when Sir Gale dismissed them from class…

Separately, they're crippled. My mother's words came to mind, my bat ears growing and folding down. They had looked so miserable…

I bit my lip, glaring at the lizard. Maybe if I caught the lizard for Alexander, just this once, it would cheer him up—?

Craaaw!

A crow suddenly soared down and snatched the lizard in its beak. The black bird alighted on the railing beside me and *crunched* into the lizard with hideous cracks before swallowing the little thing whole and politely preening its feathers.

"Ew…" I suppressed a gag, huffing at the bird impatiently, "Well, I hope it was a fine meal. Now I have to find Alexander a new gift—"

The crow's gaze whipped to my face.

Something snapped in me. I drew in a gasp, my soul filling with a radiating warmth and drawing my soul toward the crow.

Neither of us moved for a long, breathless minute. My heart was bursting so hard, it threatened to crash through my ribs to reach the new crow.

"Are…" I whispered, reaching for the crow with hesitant fingers. "Are you…?"

Craaw!

The crow flapped off the railing and perched on my shoulder, settling there proudly with its chest feather puffed out.

"Oh, you *are* mine!" I squealed with joy and hopped in giddy circles. "I-I-I have a messenger! A real messenger! I *will* be a Reaper…!"

"… keep quiet! Someone's going to hear us…"

I paused, the familiar voice catching my bat ears in the distance. My hearing was amplified when they were grown, and this sounded rather distant.

It ounded like Alexander.

I pet my new messenger from my shoulder and searched the grounds outside. There, in the royal cemetery next to my yard, I spotted two cloaked figures sneaking about, two ghosts accompanying them.

My brow furrowed. "The twins are out at this hour?"

They were heading toward the back of the cemetery where the canals led into the city.

But Mother said there were demons in the city somewhere. They couldn't go alone. It was too dangerous without any…

I straightened, an idea hitting me. *Didn't Mother say I could have scythes after I had my own messenger?*

I glanced at my new messenger crow from my shoulder. "Uhm, excuse me, but… could you help me with something?"

My crow fluttered its wings dutifully, my soul tightening with a sudden feeling of confirmation. I took that as a 'yes'.

I spread my wings and quietly soared off my balcony. After a short flight, I crouched onto my parent's balcony outside their bedchambers.

I kept low to the stone floor, and whispered to the crow, "My mother keeps her scythe blades in their spherical forms when she isn't using them. They look like little metal balls on a necklace. Can you sneak in there and get those for me, little messenger? Without waking my parents? It's important."

The crow bobbed its head, and I kissed its beak before gently cracking open the glass door. The bird hopped inside, creeping with quiet talons into the dark room.

The crickets whined all around me, my heart beating louder than normal.

Clink!

I nearly yelped in fright at the noise, but I calmed after seeing it was just my crow returning with a necklace. On its silvery chain were two small, metal spheres with rippling designs etched over its glowing-blue surface.

"That's it!" I hissed happily, clipping the necklace round my neck. I blew out a hard breath. "All right… now we're ready. We'll be back before Mother notices they're gone."

I leapt off their balcony, spread my leathery wings, and soared after the boy's retreating figures as my new messenger and I followed them into the canals.

WILLOW

Fire shredded the ballroom.

The flames climbed higher, black smoke thick and suffocating as bodies of the noble guests lay across the marble floor, blood pooling around them.

At the center of it all were the two faces with mismatched, blue-and-clear eyes.

I woke in a frightened scream, shooting upright in bed as my ashen hair fanned around me in a messy tangle.

Jewel chirped and fluttered off the blackwood headboard. She hopped onto my head and twittered at me in concern.

"Seamstress," I puffed shakily, slipping out of bed with wobbly legs. I made my way to the crystal ball set on my vanity, mounted on its dais. "Was that a vision…?"

As Jewel alighted on the crystal ball, I sat on my vanity stool and placed my hands on the clear orb, evoking my prophetic Hallows. Azure light bloomed from my palms and leaked into the crystal. It billowed into smoke, the burning scene flickering within. The twins appeared next, wafting in and out of focus until…

My Hallows cut off, prompting a sharp headache at my skull. I rubbed my temples. Jewel hopped off the crystal ball and fluttered to my shoulder, nuzzling her beak on my neck.

"Mother of Death," I cursed. "What do those twins have to do with that vision?"

I rose and drifted out to the corridors. Maybe some tea from the kitchens would clear my mind? I yawned while stepping down a spiraling stairwell, climbing down to the first floor toward the kitchens. But when I arrived at the large arching doors of the dining hall, I saw they were already cracked open and spilling with light.

"You should have seen the half-breed," a voice echoed from inside. "She *still* can only make red fire—even five-year-olds can make orange. You should have seen her at last week's training, she very nearly passed out from *one* flame."

A flood of chuckles bounced through the hall.

I peeked inside, staying hidden. There were a handful of young lords and ladies lounging around the blackwood dining table. At the head was my ashen-haired cousin:

Prince Felix.

His large Songcrow was perched on his shoulder and gave a low-pitched whistle in agreement. His crow was the size of a toy dog, like most Songcrows, which only bonded with members of the royal Death family. Felix's messenger was the same size as my father's Songcrow, as well as my uncle Yvann's, as well as… well, *every* ancestor that came before me.

I glanced at Jewel from my shoulder. My own, tiny Songcrow was an oddity. She was the smallest anyone had ever seen—so small, my father said he hadn't been sure she was a crow at all when she first bonded with me.

"She can't even resurrect a *toad* carcass," Cousin Felix snorted, his Songcrow flaring its neck-feathers from his shoulder. He speared his fork into a cube of lamb and circled it in a sneering gesture. "The rest of us have already moved on to rat skeletons. She's so far behind, it's a wonder the council hasn't revoked her status as heiress. I'm telling you now, that hybrid will damn the caves. We've never had a Relicblood this weak before. Bloods, *none* of the realms have ever had such a miserable Evocator for a ruler."

My stomach squeezed, his company's chuckles dimming as I ran off.

Jewel followed me when I dashed outside to the gardens. I rubbed my eyes raw while letting the chilled air calm me.

"I am not weak," I whispered. With a sharp inhale, I cupped my hands, focusing on the burning embers churning in my soul, pushing out red flames over my palms. "I… am… Death. I have the soul of a great Evocator. A great Relicblood… I can make orange fire."

I stared at my large droplet of crimson flames. It danced over my palms and rolled upward with a ribbon of smoke.

My fox ears grew and curled back. "I can make orange fire…!"

I shoved my Hallows harder, my focus strengthening. My red fire flickered hotter, rippling into a large roar, its hue brightening ever so slightly with a small, glorious splash of yellow—

Puff!

The fire snuffed into smoke. My soul seized with a painful, icy vengeance. I collapsed on all fours and heaved for breath over the grass.

I can't do it. Tears flooded, and I curled up. *I really am a mistake.*

Jewel twittered softly by my ear, rubbing my cheek with her beak. I scooped her in my hand, quivering from the new cold filling my soul. My fire needed time to rekindle after pushing myself like that. I was lucky I hadn't blacked out this time.

"What am I doing wrong, Jewel…?" I asked the tiny crow. "Am I just… broken?"

Jewel chirped and cocked her head. Then she lifted her tailfeathers as if sensing something. A spark of confusion strummed our Bond. She motioned her beak toward the royal cemetery in the distance.

"Jewel?" I sniffed, rubbing my eyes dry.

Jewel hopped in my palm, twittering urgently and throwing her head toward the cemetery again.

"All right, all right." I pushed up, exhaling hard as I started down the cobbled path. At least she was giving me a little distraction. "Clearly you want me to go to the cemetery. But I don't know why you're so…"

"… think there's a vendor with candied cherries down there?" a faint voice caught my grown fox ears. "They had one back home before, they were the best! Oh, oh! Or maybe roasted almonds! Or fizzy drinks…!"

Several figures were strolling through the cemetery, following the small stream that trickled between gravestones. Among my ancestors' floating ghosts, there were a pair of souls leading two cloaked boys. One boy was now pulling on his cowl, and I barely saw a glimpse of Xavier's face before it was cast in shadow.

"The twins?" My brow furrowed, and Jewel chirped in confirmation. She must have sensed them over there somehow. Messengers seemed to feel things we shifters couldn't, at times.

When the twins' group reached the grounds' tall stone wall, the two ghosts phased through in a quiet ripple of mist, and the brothers ducked into the arched opening that led into the canals.

Then I spied a bat-winged figure dressed in a pink cloak sneaking after them from above.

"And Lilli's following them…" I bit my lip. I remembered the dream I had of the twins earlier. The vision of them at the center of tall, dangerous flames…

I flicked my eyes at my little crow. "Jewel, could you fetch my enchanted earcuff and Storagesphere?" I asked, a small feeling of dread pinching my nerves. "We're going on a small trip into town."

11

XAVIER

The ghosts of Aiden and Nathaniel led us through the bustling streets of Low Rastiria.

As the Grand Capital of Grim, the city was far more crowded than our old city. There were ghosts and living citizens packing the roads, horses clopping over the stones as they pulled hovering coaches through the town. Vendors shouted from their booths and bargained with patrons, children played with sparklers and giggled with delight, bronze-skinned tourists from the surface enjoyed Grim's spicy cuisine and celebrated with bottles of our local wine.

But most stunning of all was how each gothic-spired building glittered with electric, violet lights.

The bulbs hung from every tree and gutter, outlining windowsills and spiraling down streetlamps in twinkling swirls. It looked like every Floating Light of Grim had turned purple and fallen from the cavern's ceiling. They dusted the town with their beauty in a mesmerizing sight I'd never forget.

We passed under an enormous clocktower that loomed in the center of the city. It was attached to the largest Harmonist temple I'd ever seen. The holy structure's coned rooftops shot toward the cavern ceiling like sharp claws, the deep-blue Floating Lights drifting around its shingles in the overhanging mist. Its arched windows were stain-glass murals depicting each of the five Gods of Land, Sky, Ocean, Dream and Death.

Death's deity filled the largest window at the center of the temple, featured right above the doors. In it, the Seamstress of Souls had her ashen hair flowing freely, her white eyes peering at us as a crow sat on her shoulder. With her left hand, she held a scythe whose glowing blade arched over her head. With her right hand, she delicately pinched a sewing needle with a radiant, violet thread: the NecroSeam that stitched our souls to our vessels.

Behind the Seamstress was her holy Relic: the Willow of Ashes. It was depicted as an enormous, radiant tree that towered over everything. Its white bark and leaves flaked with ash that spilled from the blue flames curling around the entire window like an elegant frame.

The Willow of Ashes... I marveled at the stain-glass artwork in wonder. It was as beautiful as the fables described it. They say the Willow was the bridge between our mortal plane and the realm of the Gods; where her holiness came to bring new souls to their next lives—and take them from their expired ones.

"Alex," I murmured to my brother as we walked by the glorious temple. "Do you think it's real? The Willow of Ashes?"

Alex shrugged. "How should I know? The clerics say Death's Relic has been lost for thousands of years, along with the other realms' Relics."

I hummed. "Maybe they just haven't looked hard enough?"

"Haven't looked hard enough?" Alex snorted. "For thousands of years?"

Aiden chuckled with a flutter of his translucent wings ahead of us. "Now, now, Alexander. Don't be so quick to doubt, eh? A mystical tree can be quite... mystifying. Of course it would hide itself from the eyes of mortals."

Nathaniel swiveled a spectral bear ear in his direction, not so convinced. "What're ye ramblin' about, feather-brains? It's a bloomin' tree. If no one's seen a trace o' it in a thousand years, then it ain't real."

Aiden muttered, "Always the cynical one, you are..."

Aiden and Nathaniel led us to the central marketplace.

Seamstress! I'd never seen so many different shifters! Most had the usual Grimish grey skin and native hair colors of black, white, and grey—but there were also an unusually high amount of surface tourists with hair of nearly every color imaginable. I supposed it made sense to have an influx of tourists two days before Death's Festival, though.

Every shifter was bursting with celebration. There were teens and adults stumbling out of taverns with giddy smiles, shop owners displaying all sorts of festive gowns and jewelry in their windows, and…

—A glinting light flashed over my eye from the jewelry shop's window.

Behind the glass, there was a round silver bell. It had delicate etchings on it, polished so splendidly I could see my mismatched eyes in its mirror-like surface.

A bell… I marveled at the glistening thing, a thought striking me.

I twisted to Alex and the ghosts. "Doesn't the God of Dreams have a bell?" I asked. "On his holy shepherd's crook?"

Aiden and Alex shrugged.

Nathaniel swiveled a misty bear ear and rumbled thoughtfully, "Aye, that be one o' his sacred symbols."

"Perfect." I grinned and went into the shop, using a bit of my allowance to purchase the bell. I walked out with it wrapped in a box, then looked around the marketplace for a tailor's booth of some sort.

When I found one not too far, I hurried over with the bell. The tailor was a man with white-and-black striped tiger ears and a long tail to match. His round ears perked when I came up to his booth, his smile wrinkling his cheeks.

"*Chanerr nohkosch*, young lord," the tailor greeted and cupped his hands. "How can I help you?"

"Do you have any ribbons?" I asked. "A long one?"

The tailor's tiger ears swiveled back curiously. "How long, my young lord?"

"One long enough to hold a *lot* of hair." I stretched my arms out to demonstrate. "Hair that trails behind you."

The tailor's smile widened, his cheeks crinkling like leather. "Ah, there's only one shifter in town with hair that long. Looking to get Her Highness Willow a gift for her *Rae'u Shelic*, young lord?"

I blushed. "Well…"

"Not to worry. I've got just the thing." He rummaged through a basket of ribbons on the counter behind him.

When he twisted back to me, he held out a very long, black ribbon. It was made of silk and decorated with silver butterflies that trailed all the way down its length.

"They say that Death loves butterflies," the tailor hummed as he slid two boney fingers over the glossy ribbon gingerly. "Every incarnation. This would normally be used as trim for a gown, but I should think it's long enough to keep Her Highness's hair up."

"It's perfect," I beamed. "How much?"

The tailor shrugged blithely. "Normally, I'd charge two silver Tallohs. But since this is for Her Highness Death, let's call it three copper rohten."

I fished out three copper coins from my Storagebox and *clinked* them on the counter. "Thank you. Could I also borrow a needle and thread? I promise to return them."

His brow raised, but he didn't object. The tailor fetched a needle and spool of black thread and handed them to me.

I opened the box with the silver bell I'd just purchased. Next, I fed the long ribbon through the metal ring attached to the bell and tied it in a strong knot at the center of the ribbon. Then I pinched the needle and thread and stitched the knot together to keep it in place, looping each stitch with a well-practiced knot.

The tailor watched me from the counter and gave an impressed hum. "My, what clean stitchwork… You'd make a fair Seamster yourself, young lord."

"I'm a Necrovoker," I said absently, focusing on the sewing. "I had to practice on real thread before learning to stitch NecroSeams."

When I tied off the last knots, I gave the bell a testing jingle and smiled. "Perfect. Thank you for the help." I handed back the needle and spool of thread.

"My pleasure, young lord." He winked. "Best of luck winning Her Highness's favor."

My face warmed, but I mumbled, "Th-thank you."

"Ah! Wait." He snapped his fingers as if having an idea. "You'll need a proper presentation, won't you?"

He rummaged behind the counter and gave me a long box to put the ribbon and bell in, then wrapped it with black paper that glittered with silver designs.

"There you are," he chuckled and spread his arms in a flourish. "A gift fit for royalty."

"Thank you again, sir." I tucked the gift into my Storagebox, bowed respectfully, and trotted off with a wave. "*Chanerr Vith!*"

I watched him return the wave with a wrinkled smile before he turned to the next customer.

After a short run, I found Alex and the ghosts again.

"Sorry," I panted. "I'm done."

Alex scowled at me. "What was that about?"

I shrugged. "Her Highness's *Rae'u Shelic* is on Festival. I wanted to get her something."

Alex rolled his eyes. "Whatever. Can we get some roasted almonds already?"

WILLOW

I peered around a corner building to watch the twins in the marketplace, squinting so hard my lids ached. "Why was he speaking to a tailor—*ouch!*"

A passing woman stepped on my long, disguised hair. Her sharp heel snagged one of the strands.

The woman stopped and gasped, "Oh, I'm terribly sorry, dear! Here, let me…" She awkwardly peeled off my grey hair caught in her heel. Then she saw the full *length* of my hair. "My goodness, Howless, you've a drapery there, haven't you?"

Howless?

I preened. She didn't recognize me with my illusion! She thought I was any regular noblewoman.

I quickly gathered my hair in my arms before someone else walked on it, and flashed her a tight smile. "Y-yes…! I… I'm growing it out, hah, hah…!"

The woman glanced round, her lips pulling into a concerned frown. "You're awfully young to be out here alone. Where are your parents, dear?"

"I, er…" I hurried to think of a reply. "I'm… looking for them. Yes, I lost them. In the crowd. Just now."

She had a pensive look. "I see… What is your name, little Howless?"

"It's… er…" My fox ears grew and burst with panic. I blurted. "Lilli. It's… Lilli."

Bloods, why was that the first name that came to mind? Lilli wouldn't be happy about that, surely.

"Well, Howless Lilli." The woman crouched down with a kind smile. "Why don't we look for your parents together?"

I gave a nervous laugh and backed away. "Oh, that's… that's quite all right. They, er, told me where to find them if we separated—I really should be going there. Now."

"Perhaps I should escort you there—*wait…!*"

I dashed off, jumping into the crowd and hurrying into an alleyway. I hid behind a barrel of potato skins, peeking over it. I watched the woman hurry through the markets to search for me.

Death, that was close.

My heart was still thumping in my fox ears, sure it would pop out of my throat. I sucked in a breath, then blew it out in a calming exhale.

Now… where did those twins go?

I peered around the markets, but couldn't find them. The crowd had shifted while I was distracted and they vanished somewhere in there.

"Drat." I glanced at Jewel who fluttered by my head. "Where did they go?"

"—that's what *I* want to know," a girl huffed beside me.

I whirled, bumping the barrel and causing some potato skins to fall on my head. The bat-winged Lilli was standing next to me with her arms crossed.

"I lost track of them, too," Lilli said bitterly. "I can't even find them from the rooftops."

I grinned at her. "I see you wanted to find out what they were up to also."

"Well, I couldn't let them go without some kind of protection." She stuck up her nose, but I caught the hint of a blush coloring her cheeks. She didn't acknowledge it, of course. She only sniffed and tucked a strand of her silky black hair behind an ear. "My mother said there were demons on the loose out here somewhere. They don't have any scythes to deal with them."

I cocked an eyebrow at her. "Neither do you."

She flicked her orange eyes away. Then twiddled with a silver chain round her neck, which dangled with two glowing spheres.

I went cold.

"Lilli," I began, "are those… scythe-spheres?"

Lilli's cheeks flushed as pink as her gown. "Yes."

"You have your own scythes now?"

She swallowed. "N… not exactly."

"You stole your mother's scythes—?!"

"Borrowed!" She slapped her hands over my mouth and hushed, "I *borrowed* them…! I was worried about the boys, all right? I didn't know you were following them, too!"

"Lilli! You're not allowed to have any scythes! It's against the law—!

Craw! Craaaw!

A crow suddenly swooped down from the air and perched along Lilli's shoulder, sitting poised there like a duchess awaiting applause.

I stared at the crow. At first, I assumed it was one of her parents' messengers. But after closer inspection…

"Wait!" I gasped. "That's not Twilight! *Or* Dawn!"

Lilli couldn't contain her elated smile now. She preened as she scratched the crow's chest feathers. "This is *my* new messenger. Willow, meet Dusk. She came just tonight. So, technically, I'm not breaking the law." She crossed her arms. "A messenger makes me an official Reaper Apprentice. So I'm legally allowed to have scythes."

I gave her a flat stare. "Your mother is still going to kill you."

She yielded to a small quiver. "N… not if she doesn't find out."

Priiiiiiiwiwiwiwi!

Jewel suddenly gave an earsplitting shriek, so high-pitched, it made Lilli and me cup our throbbing ears in pain.

Craw! Craw! Craaaaaw!

Lilli's new messenger, Dusk, started cawing and screeching something fierce as well.

"Jewel!" I shouted over her relentless hollers as the crow buzzed in circles round my head. A sudden flood of terror slammed through our Bond. "Jewel, what—?!"

Sirens blared throughout the marketplace. They were even louder than Jewel. Then a woman shrieked from the crowd.

Lilli and I shared a pale look.

Chaos struck the markets. Shifters dashed away from all directions, shoving each other aside and leaping over those who'd tripped and fallen.

My fox ears grew and dropped to my neck, pulse thundering.

"Death!" Lilli shouted, her bat ears growing as she plucked the two scythe-spheres from her necklace. She pressed her thumbs over the etched Sealing Runes on the metal balls, which melted in her palms like liquid silver. They took the shape of two short-handled, crooked scythes, which she now gripped with a panicked glare. "I knew it…!"

A boy's scream pierced through the noise behind me.

I found the cloaked boy scuttling backward on all fours in the middle of the marketplace. When his burgundy cowl fell to his shoulders, I saw his face.

It was Xavier.

A shadow loomed over him. His mismatched gaze lifted to the roof of a vendor's abandoned booth.

Where a dark, dripping creature stared down at him with glowing eyes.

Its skin slithered over its bone-thin frame like blackened worms. Its creaking limbs were stalky and disjointed, and its crooked maw peeled open to reveal a dangerously sharp row of fangs.

Skririririririiiii!

Its hideous shriek made my bones tremble.

Then it leapt for Xavier.

"Death!" I broke into a furious dash, quickly reaching into the Storagesphere at my waist and plucked out my diamond-encrusted, ebony hair-stick.

I twirled it between my fingers and pressed my thumb against the engraved Sealing Rune at the middle. The stick shimmered with golden light, radiating out from the rune.

The stick stretched in my hand. It melted outward at both ends until I held a five-foot, metal staff. From the staff's top grew a crystal, curved scythe blade. The crystal's mirror-like surface glowed with a ghostly blue light, which streaked in an afterimage when I cocked it behind me.

"Willow, wait!" Lilli shrieked.

I ignored her, my earcuff slipping off my ear and dropping my disguise as I sprinted faster toward the demon.

XAVIER

The Necrofera leapt off the booth and bounded for me.

I wanted to scream, but my throat cinched. The beast's hideous goopy limbs had me in a terrified silence. All I could do was obey the order to *move*. I scurried backward over the cobblestones, snatching up any loose stones I could find and chucking them at the nightmare coming after me. My stones barely clocked the thing in its squishy skull. It paused for a millisecond but kept returning to the hunt.

I tried shuffling to my feet, but my cloak tangled around my legs. The fabric was caught on the heel of my boot and restricting my freedom. The demon lunged for me, and I managed to kick the side of its muzzle. The blow knocked the beast aside for a moment, but the blackened skin on its snout peeled off and clung to my boot like curdled ink. I almost vomited, but there wasn't time. The beast ripped a horrendous shriek and pounced for me—

A girl's furious scream split above me.

My head snapped up.

Willow appeared out of the grey and jumped over my head in a flying leap. Her long hair flowed in wild curls behind her like a wavering river, a crystal scythe in her grasp.

She slashed her scythe into the beast's sticky chest, a blue after-image streaking the air behind her blade's path. The demon shrieked as it was sliced clean in half. A distinct *snap* sounded from its cracked ribs. Willow must have reaped the thing's NecroSeam in one cut.

The demon's pieces collapsed to either side of Willow. She flicked the creature's black blood off her crystal scythe and panted as she kept a defensive stance in front of me.

The Necrofera's slurping skin began to evaporate. The black mist made a morbid hissing sound as it peeled away from a man's corpse that hid beneath.

It was the rotten soul separating from its vessel. Now, the corpse that had once been the demon returned to his lifeless body—*before* he had transformed. This was the result of a soul that went un-reaped.

I shivered on the stones, staring at the corpse laying inches away from my shaking boots. Bloods, I'd never seen a demon up close before. Let alone, nearly been eaten by one.

And Willow had killed it. Seamstress Cleanse me, she'd *killed* it.

"B-B-B-Bloody Death…" I stuttered, marveling at her looming, scythe-wielding figure. Her hair drifted in the cavern winds as a crowd came to surround us.

I was so rattled that I barely heard Alexander shouting for me as he pushed to the front of the sudden audience.

"Xavier!" Alex ran over and pulled me to my wobbling feet, steadying me by the shoulders. "A-are you all right?! I was pushed down before I could reach you, I-I couldn't see—!"

"I'm… I'm okay," I panted, my gaze still plastered on the princess. "Willow just… S-she just…"

Willow flicked her icy gaze at me from over her shoulder. Good Nira, she looked so *fierce…*

"Are you all right?" Willow asked. She pressed a Sealing Rune on her scythe's staff, and the weapon shrank into a diamond-encrusted stick with a golden glitter.

"I'm… fine—" A dark movement caught my eye behind her. Panic split, and I threw a finger over her shoulder. "B-behind you—!"

Shhling!

Lilli flew into view like a bolt, gripping two scythe blades and *slashing* them into the Fera coming for Willow.

By the time Willow turned to look, Lilli had sliced the beast's chest, severing its NecroSeam. Lilli kicked the gelatinous form to the ground. It was certainly dead, its sticky skin evaporating into mist to reveal the woman's corpse beneath.

"*Willow!*" Lilli clipped, the demon's blood hissing off her scythe blades and evaporating clean. A new crow I didn't recognize glided onto the bat's shoulder and screeched at Willow, as if scolding her alongside Lilli. "Pay attention! Mother said there were two demons!"

Willow rubbed her neck. "Right, right… Thank you, Lilli."

Lilli beamed at that, standing taller. "You're very welcome. It *is* my job."

"—Wait," I blurted, the girl's attention snapping to me now. I hesitated, staring at Lilli's weapons. "I thought only Willow had…?"

"You didn't say you had scythes," Alex finished for me with a scowl. "And I certainly haven't seen you wear those spheres until now. Where did those come from?"

Lilli huffed and had her scythes melt into two small spheres, attaching them to the magnetic holders on her necklace. "That's not important right now. You both need to be more careful—"

"Bloody Death!" someone piped from the crowd. "It's Princess Willow!"

The market burst into a tangle of noise over this.

Shifters poured around her left and right, and Willow shriveled in the center. She tried to run, but she was blocked on all sides, her white fox-ears stuck to her neck.

Death! I quickly unclasped my cloak and threw it over her head, pushing her through the crowd. Alex and Lilli tried to follow after us, but they were swept away in the ruckus.

Willow and I sidled into an empty back alley and hid behind a stack of crates that reeked of spoiled fish. I dropped on my rear in a heavy pant as she lowered beside me, winded.

"Death." Willow hugged her knees and pulled the cloak tight around her grimacing face. "Now Father's going to hear about this…"

I gave a one shouldered shrug, still panting. "At least… at least he'll be glad to hear you managed to kill a demon?"

That made her blink. Then her face cracked with shock. "I did! I killed a demon! I actually killed my first demon!"

"—Willow!" Lilli's voice hollered from the rooftops. Lilli appeared from behind a chimney and soared down to us, helping Willow to her feet. "We need to get back to the palace! Bloods, if my mother finds out I took her scythes, she'll…!" Lilli's bat ears grew, and she ruffled her perfect hair in a miserable groan. "Oh, I'm dead, I'm beyond dead! I'll be lucky to have an Afterlife when Mother is through with me…!"

"Xavier!" Alex called from around the corner of the alley. He came trotting up to us with Aiden and Nathaniel's ghosts floating behind him. "Death, don't…" He slowed to a stop before me and panted over his knees. "Don't just run off like that…!"

I scratched my neck. "S-sorry. But we need to get Willow back to the palace before that mob of admirers finds her back here."

"And how are we going to do that?" Alex thrust a hand at Willow. "That cloak can't hide *all* of that white hair."

Lilli fluttered her wings and offered, "I could fly her back—?"

"*NO!*" Willow squeaked and shuffled behind me. "I'm *not* doing that again, Lilli! Remember the last time you tried that? I nearly fell to my death!"

Lilli snorted. "Only because you kept floundering."

A light chirp echoed through the alley. Willow's tiny crow, Jewel, buzzed around the corner and perched on Willow's extended finger. In Jewel's beak was the princess's silver earcuff, the one that held her illusion.

Willow smiled and took the cuff from the crow. "Thank you, Jewel!"

She slipped on the earcuff. Her hair bled into a charcoal grey, and her azure eyes changed to a deep onyx color. She still wore my cloak for extra veiling and tightened the cowl around her face, then turned to us in a huff. "Ready."

We all gave approving nods, then got the Void out of there.

12

WILLOW

We followed Aiden and Nathaniel back to the palace grounds and ducked under the opening of the canal's stone wall, walking along a trickling stream that ran through the royal cemetery.

I hopped from stepping-stone to stepping-stone in the stream, humming cheerily as my exciting victory from tonight replayed in my memory. The cloak Xavier leant me billowed with every leap. I was in such a blissful daze that I had absently tuned out Lilli's anxious worrying.

"… Bloods, this is terrible, *terrible!* Mother's going to be furious…!" Lilli threw up her hands, her new messenger cawing in response. "Not to mention your father will hear about this if the reporters have anything to say about it! And then *my* father will hear about it, and my *mother* will see me using her scythes, then she's going to Cleanse me and send me straight to the Seamstress on the spot…!"

"… by the Archer, we're dead!" the ghost of Aiden cried. The specter's translucent wings dipped depressively. "We're unequivocally dead!"

"We're already dead, feather-brains," chewed his wispy companion, the bear-eared Nathaniel. "What're they gonna do? Kill us again?"

"Yes!" Aiden smeared his hands over his see-through face. "When they find out we encouraged them, they'll resurrect us, drop us off a cavern pillar, resurrect us again, and feed us to a pack of demons on their next hunt!" He cupped his eyes in a bemoaning weep. "Archer shoot me, we're as good as Fera kibble…!"

As they continued alongside Lilli's panicking, I hopped onto the grass beside Xavier, strutting with pride as I gave him a toothy smile.

"I'm glad I decided to follow you all," I said.

Xavier rubbed his neck in a grimace. "So am I."

Alexander snorted beside him. "Bloody nosy is what you are—*ow!*"

Xavier jabbed an elbow in his brother's ribs. "I'd have been in that demon's stomach if she hadn't followed us."

Alexander blanched. Then he scowled and looked away, his grown wolf ears curling back.

"Right…" Alexander grudgingly flicked his mismatched eyes at me. "Sorry… er, thank you… For, you know…" He rolled back a shoulder, glaring away.

I beamed. "You're welcome—*oof!*"

I bumped into something.

It was a Flamedragon. A Flamedragon I knew.

"Raavith?" I questioned with a skeptical brow.

The dragon's long face cocked at me. Then he swung back toward a cluster of faces that circled behind the creature.

"Look who it is, Myra," my father drawled as he and Mother stepped forward from Raavith's feet.

I paled. *All* of our parents were here. Lilli and the twins jolted like I did. My father's white eyes locked onto me like a cleaver poised above fresh meat.

"Why, if it isn't our little Screen celebrity," my father said. "Finally decided to come home after our night of unscheduled publicity, have we?"

My stomach shriveled, and my fox ears grew. "*Ch-Chanerr*, Father… There's a perfectly good explanation for this—"

"No need," the twins' mother growled. "This is hardly the first time my sons have caused trouble. And in one day, at that. I'm hardly surprised."

Their father rumbled. "Perhaps we ought to give them… *incentive* to keep their new friends out of their reckless escapades?" He glared at the nervous ghosts floating behind the cowering twins.

"And perhaps give stricter orders to our enabling vassals to *prevent* these disasters again?"

Aiden's misty figure trembled behind Xavier. "A-a-ah, terribly sorry, my lord…! We saw them leaving and thought, er…"

Nathaniel swiftly came to his aid. "We thought it be a right good idea to keep an eye on the lads, we did! An' there wasn't much we could'a done without bein' resurrected an' all—"

Mother Alice and Father Lucas both waved their hands with violet-glowing flourishes. Smoky lights trailed down to two small Storagecoffins that were strapped to either of their belts. Two skeletons clattered out of the Storagecoffins, palm-sized at first until they grew to full scale once out of the coffins. The one that Mother Alice controlled had an added set of bones that she connected to the lanky skeleton's back.

Then the skeletons grew muscles and tendons, complete with veins and nerves until they finished off with fully-developed skin and hair.

Now that both skeletons had been resurrected, it was clear who these vessels belonged to. The teenaged boy with brown skin, robin-red wings, and feathered hair had the same face as Aiden's ghost. The bear-eared man with thick muscles and a wily, black beard looked like Nathaniel's ghost.

With their corpses fully resurrected, my Spirit Parents proceeded to twiddle their violet-glowing fingers. From the ghosts' chests sprouted gleaming, purple lights. They were NecroSeams, meant to bind the souls to their bodies. They weren't *pure* NecroSeams, of course. Just temporary ones. Only the Seamstress of Souls had the power to make a true NecroSeam; the Seam you're born with.

With their temporary Seams glowing bright from their chests, the two ghosts were dragged into their awaiting vessels, sucked into their pores like hissing fog until they opened their newly physical eyes.

"There you are," Mother Alice huffed and dismissed her Hallows alongside Father Lucas, the violet lights fading from their fingers. "Now you'll have no problem snagging the boys by the necks the next time they try and sneak off, hmm?"

Aiden's wings bowed stiffly. "Y-yes, *Da'torr…*"

Each of the resurrected men bowed in apology, then did precisely as Mother Alice said and snagged the twins by their necks and shoved them toward their manor in the distance.

"Wait!" I called, hurrying after them.

They stopped as I went up to Xavier and unclasped the cloak he leant me, handing it back to him.

"You may want this," I said. "For the cold. Pyrovokers don't need it. Fire-throwers have their own heat."

Xavier took his burgundy cloak with hesitant hands before donning it and clasping it at his neck. "Thank you."

Father Lucas cocked an eyebrow. "Yes, thank you, Willow…" He cleared his throat and stabbed a finger at the boys. "Now *march,* young men."

The twins jumped in fright and hurried on, and I watched the family leave the royal cemetery together.

Lilli flapped her wings in a huff. "Serves them right, sneaking about like that at such a late hour and…" Her parents shot her a strict glare, shutting her up.

Lilli's mother, Maria, held out an expectant hand and growled, "Lilli. My scythes, please."

Lilli ducked her head. Her hands shook as she took off the necklace and handed it to her mother. Her new crow, Dusk, flew to her shoulder, giving a weak caw while hiding under Lilli's tangled hair that had fallen out of her pink ribbon.

Lilli bit her lip. "U-uhm… I… got my messenger, Mother…"

Mother Maria's face didn't soften. Neither did her gritty tone. "Congratulation. Now come. We can celebrate after your punishment. I should think polishing my armor for the next month will suffice. And sharpening my blades, which you decided to dull, hm?"

Lilli's voice tightened into a terrified whisper. "Y…yes, Mother…"

She shuffled alongside her parents, her wings stiff and drooping.

Now I was alone in the cemetery with my mother and father. The Flamedragon gave an impatient chuff in the new silence.

I circled a foot over the soft grass. "So… I killed my first Necrofera?"

"Yes, we saw," Father rumbled. "On every Bloody news station in the caves. Congratulations, dear." He jabbed a hand toward the palace. "Now off with you. And the next time you decide to pop out of bed and cause a scene, just remember your mother will see you've left your dreams and report it immediately."

I walked between my parents and grumbled. "I know… but I saved Xavier from a demon! If I hadn't gone, he would've been dead."

"The twins shouldn't have been there without guards in the first place," Father emphasized. "There are always assassins lurking about. If they're ever recognized as the sons of a highlord, they could be put in danger. As could you."

I nearly pointed out that a demon was far more dangerous than an assassin, but realized any mention of *today's* danger would only prove his point further. So instead, I twisted my mouth. "Well… I think I've proven I can take care of myself—"

"But the twins cannot, Willow," Mother snapped. She'd been silent until now. I never expected such a harsh tone from her.

There was something strange in her distant stare, but her face was unreadable. Her eyes darkened as she whispered, "They aren't ready for such dangers. Not yet. And if you encourage them to seek out any more trouble, there will be *more* lives at stake than just theirs."

I wasn't the only one to slow my step. Father scowled at her just as intensely as I did.

"What do you mean, Myra?" Father questioned.

Mother massaged her eyes tiredly. "It's… never mind. Come, let's return. I'm growing far too cold out here."

XAVIER

Father slammed the front doors closed behind him after we returned to the estate.

Alex and I yelped and scrambled back, our wolf ears fully grown and folded down so hard, the skin was screaming. We backed into Mother, who glared down at us with such ferocity, we flinched away and found ourselves caught between our two furious parents.

Father was the first to snarl, "What in *Death* possessed you boys to go down there with demons on the loose?!"

"And dragging the girls into danger with you?!" Mother barked. "The foolishness! The gall! The pure, delinquent, *irresponsibility!*"

Alex and I were trapped between them, trembling. "We-we-we-we're sorry…! We d-d-didn't mean—!"

"Intentions are irrelevant!" Father bellowed loud enough to make my belly quiver. "Xavier! Come here!"

I squeaked, pointing at myself. "M-m-m… me—? *Ahh!*"

He grabbed my arm and yanked me away from Alex with a hard jerk. His thick fingers were like iron clamps over my quaking bones. Death, Death, Death, Death, Death…! Why just me? Why didn't he ask for both of us? Father hardly ever had time to pay attention to either of us, and now he was singling me out for punishment? Bloody Seamstress, what did *I* do—?

"Where are your injuries?" Father demanded.

My terror choked off. "Wh… wh-what?"

"Your injuries, boy!" Father snapped, crushing my arm tighter. "Don't pretend you weren't seconds from death tonight! We saw it on the damned screens!"

He threw off my cloak to examine me, lifting my arms and growling at every shallow scrape that marred my skin.

"Are these from that beast?" Father rumbled, his teeth sharpening.

I swallowed and shook my head. "N-no, my lord! I… I fell on the stones. Willow killed it b-before it got to me."

"Do you need a Healer?"

"No, my lord."

"You'll need something for those scrapes, at the least." He finally released me, rising to whip his gaze at Thateus, who timidly waited by the curling staircase. "Thateus! Fetch some medical supplies and see that Xavier's injuries are dressed immediately!"

Thateus's limbs locked stiff at the command—likely because it had been a direct order from Father. Thateus was magically bound to obey, as his vassal.

"Yes, High Howllord!" Thateus affirmed, quickly ducking out of the foyer to do as asked.

Father's curdling glare sliced down at me as he gave a final, ripping snarl, "This will not happen again. Am I understood?"

My lungs shriveled, my reply a tight whisper. "Yes, my lord…"

He said nothing more, stalking up the stairwell and leaving us in the foyer with Mother.

But as he ascended, something strange happened. Although I couldn't see his face, I thought I caught a glimpse of Father's shaking hand rubbing at his eyes.

13

XAVIER

The next morning, our irritated parents strode under a stone breezeway beside Alexander and me, rounding the academy's perimeter in a haunting silence. The only sounds between us were our echoing footfalls and the gentle scratches of Father's quill on rough paper as he jotted down notes in a leather-bound book.

Father wore a silken black doublet with a low collar hugging his throat. The diamond stud in his left ear glinted as he absently turned his head to scratch at his recently groomed beard. His sapphire eyes had been dedicated to that notebook all morning. He hadn't said anything past an absent 'good morning' to Alex and me while showing no indication of bringing up yesterday's incident. Instead, Father occupied himself with scribbling memos to himself, adding more items to his ever-growing list of tasks for the next three years.

Typical. One moment Father shows an ounce of affection for either of us, and the next, he was back to forgetting we were here.

I stole a glance at Mother. She didn't wear her armor for this occasion. Instead, she wore her general's uniform with thick, alabaster fabric that bowed upward at the shoulders with sharp curls and golden braids trailing the seams. Fastened to her high collar were six silver pins carved in the shape of raven skulls which marked her as the First Fangs of Grim's military. Her long, shadow-grey hair was coiled in a braided bun atop her head, her marriage-vines glittering across her brow.

She was Deathly quiet while we walked.

My steps were rigid beside Alex, stomach quivering sickly. We were on our way to speak with Sir Gale, as demanded. I wish I knew what in Bloods we did wrong. Not that it would change our sentencing. If I had the tiniest hint, though, perhaps I could better brace myself for punishment.

Skritch, skritch, skritch, skritch...

Father's scratching quill sawed through my eardrums behind me.

Skritch, skritch, skritch, skritch...

I dared a peek at Father over my shoulder. The Shadows of the breezeway's ionic columns glided over him as he walked. He never looked up from that notebook, writing feverishly as his steps subconsciously slowed.

Skritch, skritch, skritch, skritch...

His feet started drifting rightward.

Skritch, skritch, skritch, skritch—BAM!

Father ran into a column. His quill went flying out of his fingers, and he fumbled to snatch it out of the air. He missed three times before he finally caught it, blew out a breath, then readjusted his course and fell into step behind me once more.

...Before immediately returning to his writing.

I sighed, my wolf ears growing in annoyance. I supposed he didn't even deem *this* as important enough for his presence.

Then again, I considered, remembering Father's unusual behavior last night, *at least he was attentive when I was almost eaten by a demon.* Maybe compared to that, a simple conference with a teacher wasn't nearly as vital.

My nerves eased at the reminder. That's right. I could have died yesterday. The fact I'm still alive is enough of a relief on its own. Who cared that our instructor was angry?

We reached the end of the breezeway and stepped out from under its stone roof as we entered the outdoor training grounds.

It was a blackstone colosseum. Five stories high with gothic archways and iron fences barring around terraces like sharp claws.

We stepped through the wide entryway into the colosseum's dirt arena. Students of every age flooded the site, some training their Fire and Death Hallows, others running laps, some racing on the backs of Flamedragons *and* Bonedragons on the ground, many spectating students lining the stone aisles to watch…

There were also older students sparring in full armor and Crystal scythes. Messenger black birds clustered in several murders around them, croaking and cawing in a mass of noise.

Apprentice Reapers, I marveled. They must have been rather far along in their apprenticeships to already be training in full armor and scythes. I envied them, staring at the black birds that screeched encouragingly at the apprentice knights. When would Alex and I get our own messengers? How long did we have to wait for them to find us?

We'd already prepared names for them, for the day they would find us. Alex had chosen the name Mal, and I had chosen Chai. It was something we'd decided year ago. But how long would we need to wait to officially name them?

And were they coming at all?

Ahead, I spotted Sir Gale waiting for us under the shade of a tree, his arms crossed and back leaned against the trunk with a dark stare at a small group of students who spared in plain attire nearby.

There were a mere dozen students in this group. We only recognized a handful of them, from our Necrovoking course yesterday. Everyone was scattered in pairs and trios as they sparred with one another in hand-to-hand combat. Some, like Willow and Lilli, were on their own practicing form with wooden replica scythes.

I noticed Lilli was wearing a new necklace with scythe-spheres. Did her parents gift those to her because of her new messenger? I thought she was going to be punished?

No, it makes sense, I decided. After last night, I supposed it was more practical to arm her for demon encounters. Seamstress knew I felt safer with both girls having weapons. I wished Alex and I could have our own.

Lilli's crow, Dusk, was perched on a nearby tree branch, cawing and screeching in conversation with the twittering Jewel.

I sighed while watching the black birds. *When will I meet you, Chai?* Why did the girls get theirs so early?

I moved my gaze to Willow. It was odd seeing her practice with a wooden scythe. It wasn't as splendid as her Crystal blade. But Willow was just as impressive with a wooden one. Her hands bowed and swayed with the weapon as if it were part of her body, like an extension of her limbs. It was a rigid thing, but she made it look as fluid as her flowing hair that wafted and spiraled around her dancing figure. Compared to her, the other students looked clumsy.

"You must be Sir Gale," Mother said suddenly, breaking my distraction.

We'd reached Sir Gale under the tree. The wrinkled instructor pushed off the trunk and stood before my mother with an expectant gaze.

Skritch, skritch, skritch, skritch...

Father's quill kept scribbling in that book noisily, my ears scratching with every distracting stroke. I flicked him an irked glare over my shoulder. Father was muttering to himself now. I doubted he realized we'd arrived.

Skritch, skritch, skritch, skritch...

Mother folded her arms behind her back as she cast Alex and me a nasty glare. "Let's have it, then. What have these two miscreants done to warrant a summons?"

Skritch, skritch, skritch, skritch...

I scratched my wolf ear to block out Father's noisy quill, trying to focus on the Sir Gale. Even still, Father's scribbling scraped behind me.

"What they did," Sir Gale rumbled and tapped an impatient finger over his arm, "was enroll in my class."

Skritch, skrit—

Father's quill halted.

I peered over my shoulder at him. A very strange, very terrifying expression flashed across Father's face. It was a look I had never seen on him.

Mother's gaze narrowed at Sir Gale. "What do you mean?"

"You've given me two lost causes," Sir Gale clarified. "They don't belong in my Necrovoking course. They don't belong in *any* Necrovoking course."

"I beg your pardon?" Father snarled, startling me. For the first time since the morning started, Father clapped his book shut. "You will explain yourself this instant, Sir. And I suggest you choose your next words wisely."

Sir Gale gestured sharply at Alex and me. "You can't expect me to waste my time trying to teach someone like them?"

"I expect you to do your job," Father snapped. "They study with their Hallows every Gods damned day—for hours on end. I will not sit here and allow their tenacity to be met with ignorant insults from an incapable instructor."

I gaped at Father. How did he know how much we studied? He rarely noticed when we were even around, let alone what we did in our spare time.

"They may be handicapped," Father growled, violently waving his book at Sir Gale, "but they have fought tooth and claw to overcome their disability. They have every right—"

"Handicapped?" Sir Gale cut off sharply. "Disability? Have you seen your sons cast even a single Evocation?"

Father threw down his notebook, his fury exploding tenfold. "Of course, I Bloody have! When they were three, they were casting Evocations your silly class would only dream of teaching! *Three!* Alexander was raising feral hound carcasses at that age! And Xavier was tailoring the ghosts new spectral clothing for the fun of it! There isn't a single Necrovoker alive capable of such brilliance—!"

"Precisely my point," Sir Gale interrupted. He jabbed a hand toward Alexander and me. "Because of their so-called 'handicap', they've surpassed every Necrovoker I've ever met. Including those I've only read about in history texts. And they're only *ten*." He threw up his hands. "What am I supposed to teach two prodigies who can do far more than I? They don't belong in these classes. If anything, they should be teaching them—I may even pair them with Her Highness to help her along. She desperately needs it."

Alex and I flicked each other baffled looks.

Father's anger simmered away. After a long silence, Father scratched his chaffed neck under his collar. "Er, oh... Yes, erm... I suppose we're in agreement, then…" He paused, mumbling, "Then… they're not in trouble?"

"Good Seamstress, no."

Mother circled a perplexed finger over her temple. "Then why have you called us here?"

"For academic purposes," Sir Gale explained. He produced a tiny notebook and pencil from his trouser pocket, flipping it open. "You see, I've been contracted by the Grimish Evocation Association to update the archives of noteworthy Necrovokers from our era. I had just finished compiling this list and was about to send it off next week, but after *this*…" He waved his stubby pencil at us. "I'm suddenly finding my list deprived of two entrants."

My face burned, and there was no bit of grey left of Alexander's face under his blush.

Sir Gale began writing in the little notebook. "Now, to start, how did their condition happen? Halved Hallows? Split so perfectly that the other half of their magic is completely empty? Every Evocator is stronger in some areas, and this does happen with twins, but to be totally void of the other half?" He shook his head. "Never in my life have I heard of such a thing. Was there an accident? Or did they come by it naturally?"

Mother exchanged a skeptical glance with Father. Then she sighed. "Naturally. They were born this way. I'm afraid we don't know why."

Father rubbed his knuckles. "We've researched as much as we could… but we have yet to find anything, even still. We think it may have something to do with their Evocator marks, but we haven't found answers to that, either."

Sir Gale's crinkled eyes turned to slits. "What about their Evocator marks?"

Father nodded to us, prompting Alex and me to hold out our hands—Alexander's right and my left—to show Sir Gale our matching birthmarks of three, black diamonds.

Sir Gale crouched down to examine our marks. "These are their marks…?" His voice was an awed whisper. "But… these had been

Death marks when they were evoking their Hallows yesterday, hadn't they? I saw them glowing white myself."

Alex and I shrugged and replied in unison, "It changes."

"But I… this isn't…" He cupped his mouth, dumbfounded. "What *is* this mark? It doesn't belong to *any* element of Hallows… It's just the Crest of Nirus."

"We know," Alex and I said. Alex continued by himself, "Our parents have looked for the mark in history texts, but they haven't found anything yet."

"Never as an Evocator mark, at least," I added.

Sir Gale murmured in wonder. "Fascinating…" He rose in a sigh and tossed his head at us. "Why don't you boys join your classmates for fitness training? I'd like to speak with your parents on this more."

Alex and I bowed low, thanking him, and quickly left them to their discussion.

"W-well," I stammered, still rattled from the whole exchange. "At least we're not in trouble."

Alex grimaced. "Thank Death."

As we crossed the training grounds full of students, many heads followed us. They whispered in their closed little groups, but none dared approach us. Bloods, they'd heard what Sir Gale had said. Father's yelling must have attracted their ears. We heard many of the children calling us freaks as we passed.

Wonderful, I brooded. *At least it's starting to feel a little more like home.*

There were only three faces we recognized among the crowd, all from our Necrovoking class yesterday.

The first two were Lilli and Matthiel who took turns twisting the other's wrists and bringing them to the ground. The third was Willow who was off to the side on her own practicing with a wooden scythe.

Matthiel was the first to spot us. When he trotted over, Lilli and Willow noticed and hurried after him—though Willow tripped over her own hair and nearly fell flat on her face, but she regained her footing and raced to catch up.

"You're in one piece!" Matthiel cried as he screeched to a stop in front of us. "We thought Sir Gale was going to skewer you, with the way he sounded!"

Lilli put fists at her sides. "What did he want?"

"Was it awful?" Willow questioned. "What did he say?"

I shrugged. "He, er, said we're too advanced for his class."

Alex pointed his chin at Willow. "He also wants us to help you with your Hallows."

Willow flushed. "Oh. I… suppose I *do* need more tutoring in that, too…"

"Too?" I asked. "What else do you need more tutoring in?"

"Well…" She swirled her foot over the gravel. "In *every* element. I may have six Hallows, but I'm not good at any of them. My mother thinks my Hallows strength was split too many times, so…"

Matthiel laid an encouraging hand on her shoulder. "Don't worry, your grace. You're improving splendidly with your Pyrovoking."

His hand lingered there on her shoulder for a suspicious moment. There was an annoying familiarity with the gesture.

Though, now that I thought on it… They *were* familiar, weren't they? They shared at least one class together, and it sounded like they had more. Matthiel must have known Willow for years.

Were they…?

Craaaaaw!

A crow cawed abruptly behind us, making us jump. The black bird was perched on a tiger-eared woman's shoulder, who clapped her hands sharply.

"You five!" The woman shouted while storming toward us. "Why are you standing around like bumbling pups? This is not some Bloody daycare where… who are you two?" She eyed Alexander and me, the crow mimicking the gesture from her shoulder. "Ah, you must be the Devouh twins I heard about. Sir Gale mentioned you had funny eyes. My name is Sil Reia, I'm Sir Gale's assistant trainer." She cocked an eyebrow. "Which one of you is which?"

I stammered, "X-Xavier, honored Sil."

"Alexander," my brother said next. Then we said together, "It's easier if you pay attention to our blue eyes."

Sil Reia grimaced as her crow dipped its head in a groaning caw. "I'm never going to remember that. How about this: whichever one I point to first will be 'Twin One', and whichever I point to next will be 'Twin Two'. Sound good?"

Alex and I gave her a flat stare.

"Good." She clapped her hands and ushered Alex toward Lilli; then ushered me to Matthiel. "Twin One, I want you to spar with Lilli. Twin Two, with Matthiel. I need to know where to place you. I'd like you two to go through a series of control techniques—under my supervision, of course."

She placed Alex in front of Lilli, and me in front of Matthiel.

"All right," Sil Reia cleared her throat. "Show your partner the respect they deserve and bow."

We did, and she waved at Willow off to the side. Willow came to join Sil Reia.

"Now," said Sil Reia, "the first technique I want to see is the basic take-down. Like so. Willow?"

Sil Reia and Willow slid into combative stances. Then Reia stepped forward and swung an open hand down at Willow's head. Willow raised her arms, blocked, twirled her hands to grab Sil Reia's wrists and practically danced around her while twisting Reia's arm at the same time. Willow finished in a graceful yet powerful flourish as she pushed Reia's twisted arm and sent her rolling forward over the dirt.

When Reia finished her roll, she turned about and rose to her feet again. "Very good, Willow." She nodded to Alexander and me. "Now, your turn."

Alex and I mimicked the technique—though, not nearly as fluidly—then completed the next five tasks. Once Sil Reia was satisfied, she put fists at her sides in approval.

"Well done," she said, her crow bobbing its head in consideration from her shoulder. "It seems you're exactly where I need you to be. As expected of the sons of a First Fangs. Now, here is today's technique."

Using Willow as her partner again, she showed us a forward take-down that twists the opponent's wrist forward and down. Once Sil Reia was finished with the demonstration, she turned to us and clapped her hands. "There you are. Now, I want the four of you to alternate who does the technique this time, since you're all starting from square one." She nodded to Willow next. "As you were, Your Highness."

Willow grimaced. "But I want to partner with Xavier."

I cracked a grin. Then caught Matthiel squinting at me with suspicion.

"No, no, no!" Sil Reia wagged a finger. "You're far too advanced for these wee kiddies, Your Highness. You'll have to wait until they catch up to you. Besides." She gave Willow a scolding look. "From what I hear, he's already had quite the terrifying welcome, thanks to you." She paused and glanced at me. "Was that you or your brother?"

I ducked my head. "Er, that was me…"

Willow picked up the wooden scythe she'd set aside and shouldered it with a sniff. "It wasn't my fault a demon tried to eat him. *I* saved him, thank you very much."

Matthiel's glare slitted further at me. I gave a nervous laugh, coughing into a fist.

Sil Reia steered Willow away. "Saved or not, you'll have to wait. You four, practice that technique. I'll be around to check your progress in a bit."

She headed off to observe the other students, leaving Alex to train with Lilli… and me with Matthiel.

His sienna eyes were still set in a glower at me. We bowed and slid into combative stances. Matthiel began the technique first.

"So," he said while taking my hand the way Sil Reia had instructed, pressing his thumbs on the back of my knuckles and twisting downward. "You were the one her grace saved last night, were you?"

When pain split through my wrist, I was forced to my knees, straining. "Er… y-yes…" I tapped out to signal him to stop, and he let me up. Then I did the technique on him. "I didn't know she followed us down there. But Bloods am I glad she did."

"I'm sure…" He strained, curling to his knees before tapping out himself.

It was his turn again, and he snatched my hand with crushing fingers this time. "Her Highness is truly a noble soul," he growled, any hint of friendliness snuffed from his tone now. "She would save any old shifter." He twisted harder than before, making me grunt and drop to the ground in a puff of dirt. "I'd suggest you don't think yourself special for it."

He let me go, and I staggered to my feet, my wolf ears growing angrily. "I never said—"

"Ah, these are the freak twins I told you about," a voice interrupted.

The four of us, Matthiel included, turned to the ashen-haired boy who'd spoken.

Felix had come with a cluster of students, his smirk condescending as he looked down his nose at us.

They were all wearing matching black-and-gold athletic uniforms. They were the same uniforms I'd seen practicing Hallows maneuvers earlier on a different side of the colosseum. Part of some Evocator team, I wagered.

"They're an odd pair of defects," Felix explained to his teammates. "One can't raise a single bone, and the other can't even touch a ghost. I've never seen anything so amusing."

"Shove off," Alex snapped. "Sir Gale decided we were too advanced for the rest of you."

Felix laughed. "Sir Gale is a senile old coddler. He thinks anything is impressive."

"What a surprise," Matthiel cut in with a pompous scowl that could easily rival the one painting Felix's face. "Prince Felix feels threatened by someone better than him. We've never seen *that* before, have we, Lilli?"

Lilli gave a sharp flap of her wings. "Really, Felix, whenever you decide to change your routine—"

"You will address royalty *properly*," Felix snarled at her. A puff of orange flames burst from his hands. "You are speaking to the *true* heir of Grim. When the rest of those idiot councilmen realize what a mistake my mutt cousin is, I will personally remember your rude-ness when I hold the crown."

I snorted, "You'd be the mistake if you act like this—"

"Mind who you speak to, freak!" Felix flung his enflamed hands at me, his orange fire spiraling straight for me.

I cringed back—

Matthiel lunged in front of me. The fire splashed into his chest, burning his tunic to a crisp. When the fire puffed out in a lick of smoke, I stared at the still-standing boy.

"Matthiel…!" I hurried around to check on him, positive his skin would be scarred and disfigured.

But there was nothing there. There was no burn mark under the open hole in his tunic. It was just smooth skin.

"You aren't burnt?" I asked, stunned.

"Fire doesn't hurt a Pyrovoker," Matthiel said—and his hands ignited in a burst of flames, glaring at Felix.

I gaped at Matthiel. "You're a Necrovoker *and* a Pyrovoker?"

Alex breathed in wonder. "A Dual-Evocator…! Bloods those are rare—*woah!*"

Alex ducked as Felix threw a ball of flames his way. When it missed, Felix thrust another fireball—

But Willow slid in front of Alex. She jerked out a hand and blocked the fire with her palm, the flame snuffing out as smoke curled from her fingers. What do you hope to prove by melting the new highlords, Felix?"

Felix scoffed. "I'm half surprised my fire doesn't melt *you*, vermin. As cold as your fire is, it's a wonder you…"

He was drowned out by frightened shrieks that split through the arena.

His posse suddenly split apart, the young lords and ladies yelp-ing as they retreated to safety from whatever was making its way through the crowd.

Felix's scowl was confused. "What is it? What's got you all so…"

The crowd cleared away. There was a small, long-snouted creature slithering on the ground. It was covered in purple-and-black striped quills, which rattled threateningly as the reptile hissed at each shifter in its path, its spiny tail whipping left and right.

Felix paled at the thing. "Poisondragon!"

Wails cut the air from the crowd of terrified students, everyone huddling away from the thing.

Puff!

Felix and Matthiel hurtled fireballs at the little dragon.

Puff!

Puff!

Puff!

The creature slithered away from the fireballs in frightened hisses, curling into itself as if wishing to hide.

There was something painfully familiar about the dragon's behavior. It reminded me of something from a long time ago. At our old home.

When Alex was nearly beaten to death.

"Kill it!" someone shouted from the crowd of students. They started chucking stones at the trapped dragon. "Kill it before it stings someone!"

"—*Better him than us!*" I remembered the children had shouted with each kick to Alex's ribs. I didn't get there soon enough. He was already unconscious by the time I found him. I… I thought he was…

Someone grabbed my arm.

"Xavier!" Alex barked, his voice cracking with fright as he pulled me away from the dragon. "Don't just stand there! Come!"

I fumbled after him, twisting back to see Matthiel and Felix were still throwing fireballs at the little creature, everyone else still throwing stones. It slithered and dodged the volley of projectiles, its bright quills shivering in terror. One of the stones cracked against the dragon's tail and it let out a wounded hiss.

"N-no! Stop!" I dug my heels in the dirt.

"What are you doing?!" Alex squeezed my arm harder. "If that thing stings you—!"

"That doesn't mean it will!" I shouted, yanking my arm out of his fingers. "*You* were just passing through when they thought *you* were dangerous…!"

Alex stopped. His wolf ears lowered. "But… that doesn't mean—"

I rushed off before he could grab me again.

I pushed Matthiel out of the way, standing between the frightened Poisondragon and the stone-throwing students, ignoring the sharp jabs of pain when the rocks accidentally hit me instead. "Stop this! He's only lost! Let him find his way home—*Argh!*"

Someone threw a heavy stone right at my temple. Pain burst from my head. I stumbled back, slipping on a stray stone—

I fell spine-first onto the Poisondragon's quills.

A burning pain scorched through my back, the venomous tips of three quills piercing my skin. I rolled to my side in screaming agony—

Alex ripped a hideous scream beside Lilli, dropping to his knees and arching his back as if he'd been stung himself.

Lilli blinked at him. "Alexander? What's wrong—?"

"Help him!" Alex shrieked, clutching his stomach as if to keep it from spilling out. "He… he's in pain…! *Nngh*…!" Alex's eyes rolled back and he collapsed, causing Lilli to panic.

My spotting vision swerved as I saw the Poisondragon hiss at me before slithering away to safety in a nearby bush.

I stayed curled in a writhing ball, screaming as the venom spread across the rest of my back and up my shoulders. I could still feel the quills stuck in my skin.

"Xavier!" Willow rushed to help me up, offering her hand. "You need to go to the infirmary—!"

She pulled my arm so rough, another wave of pain stung through my blood like a ripple of needles. I grew dizzy, barely aware of the sudden storm swirling in my soul that leaked through my fingers in violet lights.

Willow screamed in pain. She collapsed beside me, her hair fanning around her in a messy tangle.

After a few seconds, though, her invisible pain seemed to fade.

"Wh-what… what did you…?" She stared at her hand, then gaped at me. "Was that a Sensory-Illusion…?"

Death… I was still convulsing. Although her agony seemed to have ended, mine was intensifying by the minute.

"I… I'm sorry…" I tried to sit up, but my burning muscles locked and I fell over again, seething, "I'm… sor*rrrgh*…!" I gritted my teeth against the pain. Dearest Death, my blood may as well have been fire.

"What happened?" the exasperated voice of Sir Gale demanded. He shoved his way to the front of the crowd that had formed around me. When he found me and Willow on the ground, he jolted. "Death's Head! Are those Poisondragon quills?!"

My parents ran behind him frantically, gasping when they saw me. "Xavier!" Mother shrieked.

Father knelt to pick up Alex's limp body off to the side. "It's Alexander as well! What's happened to them?!"

"Let's get them to an infirmary!" Sir Gale hurried to scoop me up, since I couldn't stand. My whole body shivered as the pain spread down my limbs, my wolf ears glued to my neck so tight, I thought they'd rip.

"Come with me!" Sir Gale shouted to my parents. "We need to hurry before…!"

Their voices faded as my vision splotched. I stole a final glace at Willow, who still stared after me from the ground with a pale expression.

Then everything went dark.

14

XAVIER

Willow's frightened stare peered at me through the smoke. She said nothing. Yet, her frightened face said enough as she stepped away, as though I were a wild beast.

"I'm sorry," I pleaded. "I didn't mean…"

Willow darted off, her long hair swimming over the hazy floor behind her in delicate curls.

"Wait!" I followed after her, reaching out desperately. "I'm sorry! Please…!"

She puffed into mist under my fingers.

"Please…" I stood there shivering. "Why is everyone afraid…?"

"—Why am I not surprised?" a woman's voice suddenly sighed beside me. "Yet another boy dreaming of my daughter? Honestly, what is that girl doing to you all?"

I yelped and shuffled back. My head snapped to the tall woman now looming over me. She had wavy, azure locks and an icy blue stare. It was the same stare as Willow's, with a fox-like face to match.

"You're…" I pointed dumbly. "Willow's mother? The queen of dreams?"

She hummed and cocked her head. "Willow is my daughter, yes. But my mother is the queen of dreams. I'm only a princess of this realm." She gestured to the smoky void around us. "Though, I am *the queen of Death* now, to be fair. It was a reasonable guess."

I frowned. "Princess of this realm… we're in the realm of Dreams? Aspirre?"

She smiled. "Yes."

"Then… I'm dreaming?"

"Oh, yes. For quite some time, now."

My nose scrunched. "What do you mean?"

"You're in the palace infirmary." She lifted a hand. "You've been asleep for a whole day. That Poisondragon really did a number on you. I'm relieved you pulled through so soon. I believe that's twice now that you've averted death—and in as many days, at that." She gave a dreary sigh and cupped a hand to her cheek. "Keeping you and your brother alive long enough will be quite the challenge, won't it?"

"Long enough for what?" I asked.

She tapped a glowing-blue finger to my forehead. "I'll tell you when you're older."

—the smoky void vanished as I woke.

My eyes peeled open, but I had to squint at the bright ceiling lights that split through my lids.

I was in a patient bed. Was this an infirmary?

The walls and floor were dressed in white, and a heart monitor bleated every few seconds beside me. I had several fluid-tubes stuck to me, so it was hard to move. I was also wearing a clinic gown with my chest and back wrapped in gauze.

I glanced down and saw Alex was seated on a chair beside me.

My brother slept at my bedside, his head laid on the edge where my arm was as he snored softly.

"Alex…" I croaked sorely and poked his skull. "Alex?"

His eyes fluttered open in a groggy rumble. When he noticed I was awake—

"You Bloody idiot!" He burst into tears and squeezed my sore ribs. "What were you doing?! You could have…! You could have…!" He sobbed into my bandaged chest.

I sighed and patted his head. "I'm fine, Alex… but I guess I *was* being an idiot…?"

"You're Gods damned right you were." He rubbed his eyes dry with a sleeve. A very formal sleeve, I noticed. Alex was wearing a silken, alabaster suit with silver trim and a rustic collar-string. The curling designs on the fabric gave off a beautiful sheen in the light, and I found an eye-mask in the shape of a wolf's face waiting on the table beside him.

I gave him a confused look. "Why are you dressed for a… ball…?" I stopped short, remembering my dream. "Oh, Gods! I really *have* been asleep for a whole day…! It's Death's Festival, isn't it?"

He rubbed his nose in a hollow laugh. "Obviously. I woke up this morning, but we didn't know if you'd wake up in time." He grumbled under his breath, "They said *I* had to go to this stupid party no matter what… said they didn't trust us to be out of their sight anymore."

"Wonderful…" I paused. "Wait, that's right. You were stung, too, weren't you?"

Alex hesitated. "Well, no. But I could sort of…*feel* yours."

He didn't seem sure how else to explain it. But he didn't need to.

"I know," I hummed softly, tugging my fingers. "That happened with me, when we were younger. When those kids were beating you and…" I pushed out a breath through my nose. "I felt everything. Even after I found you. I was starting to think I'd imagined it."

Alex's tone was grim as he muttered. "I guess not."

My stomach rumbled, and I clutched my empty belly. "Bloods," I groaned. "Does this ball have food…? I'm starving…"

I slipped out of bed, wincing slightly, and peeled off the fluid-tubes and wires stuck to my arm. I tried to take a step forward and nearly fell, but Alex caught me. My legs were a little wobbly.

"Careful," he said. "That was a Poisondragon—they can infect your soul just as much as your flesh. The doctor gave you a tonic to help speed up your recovery, but she said it would probably take a few hours to get your energy back to normal." He slung my arm over his shoulder. "If you're feeling up for the ball, that's fine, but we'll go *slowly* and *together.* Understand?"

"Y… yeah." I smiled appreciatively. "Thanks, Alex."

Alex snorted, but gave a relieved grin. "Just don't jump in front of anymore Poisondragons? Please?"

"Heh… Deal." I grimaced, letting Alex help me out to the halls.

15

XAVIER

Alex and I helped ourselves to the open buffet in the palace ballroom, scarfing down two thick slices of peppered boar, roasted turkey over grilled onions, and three *whole* cups of pumpkin gallings each. We chased it all down with spiced hot cider and filled our bellies until we were about to burst.

Maybe it was excessive, but this was the main appeal to these parties. The food was always delicious and plentiful. Given we were still recovering, more or less, one could argue we should be allowed to eat as much as we needed. For our health. Yes.

The ballroom was crowded with noble citizens dressed in festive, white garments and decorative masks.

Stringed music played from the orchestra set at the far corner. The dreary waltz was set to a minor key as the Howllords and Howlesses danced across the marble floor, many ghosts joining them. Their masks had soul-seeing Evocations, which is why it was tradition to wear them during Festival since only Necrovokers had natural soul-sight.

In the back on a risen platform, I saw Willow speaking with her azure-haired mother on the thrones, playing with the braids in her long hair. The powdery strands tumbled in playful curls to the floor like a curtain twisting round the chair legs. The princess wore a flowing, ivory gown for the Festival. A butterfly mask hid her face. She pointed to it now, asking her mother something I couldn't hear from this distance.

The blue-haired queen nodded kindly to her daughter—then the woman's eyes snapped directly at me.

I stiffened, the hairs on my neck leaping.

Then the queen grinned.

I looked away in a shiver. There was something *really* unnerving about that woman.

My eyes drifted back to Willow on her throne.

Right… the second reason I came. I reached into my vest pocket and pulled out the gift I'd hidden there. I scrutinized the long box, making sure the decorative black and silver paper wasn't wrinkled or torn. I lightly shook it next to my ear.

Trilililing!

The delicate bell jingled happily from inside.

"Do you think it'll be enough?" I asked Alex beside me, sliding the box in my vest's hidden pocket.

My brother rolled his mismatched eyes behind the white, wolf-shaped mask covering the top half of his face. "For the fifth time, she's not angry. She came to visit every Bloody hour in the infirmary. You don't need a gift to apologize."

I fidgeted nervously, adjusting my own wolf-mask that matched Alexander's.

Today was the 60th of Spiridel: the day of Death's Festival.

It was also Willow's *Rae'u Shelic.*

What if she hated the gift? What if someone else already got her one before she opened mine? Seamstress prick me, maybe I should have gotten something else—

A heavy hand clasped my shoulder.

"Xavier," my father's deep voice rasped above me. I craned my gaze up, my head ducking. My father gave me a warm, bearded smile. "We weren't sure if you'd wake in time."

"W-well… here I am, my lord…" I quickly stood at attention alongside Alex. My punctured back throbbed faintly at the motion, but even pain couldn't break my hard-taught conditioning. "I was feeling well enough to attend, so… I-I'm in attendance. My lord."

"Good, good." He coughed into a fist, hesitating. "Erm, since you seem to be in good health now, and the doctors cleared you… I suppose it's safe…" Father ushered us, gently, away from the buffet table. "At the very least, there is someone I'd like you both to meet. *Two* someones."

Father led us toward two grey-haired, identical girls who waited alongside what I could only assume was their father. Both girls, clearly twins as well, had primary cat ears.

The twin girls wore similar white gowns and masks, but one had her braided hair tied with violet ribbons and the other had hers tied with gold ribbons. Both girls gave a simultaneous curtsy.

"*Chanerr nohkosch*," the girls greeted in unison, their cat ears perked from under their hair.

"*Chanerr nohkosch,*" Alex and I replied, bowing as per protocol.

Father delicately nudged me in front of the violet-ribboned sister, who flashed me a kind smile.

Alexander was positioned before the scowling, gold-ribboned sister.

Father cleared his throat. "Erm, boys… these are Jessah and Mynnah Vrubell." He nodded to the man standing beside them. "And this is their father, Howllord Burton Vrubell. These are my sons, Xavier and Alexander."

"Lovely to meet you," the violet-ribboned girl—Jessah—said with a smile.

"A pleasure," the gold-ribboned girl—Mynnah—sighed as she put a delicate hand at her waist. She cocked her head at us. "Why are your eyes different colors?"

Her father rumbled. "Mynnah, be *polite*."

The music shifted to a traditional, Grimish waltz suddenly.

"Death, no time now," Father said to Alex and me hurriedly. "Now, er, given your recent incident… Are either of you in any condition to dance?"

We gave him a flat stare. "What?"

"Since this is your first time here," Father explained, looking uncharacteristically anxious as he dabbed at his sweaty brow with a kerchief. "You mother and I would like you both to partake in the Breathless Waltz… Health permitting, of course."

"What is that?" we asked.

"It's a traditional waltz for children your age. It's a fine way to meet your peers and decide whom you're most fond of. Once you've chosen your preferred Howless, we will arrange a partnership with them."

Alex whispered under his breath to me, "What sort of partnership does he mean?"

I shrugged and hissed back, "Perhaps some sort of training arrangement? For combat?"

"Why would we decide that from a dance—?"

"Death, they've already started!" Father cursed and nudged us onto the dancefloor with the twin girls. "Go on, go on! Ah, but don't push yourselves too hard, yes? If you feel unwell, take a rest before jumping back in. Good luck."

With that, he shooed us away as we fumbled into line with the other children.

I tried like Death to remember the steps our tutors had taught us, but the young Howless Jessah was twirling too fast for me to keep pace. I looked over her head at Alex, hoping to mimic him, but he was too busy staring at *me* for the very same reason. Desperate, I tried to watch the other young lords—

I found Willow dancing on the other side of the floor. She was partnered with Matthiel, the two laughing and striking up an engaging conversation. Matthiel didn't fumble even once. Why was Willow smiling so much?

My wolf ears grew.

"Something wrong?" Jessah asked, snapping me out of my glaring. One of her cat ears swiveled. "Your ears are showing."

I had my ears recede in a nervous laugh. "So are yours."

"Yes, but mine are primary ears." She grinned. "They're always showing. If yours are out, that means something's bothering you."

"N-no," I assured with a tight smile, trying to be polite. "I'm, uhm, recovering. From an injury. I was stung by a Poisondragon yesterday."

She started. "Oh! That sounds awful! No wonder your steps are lagging."

I blushed. "Actually, I'm just not very good at dancing… haven't had much practice."

"You didn't have dances at your old home?"

"It's not that we didn't have them. It was more that no one wanted to dance with *us*, so…"

She lowered a cat ear. "Why not?"

I hesitated. "Well… Everyone was terrified of us. Until recently, our father had been the Eyes of the Death King—His Majesty's ambassador. My grandfather is the Eyes now, but only because he wanted to relieve my father of that horrible position."

"Horrible?" she asked. "That sounds like a very high honor to me."

My wolf ears folded down in a long sigh. "It wasn't the role itself. It was how everyone treated us. There were a lot of… rumors. They were afraid of Father and said all sorts of things about him. None of them were true, but that didn't stop them from avoiding us or, sometimes, attacking us."

Jessah cast me a sympathetic gaze, fanning a hand to her chest. "Oh. I'm terribly sorry… I hadn't heard anything about that."

"All the better. No one on *this* continent seems to know about it, thankfully." I gave her a reassuring smile. "It's strange, to be honest. We weren't sure if it would be any different here, but it looks like it might be worlds better after all. It's pleasant without everyone running away at the sight of us."

She smiled back. "I imagine so."

There was a flight of high-notes from the quartet, signaling that it was time to switch partners. Jessah curtsied while I bowed, and the girls on the floor cycled to the left. I was partnered with a new Howless, and the waltz began once more.

It went on like this for some time. There was Elanor Shulth, Rathella Murr, Hannah Lovell, Heather something-or-other…

After half an hour, the names were a blur. I must have danced with over a dozen girls, even after resting several times. There were a *lot* of young nobles, apparently. More specifically, a lot of young

Howlesses. There were less Howllords our age, it seemed. The ratio was so skewed that there was a line of Howlesses at the back waiting for their turn to dance at all. It took three whole hours to get through the lot.

When the current song ended and the last song of the Breathless Waltz was announced, I was exhausted and so used to the routine of bowing to my new partner—this time, a girl with black, feathered wings—that I held out my hand preemptively in a bored sigh. She must have noticed because she gave an offended scowl and crinkled her nose before grudgingly taking my hand.

"—Excuse me, Howless," a new girl chimed beside her suddenly.

My bones nearly jumped out of my skin at that voice.

"I was sitting out for a time to give the other Howlesses a turn," a butterfly-masked Willow said as she patiently stood beside the Howless, her arms cupped behind her. "But I wished to speak with this Howllord at least once. Would you mind if I took over?"

The Howless gave a haughty flap of her feathery wings and stepped aside. "Gladly, your grace. I've already made my choice, anyway."

The Howlless strode off the dance floor in a huff.

Willow took my gloved fingers cheerily. "Lucky me."

"W-Willow," I stuttered, "I-I'm so sorry… About the sensory-illusion. I didn't know what was happening—"

"You needn't explain," she interrupted, cocking an eyebrow. "Need I remind you, I *felt* your pain? It was so excruciating, I was surprised you even noticed I was there." She hummed idly. "Mine didn't last as long as your actual injury, but I felt enough of it to 'get the gist'."

My head sagged. "I'm sorry."

She shook her head. "Don't be. I'm just glad you're awake and on your feet again."

The music started, and Willow tugged me along with the rest of the young nobles. She deftly twirled and stepped along with the quartet's song, swaying and bowing in a hypnotizing rhythm. None of the other Howlesses had half her grace. Though, her movements reminded me of something.

I grinned. "You dance like you're holding your scythe."

She chuckled. "It makes it much easier—*ouch*!"

I stepped on a lock of her long hair, making me cringe. "S-sorry."

She swept the hair away and continued in a sigh. "Again, don't be. It's been happening all night. You should have seen Matthiel's horrified face when he first did it."

I spurted a laugh. "Well, that's reassuring." It was almost enough to stave off the annoyance that he'd been partnered with her first. Almost. I mumbled, "I suppose you both… have these dances often?"

She hummed. "Actually, this is my first Breathless Waltz."

My brow knitted. "But you live here?"

"You must be between eight and twelve to participate in the Waltz," she explained. "And it only happens when new lords or ladies *of* that age move into the city."

"Oh." I frowned. "But I haven't heard about any other new children…" It dawned on me. "Is it happening because of Alex and me?"

Willow nodded. "It's the fastest way for the other children to introduce themselves. And their parents want them to meet you both to see if they'd like to form an arrangement."

She glanced over her shoulder and whispered to me behind a shielding hand. "But if we're being honest, most of their parents have already told them whom to choose. There are many status-climbing lords and ladies here, so you ought to take care with whom you choose your arrangements."

Bloods, I thought, troubled, *these partnerships are that serious?* It must have been especially significant if parents were so intent on pressuring their children into making a choice. Even *my* father had been acting strange when he brought Alex and me over to Jessah and Mynnah.

Father probably thought we'd choose them, since they're also twins, I realized. *But then… he didn't say we had to pick them, did he?*

"Regardless," Willow went on, "That's only if you choose at all. You don't have to pick anyone if you don't want to. It used to be required in the old days, but not anymore. So, don't feel pressured to choose anyone, even if *they* choose you."

"Thanks for the warning." I glanced over my shoulder and found my brother dancing with Lilli. "We should probably let Alex know, shouldn't we?"

Willow tossed a dismissive hand. "I already have. I danced with him earlier. You were partnered with Howless Greyann at the time."

"Ah." I whispered so only she could hear, "Which one was that? I think I've heard at least fifty names in three hours, they've all blurred together."

She chuckled. "She was the lizard shifter. With the scales."

"Right. You must know everyone already, don't you?"

"I do. It's part of my duties as heiress." She hesitated, then changed topic. "Actually, I came over here to ask you something… if I may?"

Why did she sound concerned? "Yes?"

"Why didn't you want anyone to kill the Poisondragon?"

I almost tripped over my own feet. "What?"

"The Poisondragon," she said again. "You had this look on your face when everyone was trying to kill it. You just seemed so…" She searched for the word. "Sad."

My wolf ears grew, remembering the scared little dragon… I didn't know how to explain the reason. I also didn't know if I wanted to explain it at all.

"Did it remind you of your brother?" she asked.

I almost choked. "My—my brother?"

"Yes." She tilted her head, her drapery of hair tumbling over her shoulder. "Did it remind you of the time he was beaten at your old city?"

"How do you know about that?"

She gave me a flat stare and pointed at herself. "Seer."

I rubbed my eyes vigorously. "Right… Could you not share that with anyone? We just want to start over and forget about—"

She pulled me into her arms, clamping my limbs stiff.

"I'm sorry," she hushed, her grip tightening around my sore ribs. "I only had to live through the vision once, but you must have relived the memory so many times." She pulled away, composing herself in a sigh. "Don't worry. I'll do what I can to see that it never happens here. Felix and his kind will do everything they can to tear all of us down, but we'll stand with you. You have family here."

I stared at her.

The waltz came to an end, and the announcer called for the boys and girls to line up on opposite ends of the floor.

Willow curtsied to me.

I bowed, my nerves still buzzing as I watched her line up with the other girls. My knees felt like rusty hinges as I took my place in the boys' line beside Alexander.

Alex cocked an eyebrow at me. "Injuries hurting? You look ill."

I was. My mind felt like a soggy puddle. My most traumatic memory had been pried into, for Death's sake. But I had the oddest feeling… I was terrified, sure, but at the same time, I felt so… well, just so…

Welcomed.

"Young Howlesses!" the announcer began with a delicate clap of his hands. "Since we have fewer lords than ladies, you all have first pick! Please go and stand before the lord of your choice!"

The Howlesses dispersed from their line, forming in clusters before certain Howllords. I was thrown out of my stupor when a large number of them formed in front of Alex and me. Jessah was one of mine while Mynnah was one of Alex's. I barely remembered any of the others' names.

Lilli was also in Alex's cluster, fanning her wings and causing the other girls to shuffle out of her way. She and Mynnah were front and center before Alex, who rolled his eyes.

Alex pointed at Lilli without a second thought. "You, obviously," he grumbled. "Are we done now?"

"Yes!" Lilli gave a victorious hop, her wings reflexively flapping— and accidentally smacking Mynnah in the face. Lilli looped her arm around my brother's before dragging him off the dancefloor to meet with our parents. I heard Alex muttering his relief that it was finally over.

There was also an impressive cluster of girls surrounding Matthiel, I noticed. Most of his Howlesses were swooning shamelessly. But his attention wasn't on any of them. He was staring at the last girl standing across the floor.

He was staring at Willow.

"Your Highness?" The announcer called eagerly. "Do you wish to make a choice?"

The room was Deathly silent now. Not a single shoe squealed over the marble floor. Not a single glass of champaign clinked in the thick quietness.

Willow denied a verbal reply. She merely cocked her head, then strode across the floor with her hands cupped behind her. This sparked Matthiel's undivided attention as she made her way over. Willow bypassed the cluster of girls and stepped in front of them.

To stand before me. She held out her hand, casting me an inviting smile.

I drew in an uncertain breath. Then took her hand.

The adults erupted in cheers. Among the crowd, I saw my parents laughingly shake hands with Willow's parents. The room was in such a buzz, I could hardly keep up with what was happening. Why were they so excited?

Willow tightened her grip on my hand and tugged me away from the crowd.

"Come with me," she hummed.

"A-All right…" I still wasn't sure why everyone was acting so strange, but I *did* know I wanted to be free of those countless eyes. Bloods, that was nerve-wracking. Thank Death Willow gave me an excuse to leave. These partnerships must have been incredibly vital.

She led me to the back through the open balcony, stepping down the stone steps toward the gardens.

"Grandfather!" Willow called into the gardens.

She was waving to a man who sat cross-legged on the edge of a lit fountain. The man swirled his hand in the glowing pool, casting quivering refractions across his body.

Wait, that's a teenager, isn't it? He looked nearly twenty, wearing a wrinkled, orange sweater and loose trousers. His bare toes scratched an itch on his other foot. *That's Willow's grandfather?*

Willow flailed her arm more violently. "Grandfather! I brought my choice, as you asked." She tugged me along, and I stumbled to keep pace. "This is Xavier."

The teenager glanced up to look at us. "Ah. Very good, dear."

He rose, pulling back his orange hood to reveal a head full of curling, azure locks that matched his—and Willow's—eyes. On his brow was a crowned Dream mark, looking like a stylized eye with three blue diamonds representing its pupil.

I stopped cold, Willow skipping ahead and leaping into the teenager's arms.

"Come meet him, Grandfather," Willow thrust an excited hand at me, the other wrapped round the teen's neck. "You'll like him."

"Oh, I'm sure of it, dear," he chuckled and set her down, crouching to look at me. "After all, this isn't our first meeting. I was there when Xavier and Alexander were born here in the palace. But you were such a small thing then." He cast me an appraising eye, waving a hand over my head as if measuring my height. "You're much bigger now, aren't you? You must be, let's see… eight?"

I stammered, "I-I'm ten. Are you… are you the King of Dreams?"

I'd only heard stories of the legendary king of Aspirre. Could this boy really be he? With that hair, and that mark on his forehead…

I glanced at the fountain. There was a white-gold crown etched with prancing foxes resting on the ledge, and a splintery shepherd's crook leaned against the pool's wall.

The fabled crook! Just like in the holy texts!

"That's right," the teen said, holding out his hand. "Dream Sandist. King of Aspirre. Grand to meet you again, Xavier."

I gave him my hand to shake—but instead, he gently peeled off my glove and stared at my birthmark of three black diamonds.

"Still the same…" he murmured.

"Sir?" I began, anxious. "They say you're the original Relic Child… Not a reincarnation, like Willow. Is that true?"

"Yes," he agreed, releasing my hand.

"But they say you're nearly two-thousand years old," I protested. "Why do you look so young?"

He held a coy finger to his lips. "Family secret. Now—Willow, dear, I'd like to try a little experiment. Would you mind playing your music watch for a moment?"

Willow squinted an eye at him. "Why?"

"You'll see, I promise."

Willow glared at me as a cat would a snake. She turned her back to me and fished something from her gown's collar. I stood on my toes, trying to see, but all I saw was glint of something shiny. A soft *criik-criik-criik* sounded, as though she were winding gears.

Music started twinkling. It was a slow melody, a dreary lullaby, wavering and tinkering in the still air.

"What is that…?" I took a step toward her—

My mark of diamonds began to gleam with a pulsating violet light.

I yelped and shuffled back.

Willow wheeled about, gasping at my glowing mark.

"What is *that*?" She ran to me, shoving the circular amulet that played the music next to my birthmark. My diamonds gleamed brighter, shining along with the strange, powdery crystals inside the amulet's silver frame. Willow gazed at it in wonder. "I've never seen that before…!"

"N… Neither have I…!" I moved my hand away from the amulet. The lights faded. Then I moved it back to watch it brighten once more. When the music died, the glow faded from my birthmark entirely.

King Dream clapped his hands. "Still the same. Very good. I suspect it would have been this way for the Orbs, if my wife didn't have them currently."

"What is this?" I asked, my brow knitting at Willow's amulet. "And what is that song—?"

Willow jerked the amulet away, clicking the silver case shut.

"It's… my music watch," she said, her glare suspicious. "*I* want to know what that mark is about. That's the Crest of Nirus, isn't it? Has that always been there?"

I lifted my left hand, showing her the Crest. "Yes… Alex has it on his other hand. It's our Evocator's mark."

Her stare went wide at me. "But the Crest itself isn't an Evocator's mark! You're a Necrovoker! Why isn't it a Death mark?"

"It is," I said, "Half the time, anyway."

I touched a finger to her bare shoulder and evoked my Hallows. Violet lights spilled onto her skin as I gave her soul the sensation of gentle feathers brushing her flesh. I hoped this softer texture would make up for my mistake the other day.

The black diamonds on my hand gleamed white suddenly, the Crest shrinking and spinning as it made room for my Death mark, resembling two scythes back to back.

Willow gasped and snatched my fingers, watching the Death mark fade back into the three black diamonds once I dismissed my Hallows.

"What in Death?" Willow rubbed her shoulder where I'd touched her. "And you can use the Sensory-Illusion… Even Sir Gale said he has trouble creating realistic sensations…"

I shrugged. "I only just learned it. I'd first tested it on a non-resurrected ghost, so you were the first time I used it on a living soul and…" I shut my eyes, cursing myself for even bringing it up. "N-never mind."

King Dream rose in a hum. "Well, it was a pleasure seeing you again, Xavier. Send your brother a due hello… Willow, dear, is your mother inside?"

Willow nodded.

"Well then." King Dream retrieved his crown from the fountain's edge and tossed it carelessly over his azure locks. He looked as if he only wore it for everyone else's sake. "I think I'd like to catch up a bit before I take my leave." He plucked his shepherd's crook from the pool's wall. A bell jingled from the hook, tied there by a black ribbon lined with silver butterflies.

My gaze narrowed at the crook. "That ribbon…"

"Hm?" Dream jingled the bell with a light shake. "Ah, this? The bell is mine, though the ribbon belonged to my sister some thousand years ago. Well, it belonged to *you*, Death." Dream chuckled and ruffled Willow's long hair. "From your first incarnation."

"But…" I touched my coat's hidden pocket. "It looks the same as…"

Dream's head cocked. Then he jammed his fingers over my scalp, making me start. His eyes glazed, and the crowned Dream mark on his brow gleamed azure.

"Interesting," he said, turning to Willow. "It seems your new betrothed has a coincidental gift for you, darling."

Willow's gaze turned baffled at me. "A gift?"

I glared at the teenaged king ruefully. *He must have had a vision of it.* Silently cursing my ruined surprise, I pulled out the wrapped box from my pocket.

"I…" I began in a mumble, "I heard your *Rae'u Shelic* was today, so…" I shoved the box in her hand and looked away in a blush. "H-here."

Curious, she peeled off the wrappings and opened the box. Her nose crinkled at the contents inside. She lifted the black, butterfly ribbon and silver bell. "A bell?"

"It's, er, for your hair," I explained, nervous. "I thought… well, you said that your other ribbons weren't long enough, so I found one that should be the right length to keep it off the ground."

Dream compared Willow's gift to the ribbon tied to his crook, musing, "How curious."

Willow handed me the ribbon, excited. "Can you tie it for me?"

She bundled her hair together in a messy twist, and my fingers fumbled to tie the ribbon into a secure bow, the bell jingling. When it was done, Willow twirled and examined the result. Her hair was safely away from her feet. The bell jingled again, making her beam.

"Thank you." She said, cheered. "I love it."

I exhaled in relief. "Thank Bloods… I mean, er, you're welcome."

"Well," Dream hummed. "I suppose I should find your mother, Willow. Xavier?" His icy eyes fell to me again, this time with an eerie look. "Do be more careful around poisonous beasts. There may come a time when you face a more venomous creature." His tone quieted to a dim whisper. "I suggest you spend these next four years wisely."

I shivered. *Four years?* Why so specific…?

Before I could ask, he walked off, disappearing into the ballroom with nothing but a half-hearted wave to Willow and me.

Part Two
Death and Poison

FOUR YEARS AFTER

KAEL

They did this…

The voice hissed in my ear, its truth ringing with an addicting cadence.
"They did…" I repeated in a whisper, clutching my arms as I sat in the empty abyss of blackness. The floor holding me was invisible to the eye, as if made of glass. I rubbed the raised lines of skin along my brow. Dream's seal. The reason I was trapped in here. How long had it been now…? How many centuries have passed?

They will bring the End…

"The End…" I mimicked as the voice rang in my mind. I didn't know if it was a real voice speaking to me, or if it was my own thoughts manifesting from my fractured subconscious.

We will bring the world Sanctuary…

"We will… bring Sanctuary…" I sucked in a deep inhale, craning my head up to look at the endless void of nothingness above me.

We will kill those who have wronged us…

My fingers clenched over my arms, claws puncturing flesh. "Death… Dream… All of them…"

Yes… and the Shadowblood…

"Shadowblood… once we're… f-f… free…" The last word was little more than a seething breath, almost foreign. "Free…"

Soon, dear Kael… We will find our freedom…

"S-s-s… soon…" My throat tightened, breaking into a sob. I screamed at the empty abyss. "You've said this for centuries…! When is morning?! When is night?! How much longer will your 'soon' last in this miserable, timeless pit?!"

I had lost my sense of time hundreds of years ago. I couldn't even tell when I was dreaming or awake in this place. Aspirre had no need of these trivial differences. Everything was real here… yet, nothing was real. What even was real? None of it seemed to matter.

Screeches sounded around me.

They were hideous sounds, like nails skidding against glass. The noise festered in my ears, which grew with fur as my cat ears folded down in fright.

I squinted, spying a faint, blackened form shifting against the dark landscape of nothingness. The form was difficult to see, but I could barely make out its sand-like features.

I scrambled to my feet. "The Noctis Golems…!"

Several more forms appeared from the darkness, the sandy creatures multiplying the longer I looked into the void. Their grains sifted and poured nauseatingly, never staying true to a single shape.

They were drawing nearer.

I broke into a sprint, rushing to get away. Their grating screeches rattled my ears—

A new pain split across my forehead—where Dream's seal was branded. The seal burned and pulsed, bringing me to my knees on the invisible floor, howling with agony. A glare spilled from the seal. A rush of energy peeled through my flesh.

I curled into a ball, screaming as the pain worsened.

My skin gleamed with an azure light. The light brightened, growing stronger, blinding me with a burning sting as it flooded the terrain in a terrible flash—

My vision returned at lightning speed, the new brightness stinging horribly.

The blackness of the void was gone.

In its place was an orange and pink sky with gentle clouds, the crimson sun barely dipping past the horizon to cast a beautiful twilight over the new city that had suddenly appeared beneath me.

Far beneath me.

I screamed, belatedly realizing I was falling downward, spiraling toward the city—

Crash!

I landed in someone's wagon, my fall bluntly cushioned by large bags of sugar that burst open on impact, white grains scattering around me. I groaned, my vision splotched.

"What…?" I rubbed my brow tenderly. "Macar…?"

—my fingers stilled on my brow.

The usual lines of raised skin—the seal that Dream had branded onto my forehead to keep me trapped in that timeless prison—was gone.

I'm… f-free…?

The thought was a dim, splash of hope. But even that faded as the rest of my vision blackened, and I lost consciousness over the sacks of sugar.

Free…

16

WILLOW

*C*lunk!

My wooden scythe struck one of my opponent's short-handled blades.

The masked boy blocked my attack in time to save my scythe from reaching his chest, and he leapt aside in a heavy pant, crouching while keeping his dual-blades in front of his hidden face.

I couldn't see his expression behind that mesh helmet. Though, he couldn't see *mine* behind my own, similar mask. My vision was slightly obscured behind the mesh wires, but it was enough for me to see the boy hurtling toward me at full speed.

I slashed my practice scythe upward, forcing him back—

The tip of my crooked blade snagged his wired helmet and peeled it off his shadowy-haired head, throwing the boy off-balance.

THUMP!

He fell on his back in a winded cough, his wooden blades clunking over the ground away from his reach.

I grinned, lowering my blade over his throat and pressing my boot over his chest.

"Terribly sorry," I chuckled and slid off my helmet. My long, ashen hair rolled out in a cascading tail, licking around me and falling past my waist in playful curls. The cavern winds brushed past my face and rattled the silver bell tied to my bundled locks.

"Looks as though I win again," I sang to the teen boy caught under my boot. "But you were quite close this time. Better luck next time, Xavier."

Xavier rubbed his eyes and groaned from the ground. "Bloody Death, Willow… that wasn't fair." He slid his hand down his face, squinting at me crossly with mismatched, blue-and-clear eyes. "If I didn't have to wear this blasted helmet, I might have won this time."

"Oh, I've no doubt." I clasped his hand, pulling him to his feet. "Even though I'm forced to wear the same helmet."

He grumbled, "That's… a technicality…"

"Match over!" called our combat instructor, Sir Gale, from the sidelines. The man gave a sharp *clap* as he approached us. "Congratulations on another win, Your Highness." He nodded to my defeated opponent. "Xavier, you must remember to take your surroundings into account. If you expect to be a Reaper one day, you'll often be required to wear far more obstructive helms with *less* vision. I suggest training more with your brother while wearing them."

Xavier sighed. "Yes, Sir Gale…"

A feminine giggle caught my attention, and I looked about the outdoor training grounds.

Standing just outside of Xavier and my dirt arena, I found a bat-winged teen with silky black hair. It was my royal Aide, Lilli. She had finished her match with Alexander and the two had been watching us.

Now that our match had ended, Lilli and Alex trotted up to us. I twirled my wooden scythe behind me and hummed to Lilli, "Who won yours?"

Lilli's chartreuse eyes rolled as she threw a thumb at Alexander. "Woefully, he did… This time. I still demand a rematch."

Alexander snorted, crossing his arms. "Cease your harping. You'll have your Bloody chance." He lifted an eyebrow at me. "Well, Willow? Are you ready for your Necrovoking exam today? I'll be the one grading you—I *won't* be lenient."

My stomach quivered, but I lifted my nose. "Of… of course I'm ready."

His lips pulled with a grin. "Splendid. I'll see you in class, then."

He walked off with Lilli, leaving me with wobbling knees and deflating confidence.

—Xavier clapped a hand on my shoulder, making me jump.

"Don't worry," he chuckled. "He's being dramatic. Don't let him toy with you."

I nodded, attempting a smile… but my nervousness doubled.

"Your Highness!" a new voice called.

It was Matthiel Inion. He ran to me in a rather large hurry, bowing respectfully before lifting his sienna eyes.

"How was your match, Your Highness?" Matthiel asked, slicking back his sweat-ridden, black hair. "I was busy with my own partner and wasn't able to observe…" He shot Xavier a deadly sharp glare. "He didn't hurt you, did he?"

Xavier matched his glare. "She won. Again."

Matthiel pushed out a relieved breath. "Oh, thank Bloods! I was so worried… Are you ready for our Necrovoking exam?"

I suppressed a groan. It seemed *everyone* was reminding me how difficult this exam would be.

I swallowed the knot in my throat. "Ready enough. I hope."

Matthiel nodded, as if having expected this answer. "We have some time yet before the next class. Would you like a bit more practice, to be sure?"

I exhaled a hard breath, the suggestion already calming my thrashing anxiety. "Please!"

Matthiel stood taller and walked ahead, waving for me to follow. "Very well! Come, we'll have to hurry."

I followed him alongside Xavier, who was brooding over something with an irritated visage… but I didn't have time to ask of it. I needed to focus on the exam.

The exam I could not, under any circumstances, fail.

"Your Highness Death." Alexander's voice echoed in the catacombs. His mismatched eyes flicked to me—straightening my spine from beside Lilli. "You're the last examinee. Please come up."

I clutched my shaking fingers, rigidly approaching Alexander.

The chamber grew Deathly silent. It became suffocating, all eyes turned to me as I stood at the edge of the gleaming waterway by the looming statue of the Seamstress.

Xavier stood off to the side to observe everyone's tests in silence. He couldn't perform this particular test since it involved resurrecting a physical skeleton.

There weren't many others in the class, even still. After four years, we hadn't gained any more Necrovokers in the academy since the twins arrived. Only Matthiel, Lilli and my cousin Felix occupied the other desks, as usual.

They had all passed their resurrection exams—having been approved by Alexander, who Sir Gale had appointed as his assistant instructor in vessel construction.

Cousin Felix snorted, his lips curled in a wry grin as if looking forward to my amusing failure.

My teeth sharpened, fox ears growing. *Sorry, Felix*, the thought was vindictive. *You'll have to be disappointed today.*

I defiantly glanced down at the contents of my exam.

Between Alexander and me lay a pile of scattered bones on the floor. It was the same bones all the other students in had already successfully pieced together with their Necrovoking.

And now it was my turn.

Alexander gestured to the bones. "When you're ready, Your Highness."

I drew in a deep breath… and raised my hands. My fingers gleamed with violet lights, which stretched and glittered over the pile of bones at my feet.

Very, *very* slowly, the bones lifted off the ground.

Steady, I reminded in silence, carefully arranging the bones where they were meant to go. *Don't lose focus.*

Sweat beaded my brow and trickled into my eye. I squinted from the sting, but kept my glowing hands raised and pouring with magic.

Then, at long last, the final bone *popped* into place, and standing before me was a fully assembled skeleton.

"Very good placement," Alexander grunted beside me.

I gave a strained smile, keeping my magic Hallows flowing so the bones didn't scatter to the ground while Alexander judged my progress with a critical eye. I wished he would hurry. My arms were starting to tremble as my stamina drained under all this effort.

"And for the rest?" Alex urged, crossing his arms.

I refocused on my assembled skeleton. In a hard breath, I pushed my violet Hallows *into* the bones. Muscle and tendon grew around them. Then veins and nerves… skin… hair…

I gave a final *shove* of magic—

The resurrected corpse's heart was beating strong, and its lungs inflated.

I nearly collapsed from the throbbing headache it caused, but I quickly spread my feet to stabilize my footing, puffing for air.

The others fell into congratulatory applause, and Alex nodded his approval.

"Well done," Alex praised gruffly. "You pass."

"Glorious Nira…!" I dropped to the stone floor, heaving straggled breaths.

Sir Gale clapped in a chuckle. "Wonderfully done, everyone! Now that you've all passed your resurrection exams, be prepared for *tomorrow's* test. Sensory-Illusion. Xavier will be grading you this time. Rest well."

Everyone broke into fervent chatter as they left in a herd down the catacomb's tunnels, leaving me behind as I puffed and wheezed by the waterways.

Bloods, my lungs were on fire. I wobbled to my feet, trying to take a step. But my knees buckled, and I tumbled toward the water—

Someone snatched my arm to keep me steady.

"Careful," Xavier warned by my ear.

My head twisted—and my lips nearly brushed over his.

I snapped my head forward, hoping he hadn't noticed. I knew it was foolish to be shy after so many years, but damn me, that didn't make it any less terrifying. We were engaged, for Death's sake. Shouldn't we have done something by now? Anything? Seamstress prick me, why couldn't I do something bold for once…?

Xavier must have noticed because he quickly released my arm and cleared his throat. "Will, er…" he began, flushing. "Will you be all right? If you need the infirmary again…"

"I'll be fine," I insisted and led the way down the tunnels. We reached the curling stairwell and climbed up together. "I've improved enough that I can last longer during Evocations now."

He followed beside me and smiled. "So I saw. Then, are you ready for your Sensory-Illusion exam tomorrow?"

"I should hope so." I stared at my bandaged fingertips. They were still sore from all the needle pricking they'd endured, the puckered scabs throbbing from under the bandages.

Finger pricking was to be one of the sensory-illusions on tomorrow's exam. For one to cast a sensation on other souls, one had to have experienced that sensation physically themselves and committed it to memory. The pricking had been the most painful sensation to study. It was frightening to think this would be a meager ache compared to future training in the coming years.

Xavier took my bandaged hand with tender fingers. "Did you not have a Healer tend to your wounds?"

"I did." I bit my lip. "Well, except for this last round… there wasn't time before classes."

Xavier's stare flattened at me. "How many times have you pricked them?"

I took back my hand and cupped them gingerly. "I… lost count…?"

Xavier rubbed his eyes. "Willow, these aren't flower petals we're working with anymore. We're introducing pain, now. You can't risk over training with these techniques. The farther you get in the coming courses, the more dangerous the training will be."

"Fine," I sighed. "I'll be more careful."

"Thank you." He crossed his arms and leaned back against the railing. Then he winced and pushed off.

"What's wrong?" I asked.

He rubbed his back in a small seethe, forcing an assuring smile. "I'm all right… I suppose the scars are still sore from my own training."

He pulled his hand away from his back. The fingers were stained red. "Blast, one reopened…"

"Here, let's get a better look in the light outside."

He let me help him up the rest of the stairwell. Once we reached the mausoleum at the top of the steps, we strode out to the academy's graveyard under the overcasting gleam of the white-and-blue Floating Lights.

I eased him onto a stone bench and circled behind him to examine his back. His cloak sported small splotches of blood near his shoulder blade.

"Come on, then," I huffed, helping him unfasten his cloak. "Let's have a look."

He lifted his tunic, revealing his scarred back. There were far more than last I'd seen. Some were older and fully hardened while others were still fresh and puckered. The slash by his shoulder blade was one of the fresh scars. It seemed it hadn't hardened enough to keep closed yet and was torn in small slits, beading with blood.

"Death, that's a lot of scars…" I hushed. "No wonder you were slower than usual during our sparing. What in Death did you use this time?"

He shrugged, wincing when the motion pulled at his opened wound. "A dagger slash again. I asked Sir Gale to cut deeper this time to try and emulate a Fera's claws."

"Bloods be good…" I shuddered. "When will I get to that level?"

"Don't worry, you all have another year or so." He yielded to a shiver, the chilled air pimpling his bare skin. "I suppose I should get inside and find a Healer to reseal it… Wait." An idea seemed to strike him. He twisted back to me eagerly. "Could you cauterize it? With your Pyrovoking?"

I started. "Why in Death would you want me to do that?"

"For one, I need to reseal this wound," he said, "and for another, I've been meaning to collect the sensation of being burned by fire. Cauterizing would achieve both. Like killing two demons with one scythe."

I gave him an uncertain grimace. "You're sure you want this?"

His laugh bordered on maniacal. "Oh, I'm sure. I've been looking forward to this one. I'd rather it be your fire, anyway."

"Why?"

He shrugged again, as if it should have been obvious. "Because I trust you."

I blushed, rubbing my knuckles. "I… I suppose, if you're sure…"

"I'm sure."

"Just… raise your hand if you want me to stop?"

He balled up his tunic and stuffed some of it in his mouth to use as a gag. Then he hunched over the bench and threw me a thumbs-up.

I reached a hesitant hand to his shoulder blade and evoked my fire Hallows. A small puff of orange flame ignited from my fingertips, burning away a few of my bandages.

I dragged the flame over his opened wound.

His muscles tensed on contact, grunting at the pain from beneath his makeshift gag. The stink of melting skin hit my nostrils. His flinching made me nervous, but his hands never left the bench, his claws scraping the stone to keep them firmly set. *He would signal if it was too much*, I reminded silently. I kept a steady breath and dragged my enflamed finger over the rest of the wound. When it was finally finished, I dismissed my Hallows, staring at the new scabs coating his skin.

Xavier spit out his gag and gasped for breath over his knees. "Bloody Death…!"

I hurried around the bench to check his face. "Are you all right?"

He wheezed out a chuckle. "Well, I'm not cold anymore."

I slipped a laugh, setting a hand at my side. "Happy to be of assistance… Part of me envies I'll never have a way to collect that sensation myself, though."

He retrieved his crumpled tunic from the ground and pulled it over his head, grimacing at the saliva stain with a twisted mouth. "Isn't it only your skin that can't be burned?" he asked. "What of blood?"

I stopped to think on it. "I suppose if it melds the blood *to* the skin, perhaps it would be effective for scabbing over." I lowered to the bench beside him. "If I ever get that far with these tactile illusions to begin with… But I suppose I should focus on passing tomorrow's exam first, hadn't I?" I stared at my fingers. The burnt bandages were charred in some places, exposing the puckered scabs from my training. "Bloods, I hope I'm ready."

Xavier gave a teasing grin. "We'll have to see tomorrow, won't we?"

His tone was playful, but it still ripped my nerves. I dropped my face in my hands. "I can't afford to fail, Xavier… What sort of Death Princess would I be if I failed at Death Hallows?"

Xavier's cheer drained, seeing I wasn't in the mood for jesting. He scratched his neck. "If you're that worried… shall we have another study session tonight?"

I eyed him warily. "Would you be all right with that? I fear I've taken up enough of your time with these lessons already."

He gave a sharp laugh. "Nonsense. I'm supposed to be helping everyone with my half of Necrovoking, and that's precisely what I intend to do. We'll meet at the usual place?"

I blushed, but nodded. "Very well… the usual place."

"Brilliant." He hefted to his feet, newly enthused. He only winced once from the scars on his back before flashing me a smile. "I'll see you tonight."

I watched him leave, then hunched over the bench with a heavy sigh.

"How quaint," a languid voice mused behind me. "The mutt thinks simple tutoring will cure her defect."

I glared up at my ashen-haired cousin. Felix was leaned against a large tombstone while crunching into an apple. His colorless eyes were stale with pity.

I grumbled, "Your time would be better spent fretting over your own studies, Felix."

"Fretting?" He took another popping bite of his apple and pushed off the tombstone, coming to tower over me as if to accentuate how much taller he was. "I think it will be amusing seeing the heiress fail at the simplest exam in her own Hallows. No, I needn't fret. I trust the council will make the right decision once they see the depressing future you hold for the realm."

I snorted. "We aren't children anymore, Felix. We've both improved. Were I you, I'd take care not to let my heckling expose my fear that my 'mutt cousin' is becoming a viable threat to my ego—"

He tapped a single finger to my shoulder. It gleamed with violet light that sank into my pores. Pain suddenly slashed across my back. It ripped and burned and pulled with such heat, I thought my flesh was tearing open across my spine.

I screamed and crumpled to the ground, writhing in agony. As the seconds passed at a sloth's pace, the stinging ache began to fade from my back. I puffed over my knees, shaking.

Felix's chuckle bubbled from around the apple piece he chewed. "Interesting. It seems you haven't even begun your self-torture training." He swallowed and crouched down as his lips curled in a patronizing smile, gesturing to my bandaged fingers with his apple. "Do have fun with your little exam tomorrow. I'm sure finger pricking will impress the council in a few years. Enjoy your throne, while you have it, Cousin."

He rose and left me there on the ground. As I watched him leave, I caught sight of the hardened scars running across the back of his neck that peeked above his high collar.

My teeth sharpened, fox ears growing as a growl ripped through my throat. "I… am *Death*…"

I threw off my cloak and plucked the glittering scythe-stick out of my hair in a vicious snarl. My scythe materialized in my grip. I poised the crooked blade over my shoulder, holding the sharpened tip to my back.

I took a shaking breath, whispering, "I will not fall behind… This is my Hallows."

I ripped the blade over my back.

XAVIER

In the midst of the royal gardens, under the cover of Dim Light hours, I waited in the usual grove of dwarfed willow trees where the princess and I often held our private study sessions. The drooping branches swayed in the breeze that swept over the soft patch of Candle Lilies.

I sat cross-legged in the lily patch with a fist shoved to my cheek. While I waited for Willow to arrive, I occupied myself with plucking lily after lily angrily, my wolf ears grown and curled back.

Bloody Matthiel, I fumed in silence, the whine of crickets filling my grown ears. *Always taking up her time with THEIR study sessions...*

One of my ears twitched. I'd hoped to gain some traction with tonight's meeting. Though, admittedly, not the sort of traction with her studies. She knew the material. She'd have no trouble with the exam, not after her progress from our last session. She was ready.

What I wanted to do tonight was tell her... well, tell her... Something?

What did I even expect to say? Maybe I shouldn't say anything.

No, Gods damn it! I pounded a fist to my head. I'd avoided this for four Bloody years—what was I waiting for? A damned invitation?

My stomach churned, and I resumed plucking lilies with more vigor. How long was I willing to pretend being her friend was enough? It was driving me mad. Our study sessions had been growing unbearable. I was painfully aware of her shrinking the distance between us each night here. Did she notice? Was it intentional? Gods, the last time we were here, she fell asleep on my shoulder before I finished reading the chapter I was teaching. She'd been so warm...

"—Forgive my tardiness," Willow's voice panted behind me suddenly, making me knock over my lantern in fright. "I... I had a few things to... see to..."

"W-Willow!" I hurried to right the lantern and swept aside the many Candle Lilies I'd plucked. My laughter was nervous. "I, er, was worried you decided my help wasn't needed."

"No, no," she insisted, still winded as she seated herself across from me. She wore a dark indigo cloak with the cowl lifted over her head. There was something strange about her face, but it was difficult to see under her hood's shadow. "I... I was just caught up with some... extra training."

My brow crinkled. "Extra training? With… Matthiel…?"

She lowered her cowl and shook out her long, curling locks, the bell tied to her hair giving a flighty jingle. "No, not that sort of training… this was, er, self-training. It was a… p-personal matter."

"I see… Er, are you well? You look a bit sickly."

She looked far more than sickly, but I didn't want to sound rude. She looked like a downright ghoul. Her grey complexion had grown paler than usual, her eyes heavy with dark circles and sweat coating her brow.

"I'm fine." There was a concerning crunch to her tone. She exhaled sharply and lifted her hands impatiently. "Shall… shall we begin? I need to be sure I pass this exam tomorrow."

Biting down my nerves, I gently placed my hands over hers. "Very well… If you're sure."

The touch of her palms sent a delightful burn over my skin. Willow always radiated with her own personal heat, like other Pyrovokers. Her soul's fire made any contact dangerously noticeable. But Gods, was it addicting. It was all I could do not to flinch. But I gave a practiced swallow and shut my eyes, focusing on the task.

"Let's begin with the simple textures," I said. "First, a bed of down feathers."

A soft sensation bloomed over my back, lightly squeezing me. It was faint, not truly tangible, but it was as strong as what the others could produce.

"Good," I commended. "Now let's feel a cat's tail brushing against your arm."

Something fluffy brushed over my arm in response.

I chuckled. "Very good. Now… a pin prick on your finger—*ouch*!"

A sharp stab of pain stung my finger, so quick I hadn't been prepared for it and flinched out of her hold, my eyes flying open.

She opened her own eyes in a cringe. "Sorry."

"No, no," I assured in a laugh. "That's the response you want. Well done."

She loosened her lungs in relief, then closed her eyes once more and laid her hands over mine to continue.

"Ice melting in your hands," I called, closing my eyes.

A wet sensation trickled between my fingers and pooled over my palms. It chilled my skin until I shivered and…

"Sorry." She quickly squeezed my fingers, letting her Pyrovoker's heat warm my hands.

I sighed. "Willow, don't feel guilty about these sensations. The point of the exam is that I feel them. You can't keep apologizing and take it back after every discomfort."

Her fox ears grew. "I-I know…" She dropped her hands over her lap in defeat. "Bloods, I'm going to fail…"

"You're not going to fail." I insisted. "You're doing splendidly. Like you do with everything."

She scowled at me, her forehead creasing with disbelieving wrinkles. "You don't have to patronize me, Xavier."

"I'm not." I crossed my arms, Deathly serious. "You must stop chastising yourself, Willow. You may have less stamina than the others, true, but only because you have *six Hallows*. No one else in the world has more than three—do you understand how world-shattering that is? Especially to a Hallows-crippled defect?"

Willow's gaze sharpened. "Excuse me?"

"Do you have any idea what I wouldn't give to have even one *whole* element?" I sighed wistfully, leaning back and circling a hand in the air. "Bloods, that would be something. Death, even being Hallowless would be an improvement. At least then it wouldn't be a mistake, it would just make me normal."

Willow scowled at me. "There is nothing *ab*normal about you."

I snorted and leaned my arms on my crossed legs heavily. "Willow, please. You and I both know I'll never be a real Necrovoker. If I'm remembered at all, hundreds of years from now, it will be because of my defect. But you? The entire world will always know you as the most noteworthy Evocator to ever live—"

"You are *not* a defect."

I stiffened. She was casting me an unexpectedly dark glower. The bags pulling down her lids made the look all the more ominous.

"You will not use that word again." Her fox ears curled murderously. "If you don't wish for me to pity myself, you aren't permitted to do so either."

I blinked at her, flushing.

"Xavier." Willow's voice was hauntingly soft. She took my hands in her warm fingers, lacing them together. "Never let me hear you condemn your gift again. Please. You insult my admiration."

"Y… yes, your grace…" I whispered, too nervous to say her name after a command like that. "I'm sorr—*hrch*…!"

She crushed my fingers in a perturbed gasp. "Good Seamstress, why would you call me that?"

"B-because that's what everyone else calls you," I stammered. "All the vassals, the citizens, the servants, the teachers… Even Matthiel—"

"You aren't Matthiel." Willow shuddered. "Bloods, it's disturbing coming from you. Don't ever do it again."

"S-sorry," I mumbled, mortified. Desperate for a distraction, I cleared my throat. "Sh-shall we, er, continue the lesson… Willow…?"

She gave a contented sigh at the sound of her name, her grip on my fingers relaxing. "Much better."

Crickets whined around us in the sudden silence. Our fingers were still laced together. Mine were shivering so much even her Pyrovoker's heat wasn't enough to quell them. What was that look about? Gods damn it, how was I supposed to concentrate with those eyes fixated on me? They were hypnotic when this close, like icy crystals…

She suddenly collapsed in my arms.

"W… Willow?" I breathed in a start.

She didn't stir.

"Willow, what's wrong?" I hurriedly pulled her hair away from her neck, laying a hand on her back to check her breathing.

Something wet squished under my hand. My fingers were now seeping with thick blood.

Panic splintered. "Willow?!"

A faint hiss of pain escaped her lips, her mumbling words incoherent. I fumbled to unfasten her cloak and grew my claws to rip her high-collar open, tearing it down her back.

Her bandaged spine was absolutely drenched with dark blood. Peeking through the cracks of the messily wrapped gauze, I saw fresh scars and open wounds lacerating her skin. They were all drastically deep.

Self-training. Her words rang through my head like funeral bells. My wolf ears grew. "Willow…! Were you conducting self-torture? Without a Healer?"

Her breathing intensified, and she let out a weak whisper, "I… I can't… fall behind…"

"Death's Head, Willow!" I scooped her in my arms and leapt to my feet, rushing her out of the veiling branches of the dwarfed Willow trees. "You daft girl…!"

17

WILLOW

I woke in a haze, my spine burning like Death.

I sat up. Apparently, I was in my bed. When had I gotten here?

Bloody Void, my head was throbbing like mad. I winced and peeled off the comforter. I was in a new sleepgown. The bandages I'd tried to wrap around my wounds earlier looked fresh and clean… and far more professionally dressed than my amateur attempt from before.

I glanced out my open stone balcony. It was still night, the cavern's Floating Lights still a dim indigo hue in the ceiling mists. Then I caught sight of something—someone—sitting on the rail of the balcony. His legs were hanging over the outside with his back facing me. He was cursing and wincing at a small blot of blood lining his tunic near his shoulder blade.

My sore throat slipped a croak. "Xavier…?"

Xavier's head snapped to me. He loosened his lungs and hopped off the balcony to approach, seething from his newly split wound again. "Thank Death, you're awake. How do you feel?"

"I've been better." I massaged my temples. "What happened?"

"You went into shock from the pain." Xavier explained. "I took you to the palace infirmary to find a Healer."

My brow furrowed. "The infirmary? Then why am I in my chambers?"

"They brought you here after seeing to your wounds. Said you would recover well and ought to be comfortable when you woke."

"I see… then what are you doing here?"

He scratched his neck. "I sort of… snuck up your balcony to check on you. Climbed up the vines."

I gave him a coiled glare. "Why would you make a climb like that after I just finished closing your wound? Now look what you did, it's split open again."

"You are *not* allowed to reprimand me for being reckless, Willow," he chewed. His grown wolf ears curled back angrily. "Not after that foolish stunt you pulled."

"I… suppose not…" I slid my legs over the edge of the mattress. My vision spun slightly, and I gripped the headboard for stability. "Perhaps I over did it, didn't I?"

"You think?" Xavier crossed his arms. There was an uncharacteristic scowl creasing his face. "What in Bloods were you thinking? Self-torture? Unsupervised? You know how dangerous that advanced study is. Especially without a Healer. You could have died if your wounds were infected, Willow. What if you hit an artery by mistake?"

My claws pierced the mattress as my arms shook. "I… I'm sorry. I needed to pass the exam and…"

"Damn the exam, Willow!" Xavier shouted. "A Bloody grade isn't worth your *life*!"

"It isn't about the grade!" I barked. "You *and* Felix have already advanced to that training while I'm falling behind! Again! I'm supposed to be the damned heiress of Grim! I'm supposed to have *the soul of Death!* I'm supposed to be the *one* shifter who excels at this Gods damned element, yet I can barely skirt by with the simplest task…!" I gritted my teeth, tears spilling. "I know I'm a mistake. I know I don't deserve these Hallows. Bloods, I shouldn't even exist… But I have to try and keep up with you all… anyway I can."

Silence strangled the chambers. There was naught but the ticking grandfather clock in the corner to disturb the space between us.

Xavier's voice was quiet. "Willow…"

"Just leave." I stared at the wall. "I'll not waste your time further."

"Waste my time?" He sounded irked suddenly. The bed dipped with his weight when he sat beside me on the edge with a long, hollow sigh. "Very well… You're right. This *has* been a waste of time. Every session we've had hasn't brought you any further along in your training even the slightest."

Tears stung. I shut my eyes, the truth of it slamming harder than I was prepared for. I'd been hardened to Felix's constant criticisms, but to hear it from Xavier, of all people…

"—Because you've already excelled at every lesson before we even started."

I felt a cold hand on my fingers.

"Willow." He let out a soft breath. "You don't need extra tutoring. You might have been behind the others a long time ago, but you've been on course with them for years now. You don't need Matthiel, you don't need Alex, and you certainly don't need me."

My face twisted at him. "Then why have you been offering to tutor me?"

"I… well, I may have wanted an excuse to… to see you…"

Silence again. His face turned an impressive shade of red.

I hesitated. "Why?"

"Because…" His tone dwindled. "Because I'm selfish. All right? I'd take up *all* your time, were I allowed, I…" He smeared a hand over his face. Then he quickly lifted to his feet. "I'm sorry. We can stop these useless sessions now. You're more than ready."

He started to leave.

I snatched his fingers. "Wait."

He kept his gaze on the wall, his wolf ears folding down. "You don't need me, Willow. I'm sorry I made a mess of your confidence… I won't waste your time anymore—"

"Perhaps I want you to waste my time," I blurted. My pulse roared when I realized I'd said that aloud. My soul's fire writhed like hungry fangs, strangling my voice into mortified silence.

He paused. Twisted back. "You… what?"

Death… I silently cursed myself. But it was already said. He'd heard it. *Well, nothing for it, now.*

In a shaken inhale, I rose to my feet. Interlaced our fingers. "Please," I said, squeezing his hand. "Do waste my time… As much as you like."

He went still. Floundered for a reply. "I… ah… i-if you wish…" He had an afterthought and added, "But no more unsupervised torture. Please?"

I flicked my eyes down, blushing. "Y-yes… I promise. But there was one sensation I've been hoping to collect…" My chest thundered deafeningly, heart splitting through my ears. "And… I want it to be from you."

He looked quizzical. "Of… of course. What sensation—"

I yanked his head to me and pressed our lips together.

His self-restraint was swiftly abandoned, pulling me closer and cupping my chin to deepen the kiss, as if relishing the warmth that radiated from my lips. He matched my growing pressure, his fingers touching my face with a cold tenderness light enough to send me floating through the cavern's ceiling all the way to the surface lands.

When we finally parted, my vision spun. The only thing I could see were his entrancing mismatched eyes.

"Willow…" he breathed so, so softly. With my pulse still screaming, and my face still close enough to feel the heat of his breath, I barely heard him hush, *"Myel ma amya, Willow."*

I traced his grey face, whispering, *"Myel ma amya… Xavier."*

Our lips burned together again, and I let my mind drift into bliss.

18

WILLOW

Fire raged the ballroom. Columns crackled and splintered as they were burnt to char, the smoke thick and suffocating.

Corpses piled round the ballroom floor. Blood pooled around them, their faces melted and burnt, cheekbones and skeletal teeth gleaning through as the fire raged in the reflection of their empty stares.

And in the veiling haze of smoke, two faces with mismatched eyes cowered under a man's looming shadow.

I awoke in a sweat, the heat of the palace fire still warming my skin from the dream. But there was no fire. There was no smoke. I was still in my chambers lying in bed.

I threw off the comforter and hurried to the crystal ball on my blackwood vanity. I took a deep breath and let it out in a smooth stream, lightly touching my fingers over the orb as they gleamed azure.

Fire crackled in the crystal, smoke pluming all throughout the ballroom… It was the same as the dream. Which meant it *was* a vision. The same one I'd had years ago.

I focused on the crystal and tried to push further with my Third Eye—but was met with a sharp throb to my temple, making me wince and knuckle my forehead tenderly.

"Are you all right, love?"

I jumped at the familiar voice from my open stone balcony.

Xavier had climbed up the vines, as he often did these past few weeks, and pulled his arms over the railing to peek inside.

When he saw me at my crystal ball, Xavier furrowed his mismatched gaze. "Did you have a vision?"

"Apparently," I sighed and went to the balcony to meet him.

He pulled himself the rest of the way up and sat on the railing. "You rarely have those anymore. What was it about?"

I hesitated. While I was excited to finally have another vision, it wasn't one I was comfortable sharing—especially since he and his brother were at the center of it. How was I going to explain that?

"I'm not sure," I said and sat on the balcony's floor with my back to the railing. I wasn't nearly brave enough to sit on the rail with him. We were three floors up. Looking down at the gardens below often made me dizzy, so I found it was best to take the floor during his private visits. "I'll have to sort through it to know what it means… Give me some time?"

He seemed disappointed, but slid off the railing to sit on the floor beside me. "Oh, all right. If you insist on being cryptic." He grinned and flicked me a teasing glare. "You're turning into your mother, you realize."

"Oh, am I?" I chuckled and pushed his shoulder playfully. "Then you'd best watch what you think, lest I have a vision of it and ruin any surprises you may have planned."

"With the few visions you have," he laughed, "you couldn't ruin any surprises if I wrote you a Bloody note entailing them alphabetically."

I shoved him onto his side. He grabbed my arm and yanked me on top of him, pulling my chin to his face and brought our lips together in a chuckling kiss.

—A knock came at the door.

We shuffled off each other.

My mother's muffled voice called from the other side of the door. "Willow? Are you in there?"

The knob rattled.

Xavier fumbled over the balcony rail and climbed down the vines, clinging tight to hide from my mother—just as she opened the door.

"Mother," I greeted with a quick smile and walked inside to meet her. Hopefully if I came to her, she wouldn't feel the need to go out to the balcony. "*Chanerr machet*, good morning. Did you wish to discuss something?"

With a haunted look, my mother went to my vanity and sat before my crystal ball, her gaze pensive. "I Saw your vision in Aspirre."

My good mood snuffed. The memory of my dream came crackling back. The fire, the smoke, the twins' faces...

"Oh," I said softly. I looked over my shoulder toward the balcony. I was sure Xavier's fingers would start cramping soon if he hung there any longer. I cleared my throat. "Er, could we perhaps discuss this another time, Mother? I'm, er, still tired and would rather be... *alert* for this topic, and..."

Mother's gaze snapped to the balcony suddenly. Her Dream mark gleamed from her neck as her eyes grew distant, as if having a vision.

"Ah," Mother hummed, her tone brightening. "Good morning, Xavier. Why don't you come up here before your screaming knuckles snap off?"

Death.

There was silence for a long moment. Then I heard Xavier sigh from beneath the balcony, and he climbed up to fold his arms over the railing with a nervous smile. "*Chanerr machet*, Your Majesty..."

Mother placed a delicate hand on her hip. "I suppose you intend to bring my daughter into town again?"

Xavier cleared his throat. "Erm... well, I..."

"Will be more than happy to meet my daughter at the palace gates where you will be escorted by an honorguard, as is proper," my mother finished with a smile while wafting a shooing hand at him. "Goodbye, Xavier."

Xavier sighed and climbed down once more, grumbling to me, "I'll see you down there, I suppose..."

He descended back to the gardens. After giving him enough time to climb out of earshot, I turned on my mother and gave her a sharp glare.

"Thank you for ruining what could have been a romantic outing, Mother... Again."

She looked right proud of herself. "It can still be romantic with a few chaperones, dear."

"You mean babysitters," I grimaced. "Honestly, I can take care of myself—*and* Xavier."

"Oh, I'm not worried about any danger," Mother clarified, "I'm worried about bad publicity at this point. So long as you stay clear of that, I wouldn't even mind looking the other way if you both decided to explore more intimate endeavors—"

"Mother!" I squeaked, my face blazing.

Mother lifted her hands in a shrug. "What? I know what it's like. I was your age once—for a few hundred years, actually—and that's about the time I started getting *curious*, at the very least." She tapped a thoughtful finger to her lips. "Although, I suppose I wasn't successful until I met your father... and our first night together did result in *you*, so perhaps you ought to wait a bit longer—"

"We are not having this conversation." I clasped my hands over my ears in a groan. "Can we *please* change the subject?"

Mother sighed and sat on the mattress beside me, folding her hands neatly over her lap as her expression grew dire. "Very well... I do wish to speak about your vision, Willow."

My bones shuddered. "I... don't know any more than the small fragment."

She lifted her hand toward the crystal ball on the vanity. "Could you show me again?"

I hesitated, but went to sit at my vanity. Mother loomed over my shoulder as I touched the crystal with glowing-blue fingers and poured my prophetic Hallows into the ball.

The flames rose within its surface. Smoke in the ballroom, screams ripping, the faces of the guards and guests melting away as if burnt from a black, veiny acid... and finally, the twins cowered under a shadow that came for them.

When the vision ended, I glanced up at Mother. Her face was creased with a dark expression.

I shivered at that look. "What does it mean?"

She was silent. Her azure fox ears grew as a growl slipped from her throat. "It means I must speak with your grandfather."

She abruptly turned to leave.

I called after her, "It—it's only a possibility, isn't it? The future has many paths…?"

She opened my doors and flicked me a sidelong glance over her shoulder. "Don't dwell on such things, darling… you don't want your 'romantic outing' to be burdened by the infinite possibilities of what may—or may not—be." She offered a smile, but it was placid. It was as if she wasn't looking at me anymore. "You'd best get dressed. You don't want to keep the poor boy waiting out in the cold."

She closed the door behind her with a soft click.

The markets were bursting with lively music and chatter today. My little crow, Jewel, fluttered by my head while Xavier and I rode on horseback side by side. We were trying our best to enjoy the outing despite some minor… obstacles.

Mother had sent for an entire ring of guards to escort us. Their silver helms glinted under the bright, Floating Lights as they rode their own mounts around us and blocked our view of the streets.

It can still be romantic with a few chaperones, my mother's words bounced in my memory. I hunched over my horse in a bitter scoff. *So much for that theory, Mother.*

Xavier looked just as irritated, scowling at the guards with his wolf ears already grown.

"Erm, Mother Maria?" Xavier called to the captain of our intrusive honorguard.

Lilli's Mother, Maria Tessinger, rode at the front of our escorting company. Her bat wings bowed out from the open slits in her armor, and they tucked politely when Xavier called her. She twisted over her shoulder to lift her helm's visor.

"Yes, Xavier?" Maria inquired, her chartreuse eyes as sharp as ever.

Xavier's cheeks bloomed pink. "I, er… I was hoping to have a… private… conversation? Only for a few moments?"

Maria snorted a laugh, clapping her visor back down and turning forward. "I'm hardly about to fall for that trick again, Xavier. There will be no slipping away from us this time."

Xavier's wolf ear twitched. "I'm serious—"

"You were serious last time," Maria huffed. "You may carry on with your private conversations as you are."

Xavier glowered, but ceased his protesting.

I sighed, looking at Jewel flying beside me. Perhaps we'd eluded Mother Maria too many times.

"Well, then," I began, looking at Xavier curiously. "You may as well come out with it. What did you want to speak with me about?"

Xavier rubbed his neck, muttering, "It's, er… some news Alex and I received this morning."

I cocked an eyebrow. "News?"

"It's about your *Rae'u Shelic*," he explained. "For the ball on Death's Festival. I know we made plans for the day after but… well…" He sucked in a breath to announce solemnly, "Alex and I are returning to Low Drinelle."

I screeched to a halt in the middle of the street, causing the pesky guards and their horses to fumble to a clopping stop. Jewel nearly fluttered ahead and had to backpedal.

"What?" I demanded. "You're leaving?"

At the front, Maria twisted back to us again, her tone brooding. "Ah… Alice told me this yesterday as well."

I jerked my gaze from her to Xavier while Jewel twittered harshly at both of them. "But why?"

Xavier gave a glum shrug. "My grandfather Edric is resigning as the Death King's Eyes. He only accepted the role back then to relieve Father of the constant torment, but now *he's* going mad and quitting immediately." He flopped onto his horse's neck. "So now, Father is going back to interview new candidates… and he wants Alexander and I to be there to 'learn from the experience'."

Maria lifted a gauntleted finger. "Oh, don't be so dramatic, Xavier. It's only for a few weeks. A month at most."

Xavier blanched. "The last time my father went to interview candidates 'for a few weeks', we stayed for nine years."

Maria's face fell. "Ah… right. I'd forgotten that bit."

"Exactly." Xavier flicked me an apologetic look. "I know we made plans after your birthday, Willow, but… well, I thought we could reschedule it for today. So…" He gestured around us. "Here we are. It's not as exciting as Festival would have been, but it's better than nothing."

"I see…" I bit my knuckle. Then glanced at Jewel. An idea struck. "Then, I suppose we should enjoy it, shouldn't we?"

I discreetly nodded at Jewel. The little crow gave an affirmative twitter, feeling my desire through our Bond. Jewel buzzed over the wall of guards without notice and zipped around a corner street.

One… I counted my heartbeats, determined to act casual as our entourage rode onward. *Two… Three… Four…*

Pwririririririririri!

An earsplitting shriek pierced the air, rattling everyone's ears at once. I knew the shrill alarm was Jewel. She may have been the smallest of her species, but she was still a Songcrow. They possessed a unique ability to project their calls at an exemplary volume, carrying for half a mile at times to sound alarms of danger to other black birds in the area.

Or in this case, create a distraction.

The Reapers surrounding us ripped off their helms to block their ears against the grating noise. Jewel's cry was especially disorienting with its high frequency. Perks of being small for her kind, I supposed.

The guards weren't the only ones in distress. Their black birds that had been following us overhead began screeching and croaking like mad, flying around the guards in a feathery cyclone of pure chaos.

I couldn't stifle my sly cackling, slipping off my horse in the confusion and grabbing a very startled Xavier off his mount.

"Come!" I tugged him by the wrist, then reached into my Storagesphere and pulled out my enchanted earcuff with my usual illusion.

I slipped the cuff onto my lobe and let my white hair bleed grey as the disguise took effect. We snuck away and ran into the nearest alleyway, our laughter echoing as we made our escape.

19

XAVIER

"So, how exactly will these interviews work?" the disguised Willow asked as we strolled through the night-dressed city hand in hand.

The Floating Lights swirling in the ceiling mist had dimmed to a deep indigo almost an hour ago. We'd made the most of our freedom while we had it, knowing we were in for a world of punishment when we returned, but we didn't care. Tonight had been worth it.

I crunched into my half-eaten candied apple in an obstructed hum, "Ahm nah' 'hur…" I swallowed and went on. "I actually have no idea what to expect, to be honest. All I know is, I'm not looking forward to being treated like a murderous demon again." My stomach knotted sickly. "When I first moved here, I was *sure* it would be the same thing all over again… but it wasn't. I *liked* it here. I don't want to leave. What if we end up staying for years all over again— what if we stay there *forever?*"

"It won't be forever." She tightened her grasp on my hand in a chuckle. "Let's pretend, for humor's sake, that you *do* stay for years. What would you do while there?" She tilted her apple back and forth. "Return to the academy where you were miserable before? You survived that. Endure the hatred all over again as you'd already done for years? You survived that. Then when you turn sixteen in two years and you finish your schooling, take up an apprenticeship as a Reaper perhaps, and when you finally turn twenty and are of age to do as you please… What would you do then?"

"Come straight home." I answered swiftly. Then I paused in an afterthought. "Assuming you're still here. There wouldn't be much point in it otherwise, would there?"

She laughed and shoved me lightly with her shoulder. "Why in Death would I be anywhere else?"

"What if you sneak aboard a ship to live with me and find yourself lost on an unfamiliar continent?" I teased.

She snorted. "I suppose this is a fantasy of yours, is it? Why on Nirus would I do a thing like that when I know you're coming back eventually?"

"Mind you, your little 'worst-case scenario' spans six entire years," I pointed out. "Do you understand how long that is? Take the four years we've spent together, for example. Now imagine those same four years without me in them."

She halted at that, her cheeks paling. Her fox ears grew, though they were a fake charcoal color thanks to her earcuff's illusion.

I held up two fingers. "Now add two more years to those four, and you can start to see how so much time apart can—"

"You can't be gone that long!" She shrieked. Her apple *thunked* to the cobbled street, and she shook me by the shoulders, making me drop my own treat. "What am I supposed to do for six Bloody years while you're gone? Princess duties? Without *this*?" She threw her hands all around us. "I need these outings, Xavier...! Being an heiress is stressful enough—I'd have a heart attack without them!"

"Calm down!" I sputtered. "Bloods, what happened to 'it won't be forever'?"

"I was an idiot! That may as well be forever!" She clung to my chest. "You can't go...! Tell them you're sick! Tell them you have an exam! Tell them I ordered you to stay, anything...!"

Bloods, her little pep talk certainly backfired, didn't it?

"Willow, be calm." I grabbed her shoulders firmly. It seemed it was her turn to be reassured. "It... it won't be that long. It will only be for a month—at most—and then I'm coming straight back. All right?"

Her fox ears folded down. "You're sure…?"

"I'm sure," I said. Though, I only half believed it myself. Now wasn't a grand time to mention that, though. "But, er… that's why we're having this outing, you see? It's even more important not to waste it by worrying now."

She deflated, but nodded. "Y-yes… you're right."

I smiled as she took my arm to proceed with our stroll—

Clack! C-Clack! Clack!

A cracking noise struck my ears.

There was a trio of young gutter boys throwing stones at the ground. Since they were blocking my view, I couldn't see precisely where the rocks were landing, but I could hear the sharp *clack, clack, clacks* they made on impact.

Odd, I thought, craning to get a better look. *Is that some sort of game—?*

I went cold.

The boys weren't hitting the ground. Their rocks were pummeling a little wolf pup.

It was a tiny thing, squealing and whimpering as the torrent of stones cracked his bones and cut his skin, his fur knotted with clumps of dark blood.

I broke into a sprint.

"Xavier?!" Willow called after me, startled. "Where are you…!"

I shoved the first boy to the ground and snatched the other boys' wrists before they threw their next rocks.

"Stop!" I roared, my teeth sharp and wolf ears fully grown.

The three boys cowered, prying out of my hold and stammering. "It-it's a feral! It was gonna bite us—!"

"And that gives you the right to take its life?!" I snarled.

The gutter boys scrambled away, ducked into an alley, and disappeared. A crowd began to form. Their questioning murmurs rippled around me.

I ignored them, fumbling to the mangled wolf pup.

It was already dead.

I sank to my knees, staring at its limp carcass. Silent.

Willow crouched beside me, hugging her legs as her heartbroken gaze fell on the pup. She said nothing. She only sat there with me. The crowd's murmurs faded next, as if a wave of sorrow had washed over them as well.

The stink of death swelled from the slumped wolf. Its blood stained its fur along with the cobblestone beneath it. It couldn't have been more than a few weeks old.

Several minutes passed before I finally found my voice again.

"Why is it like this?" I whispered to Willow. "Why is this always the first response...?"

Blood crawled along the cracks in the street toward my boots. My stomach churned. I couldn't stop a nauseated sob from spilling, my lungs choking like needles.

Willow shed her cloak and swaddled the pup, cradling it in her arms.

"Come," she hushed. "It deserves a proper burial."

I nodded, forcing myself to stand as I followed her through the crowd. They all parted for us, their heads bowed in respect. The gesture was enough to calm me, but only slightly. It was comforting to see that, at the very least, someone else cared.

We were met with no resistance as we left the city behind. Soon, Willow and I walked along the canals leading to the palace grounds, alone. The night was quieter than usual. With the autumn season rolling in, even the crickets had gone silent.

Willow veered away from the canals, still cradling the wrapped pup. I wasn't familiar with the new path, but she seemed sure of her destination, so I didn't protest as I followed her.

We stopped at the edge of the Weeping Woods. It was a misty forest of willow trees that began at the palace grounds and stretched for miles around various mountain paths in the distance.

Willow knelt and gently set down her bundle. Then she grew her claws and began digging a small hole in the dirt. I helped her dig, and once we were finished, we lowered the bundle inside together.

I drew in a long, solemn breath, staring at the hidden remains of the pup. A sudden warmth blotted against my wet cheek. It was

Willow, drying my tears with her sleeve. I hadn't noticed they'd spilled anew.

"It will live again in your spirit," Willow whispered. She pulled my head to her shoulder, letting me sob over her heated neck. "It will live in your memory, now. When the Seamstress delivers its soul to its next vessel, it will meet a better fate… for she knows of your grief. She will not allow that sorrow to be unheard."

She sat with me in silence for what felt like an eternity. Slowly, painfully, the pain quelled. I pulled her close, her warmth relieving.

Willow slipped off the music watch dangling from her neck, winding back the dial and clicking it open.

Its music twinkled alive, slow and delicate as it rang through the night.

My Crest of black diamonds began to gleam from my left knuckles, as it always did around her amulet. I had grown so accustomed to it, I barely noticed. Willow took a deep breath, held the watch close to her heart, then began to sing her usual prayer in the Grimish tongue.

Still and cold, feel the winds run slow
Start anew from the ashes that trail and blow
Lo, the voice of lamented tones
For the names engraved in new stone

With breathless sighs and darkened sight
Embrace the silence of hollow life
May She appear to release your plight
To rid you of sorrow and blight

Do you hear the bells that ring?
The crows that have begun to sing?
Heed their songs as you lay to rest

'Tis the tune for the honored and blessed
'Tis the tune for the honored and blessed

Hours after we'd buried the pup, I helped Willow return to her chambers.

Now I wandered the halls absently, my mind still dampened by the solemn ceremony. I understood why Willow said she needed our pleasant outings. Between the lost pup and my imminent departure, I didn't think I could take any more ill events. It made our cheerful time together all the more precious.

I exhaled a hard breath and climbed down a curling stairwell.

"… heard her fiancé is supposed to give her vines on her *Rae'u Shelic*," I overheard a passing ghost gossip with another specter.

I paused on the stairs, my ears perking as the two souls floated down the hallway ahead of me.

The second ghost sounded delighted. "Oh, that's right! Her Highness will be thirteen, won't she? The proper age to receive her vines—especially when she'd been arranged with the Howllord for so long."

The first ghost murmured, "One has to wonder why Howless Lilliana's betrothed hadn't gotten hers last year…"

They passed me unnoticed. I stared after them.

Her Highness? Fiancé? I replayed their conversation a million miles a minute. *Her parents have… arranged her with a betrothal…?*

No, that couldn't be right. I would have heard about this. She would have told me, she would have…

I squeezed my temples, trying to recall something—anything—about Willow being betrothed to anyone. Nothing came to mind.

My wolf ears grew, teeth sharpening. I stormed out of the palace and ran home.

With everything that happened today, I'd be damned if I allowed another misfortune to ruin it more. If I was leaving in a matter of weeks, I wasn't going to lose Willow along with everything else.

I ran straight for my estate's front gates—

Someone yanked me behind a tree.

"Xavier!" Alexander hissed, pushing me down to the grass as he crouched next to me. My brother glared over his shoulder. "What in Bloods did you do this time? Mother *and* Maria are on a war-path for you!"

I shoved to my feet. "I'll deal with it later."

"There is no later!" Alex pulled me back to the grass. "The whole staff is looking for you! Fifty vassals! They've been ordered to lug you by the ankles straight to Mother if they find you!"

I stopped. "Death."

"Now what did you—*duck!*" He shoved my head down and clung to the tree, his gaze cranked upward at the cavern's ceiling.

The sound of flapping wings rushed above us. My mother's winged vassal, Aiden, soared overhead. He didn't notice us as he flew off in the distance.

Alex and I peered around the tree. My father's bear-eared vassal, Nathaniel, was stomping through the courtyard back and forth, muttering obscenities.

I smeared a hand over my face. "Death, this is bad... But I need to speak with Father. Can you buy me time?"

Alex grumbled, "I'll try... but this better be worth it."

"I'll fill you in after," I promised. "It's urgent."

Alex shed his vermillion cloak and handed it to me. "Wear this. Give me yours. I'll draw Nathaniel away from the doors."

I took off my burgundy cloak and switched with him, throwing his orange cloak over my shoulders and pulled the cowl over my face. "I only need a few minutes. Where is Father?"

"In his study. He's on a conference call."

"Of course he is," I sighed, flicking my brother an appreciative glance. "Thanks, Alex. I owe you."

He pulled on my red cloak and tugged the cowl over his face. "I'll put it on your tab."

Alex dashed out of the tree's cover, the burgundy cloak billowing behind him as he ran through the front gates.

Nathaniel spotted him immediately.

"'Ey!" Nathaniel's bear ears perked straight up, and he barreled for Alex. "Ye better run, lad! Ye best think twice a'fore givin' yer Spirit Mother the slip next time...!"

Alex's boots skidded over the cobblestones as he darted back out the gates. Nathaniel hustled after him, shouting and attracting Aiden's attention above them.

With the vassals distracted, I rushed under the gates and sprinted inside the manor.

Thateus was waiting in the foyer. The ram-horned butler jolted when I'd entered.

"Xav...! Ah, Alexander," greeted the butler, his tension relaxing when he registered my vermillion cloak. I still had my cowl drawn, so he couldn't see my eyes.

"What a relief," Thateus deflated, letting out a hard breath. "Your father has me under orders to apprehend your brother should he arrive. It is not an order I'm particularly fond of."

"I-I see..." I grunted, thankful my throat was hoarse from so much stress today. I sounded more like Alex this way. "Well, I wish you luck in the hunt. I'm... retiring early tonight. I've class in the morning."

"Of course, Young Sir. Have a good rest." Thateus bowed, then returned to his watch of the door.

I tried to calm my nerves as I walked past him, stepping onto the curling staircase.

"—Wait." Thateus twisted his gaze to me again, puzzled. "Why would you wish me luck with hunting your brother, Young Sir?"

I stiffened, my foot still on the first step. My gaze flicked to him from under my cowl.

Realization dawned in Thateus's eyes, and his grey skin blanched.

His hand snapped for me like a viper, his bones driven by the order of his Necrovoker; the order he physically couldn't disobey.

I bolted up the stairs.

Thateus's fingers snagged my cowl, pulling it down to free my face as I raced up the stairs in a frenzy.

"Y-Young Sir!" Thateus shouted after me, fumbling close behind. "I'm sorry! Please hurry! I don't want to be the one to catch you...!"

He swiped for me again. I ducked and rolled onto the second floor—*thunking* my head against the wall and gaining a sharp throb. I gritted my teeth against the pain and scrambled down the carpeted hall.

Three cleaning vassals waited up ahead. When they spotted me and saw my mismatched eyes, their joints cracked into action.

I dodged one, ducked under the second, and slammed a shoulder into the wall to evade the third.

Now all three of them chased me alongside Thateus.

The door to Father's study was within sight. The path was clear. If I could just reach it—

Crash!

One of the windows on the right shattered right in front of me. Aiden flew inside, tucking his wings to fit in the cramped hall.

"Aiden!" I yelped and scrambled back. "Was that necessary?!"

Aiden looked glum as he stalked toward me. "Sorry, Young Sir… but you have no idea how livid *Da'torr* Alice is."

I staggered—

Thateus and the three cleaning vassals caught me by the waist simultaneously. They heaved me back, my boots sliding on the carpet as I resisted. Aiden grabbed my wrists and tugged me the other way. I felt like I'd snap in half if they pulled any harder.

"Please…!" I strained against their tug-of-war. "I just… want to speak… with Father…!"

I dropped my weight and swiveled my hands in Aiden's grasp. My fingers clutched his arms. I evoked a Sensory-Illusion into his soul. I didn't want to bring him too much pain, so I decided to make each of his fingers feel like they were pricked with needles.

Aiden released me in a wince, shaking his hands desperately.

I slapped my glowing-violet palms over the four vassals still stuck to my waist, sending them the same illusion into their souls. They freed me in shrill gasps. Their confusion only lasted for a few seconds, but that was all I needed.

I dove for the door, swinging it open and slamming it shut behind me. I turned the latch to lock the door and panted over my knees now that I was safely inside the study. The vassals pounded at the door from the other side. Their muffled voices pleaded for me to run while I had the chance.

Sorry, everyone, I thought. *I'll face my punishment once I see to this.*

"…would have to consider the possibilities, if such a treaty were to be made," Father's voice rambled behind me, perking my wolf ears.

I found him pacing the bookshelves of his study, holding his communicator. Father spoke to a scale-skinned woman on the screen of light that projected from the device's center gemstone. Father was deep into his conversation. He hadn't even noticed I'd pried my way inside.

Typical. Leave it to Father to be oblivious of the world burning around him.

"My lord," I said sternly and stalked toward him. "I must speak with you about—"

"—should think there would be no foreseeable dilemmas, given the circumstances—"

"My lord, this is urgent—"

"—No, no, I'm not saying it's impossible, I'm simply saying there may be some complications if—"

"FATHER, PUT DOWN THE DAMNED COM!"

I snatched the blasted thing out of his fingers and threw it at the wall. The communicator burst in a mess of springs and gears, the screen of light disappearing as the gemstone popped out and bounced over a table before dropping to the carpet.

Father stared at his empty hand, stunned silent. Then he slowly turned his gaze to me at last, fury creasing his brow so low they cast dark shadows across his face.

"Alexan…!" He realized I wasn't Alex, and blinked. "Xavier? Blast, boy, what in Death's name do you think you're doing? Explain yourself! And that com is coming out of your allowance—!"

"Fine," I snapped. "I'll pay for it after you explain something. And you will Gods damned listen this time. I will not be brushed aside again. Not for this."

Father's look skewed. "What in Bloods are you on about?"

"Is she really engaged?" I growled, my wolf ears curling into a snarl. "Is Willow engaged to be wed?"

His confusion melted into downright bewilderment now. "Of course she is. You don't remember—?"

"You must tell her parents to call off the arrangement."

Father grew hauntingly still. "Wh… But I… wh-whatever for…?"

"The one she's arranged with," I began. The idea that it could be Matthiel made my blood simmer. "She doesn't love him."

Strangely, I saw a pang of heartbreak strike Father. "Why do you say that, Xavier…?"

"Because she… she…" It was everything I could do not to scream. Why couldn't he understand? If he'd been paying an ounce of attention, he would have known the damned reason. But what did I expect? This was Father. The only way he understood anything was by being told in the bluntest method possible.

"Be-because…" I flushed. It was humiliating to say it so directly, but right now, anger outweighed my embarrassment. I blurted, "Because I love her. And she loves me."

Father was still for a long moment.

Since he made no attempt to reply, I went on, "We've been courting for some time now, and I… I can't lose her. It's hard enough that I have to leave her here for our trip, but this is too much. Tell them to call the arrangement off immediately. Anything. Please, my lord, I'm begging you…"

Father started laughing.

My anger burned hotter. "What part of this do you find humorous?! I will not stand by as she's forced into a marriage she doesn't want—!"

"Xavier," Father interrupted, still chortling as he wiped away an entertained tear. "Be calm. I guarantee you, after what you've just told me, she certainly wants this marriage." He nodded to me, chuckling. "She's betrothed to *you*."

I clicked my teeth shut. "What?"

"You two have been engaged for four Bloody years, Xavier." Father lowered into a leather chair and rested a hand over his knee. "You didn't know?"

"I… but I thought…" I scratched my head.

Father perked an eyebrow. "Do you still wish to cancel the arrangement?"

"N-no!"

"You'd like to keep your engagement with her, then?"

"Y…yes, my lord…" My face may as well have melted off my skull, mortified. "U-unless she, er, disagrees…" An afterthought struck me, and I asked meekly, "Erm, does she know…?"

"Of course she knows! She chose you at the Breathless Waltz when you first arrived here. And *you* chose her!" He threw up his hands. "How do you not remember?"

I cleared my throat. "The Waltz… hang on. We were choosing *marriage* partners?"

"Yes!" Father exclaimed.

I lifted a hesitant finger. "Not combat partners…?"

"Bloody Void, boy, what made you think that?"

I loosened my collar awkwardly. "I suppose… Alex and I didn't think to clarify back then…"

Father gave a long sigh and rubbed his eyes. "Seamstress, give me strength… Your mother and I will need to speak with Alexander as well, surely…"

"So then…" My brow knitted. "If Willow and I are engaged… and *I'm* her betrothed… What's this about me giving her vines on her *Rae'u Shelic*?"

Father paused. "Oh. Is she turning thirteen already? Blast, how quick that came and went." He frowned as if realizing something. "That means we'd forgotten Lilli's vines last year. *And* this year… Hrm…" He shook his head. "For another time, I suppose. As for you and Willow, yes, thirteen is the traditional age that an engaged girl and boy exchange their Ornaments of Endearment."

"But I'm fourteen," I pointed out. "Doesn't that mean we should have exchanged these Ornaments last year?"

"You may be a year older than she," Father explained, "but the ceremony waits until the youngest party reaches the proper age. It's not as common anymore in these modern times, but since you and she have been affianced since you were young, it's only appropriate to adhere to the old Grimish custom. Willow will give you an engagement ring, and you will give her engagement-vines." Father twirled a warning finger in the air. "Although, a word of advice? Since she

is the heiress to Grim's throne, might I suggest making her vines…
special? The ceremony will be broadcast throughout the caverns, so
best make them worthy of such publicity, eh?"

A shudder ran down my spine. "B… broadcast? To the whole
realm…?"

"Precisely," Father chuckled and *thumped* my back. "As I said.
Make them special."

I gulped and nodded hauntingly. *Oh, Bloods…*

—SLAM!

The study's door was kicked so hard, the latch broke off.

Under the newly opened doorway, my armored mother glowered
Bloody murder at me.

"*XAVIER MADISON DEVOUH…!*" Mother roared and stormed
over to me.

I cowered back. "Oh, Death…!"

She snatched me by the neck and *yanked* me out of Father's study,
her claws pricking my skin. "You'd best get your sleep because first
thing tomorrow, you will be scooping dung out of the dragon stables
until we leave for our voyage!"

I trembled in her grasp, tripping over the carpet to keep pace
with her. "Y-yes, my lady…"

20

QUEEN MYRA

I paced the darkened ballroom with anxious steps as my clicking footfalls echoed in the empty chamber.

Everyone had gone to bed hours ago. Even the ghosts had disappeared into Aspirre to dream and wouldn't resurface until they woke in the early morning. The night guards were the only shifters still awake in the palace, patrolling the corridors outside the ballroom and leaving me to my thoughts.

"—Myra," a boyish voice suddenly sounded behind me.

I whirled. My azure-haired father had appeared out of thin air. It was an entrance I had grown stale toward after 500 years. My father looked like a teenager even still, while I had surpassed him physically into my middle-aged visage.

Father's young face was brooding as he murmured, "Why have you called for me? You said it was urgent?"

"It is." I stalked toward him and clasped his hand. My prophetic Hallows leaked out of my palm in an azure light. With this, I showed him the disturbing vision my daughter had Seen this morning.

Father's gaze was unreadable as he watched through his own Third Eye. Then, at last, his azure fox ears grew, and he whispered, "Those burning faces… Those were not caused by any fire."

"I thought not," I growled. "I've only seen one element capable of such horrors. And barring Serdin's Bloodline, there is no other Evocator with that Hallows anymore. It's been extinct since I was a girl." I sneered. "Which means it was *him* in that vision. And it was this room." I raised my hands to the arching ceiling and tall walls around us. "It was *this very room* full of flames and rotted corpses, with the twins cowering under his shadow—and *my daughter* had the vision."

Father was silent. Pensive.

"What do we do?" I asked. "How do we stop this…? I will not let him near *my* daughter!"

The echoes of my voice died into silence.

My father lifted his gaze to me. "I'm sorry," he whispered. "I've just looked ahead through the possibilities. He comes in all of them."

My voice trembled. "All of them…? Even if we increase the guards? Cancel the ball…?"

His nod was grim. "All of them. It doesn't matter what we do. What choices we make… he will come. And he will slaughter anyone in his way."

"Is there nothing we can do…?" I whispered, the fear suffocating. "Must we allow history to repeat itself? For *my* family, this time…?"

Father closed his eyes and drew in a long, long breath through his nose. "No. I won't allow it this time. Not for my kin." He paced around me and hit a knuckle to his chin. "If we cannot avoid his coming, then we will push the timeline toward the *least* devastating outcome we can find. But…" He sighed. "You and I can only manipulate that timeline to a certain point. After we've reached that point, I'm afraid the rest will depend on the choices made by others…" His icy glare sharpened. "Choices made by the children."

21

WILLOW

The morning of Festival, my ashen-haired father and I sat in the palace library.

He wore a formal, alabaster suit and silver collar-strings as he peered down his nose through his reading spectacles. He read from the instructional Evocation book he'd given me to study the third element of Death: the Hallows of infection.

I waited on the cushioned seat beside him patiently, smoothing out the wrinkles of my silken, white gown with a silver sash and long, lace sleeves. Two layers of gossamer, chiffon skirts draped over the floor in a lovely train and met at a cross-intersection at the front of my waist in silver-trimmed waves.

It was the finest gown I'd ever worn to Festival. But then, today marked a special year. I was thirteen now. The proper age for Xavier and I to exchange our Ornaments of Endearment. He was to give me my vines, and I was to give him his ring, which was currently tucked behind my sash inside a velvet box.

I patted the hidden box for assurance, making sure it was still there, and blew out a nervous breath. I'd waited four years for this. And we had six years more before we'd officially marry. It was such a long time from now… but why did it feel like no time at all? Even for this small, silly ceremony today, I felt horrifically unprepared. How was I going to feel at our actual wedding?

Father cleared his throat as he read from the Infeciovoking book laid on the table before us, adjusting his reading spectacles.

I banished my worries and focused on the rest of today's lesson. It was nearly over regardless. We'd spent most of the morning reviewing my assigned chapters from this week. This was the last chapter: *Poisons for the Soul—How Infeciovoking Can Benefit the Extermination of Rotted Demons.*

The author of the text explains that while he himself found no opportunity to test such an Evocation—as he was only a surgeon and demon hunting was more suited for a Reaper—he interviewed several Death Knights with the element to write this chapter on its real-life application.

Death Knights with Infeciovoking… This was an ancient text indeed. There were no more Infeciovokers today. There hadn't been for five hundred years. The Death Bloodline was the only one to have the element of infection, but we had all three of our realm's elements. To imagine a time when Evocators had that element alone, and were ordinary shifters carrying out their daily lives, using it to destroy a demon's rotten soul or, as the author of this text explains in his biography, using it to *feel* infections in his patients as a surgeon… It was a whole different world back then.

"Now," Father said as his grey-ringed eyes scanned the words tentatively. "Concentrate on targeting the soul as you evoke the poison… we'll begin with a single finger and then—"

I evoked my infection Hallows and had black, squirming tendrils rise from both my hands. I raised them with pride and gave Father a smug grin.

Father laughed and pulled off his reading spectacles. "You've been reading ahead! Well done, Willow."

I dismissed my Hallows and beamed. "Of course, I read ahead. There aren't any Infeciovokers anymore. Since you're my only tutor on—quite literally—the planet, it's the easiest element to fall behind in." I sighed and closed the book, running a hand over its tattered, ancient cover.

"Father?" I began quietly. "Why aren't there any more Infeciovokers?"

Father combed a hand through his ashen hair and hummed. "No one really knows, Willow. All we do know is that there once were many Evocators who possessed the third element of the Death realm. And then, over time… they vanished." He shrugged. "There is no explanation. There may not even be a single reason for it. It may have simply been the work of nature itself."

My mouth twisted. That hadn't been a very satisfying answer. If nature wanted the Infeciovokers gone, why would they spare the element within *our* family? It didn't make sense.

"—Willow?" My mother called suddenly from the library's doorway. Her azure-haired figure stepped under the frame, her gaze apprehensive. "Serdin? Are you in here?"

My father called to her, "Over here, Myra."

Mother blew out a breath, as if relieved, and strode toward us. "Thank the Shepherd… I was looking everywhere, but I was beginning to worry." She glanced at the tattered book on the table.

Mother's eyes split with horror.

She ripped a terrified scream and swatted the book to the floor as if it were a fang-baring serpent.

The book fluttered open upside down, bending some of the delicate pages.

"Myra!" Father clipped. "What in Death has gotten into you?"

"*That* is what you've been teaching our daughter with?!" Mother demanded as she stabbed a disgusted hand at the book, her blue fox ears grown and curled into a snarl.

Father's brow creased desperately. "Of course. It's what the Death Bloodline has read since it was published. It's the only Evocation book that still exists for that element—"

"Burn it." Mother spit on the book and stormed away. "Better it be used as kindling for the hearth."

Father and I exchanged perplexed glances.

I bent to retrieve the text and closed it with gentle fingers, frowning. What in Death did my mother see to make her react so strangely? All I read was the title, written in curling, silver letters:

Evocations for the Practicing Infeciovoker.
Scribed by Doctor Kael Treble.

LILLI

"And then she tossed it to the floor and told Father to burn it," Willow explained with an exasperated gesture.

She and I stood by one of the ballroom's many refreshment tables, sipping our sparkling cider as the celebrating lords and ladies bustled around us. "Bloods, Lilli, you should have seen the *look* on her face… I've never seen my mother so upset before. And over a book, of all things."

My brow furrowed skeptically, bat wings lowering. "That *is* strange… and you said nothing prompted it save for the sight of it?"

"Precisely." Willow shook her head, making the bell tied to her hair jingle. "Even Father doesn't know what to make of it."

My wings folded down as I stole a glance at the queen. The woman sat at her throne beside Willow's father, fixated on the northern entryway where the usher was announcing each guests' arrival.

I murmured, "I see what you mean… She's acting strange even now."

"Exactly!" Willow lifted her hands at her mother sharply—and spilt some of her cider with the motion. "Look at her! I've never seen her like this. Something is going on, and she isn't telling me *or* Father. But what is it?"

My face pulled into a distraught grimace. "Bloods if I know, Willow… have you asked?"

"Of course I've asked," Willow snorted. "Do you want to know what she said? *Don't fret about it, darling. Go find Xavier and everything will be fine.* Argh!" Willow stamped a foot—spilling the rest of her cider. "She's just like grandfather Dream! Always so Bloody cryptic, leaving the rest of us to worry and obsess about everything…!"

I sighed and carefully sidestepped around the puddle of spilt cider. "If she won't tell you now, perhaps she's waiting for the proper moment? She *is* the daughter of the Great Oracle. If something were cause for concern, she would tell you."

Willow grumbled irritably, her fox ears grown and twitching. "I suppose…" Her mouth twisted. "But I still have this terrible feeling. And *I* had an… *alarming* vision some weeks ago myself."

"You did?" My wings stiffened. "Why hadn't you told me? That sounds like something your Aide should be aware of."

"I'd forgotten about it after my outing with Xavier," she said, dismayed as she massaged her eyes. "He distracted me with more terrible news… The Devouhs are apparently leaving for the other Undercontinent tomorrow."

My heart sank at the reminder. "Ah… that's right. Alex told me as well."

Yet he STILL hasn't gotten me my engagement-vines, I brooded. I was fourteen for Death's sake. He should have given them to me last year—or at least as a *belated* gift this year! I swear, with the way he acted, it's as if he didn't know we were betrothed. The Bloody idiot.

I shook my head, dropping it. That was something to deal with later. For now, something more pressing needed my attention.

I turned to the princess. "Willow, considering your vision, and the way your mother is acting, perhaps it's time we talked about the… other… duties of my role as your Aide. You know, if certain *situations* arise."

Her brow furrowed. "What situations?"

"Dangerous ones." I set down my cider on the table. "You know it's part of my duty to protect you should something happen. I've thought of several strategies in case of a catastrophe, but I wish you'd told me about this vision of yours sooner so I could have come more prepared. I suppose in the meantime, perhaps *this* will do…"

I slipped off a silver bracelet I was wearing and held it out to Willow. "Could you please seal an illusion into this? I will need it to contain your hair color and eye color."

She didn't take the bracelet, but eyed it as one would a hornet. "Why?"

"So I can serve as a decoy for you," I said flatly. Wasn't that obvious? "That way, you can escape elsewhere in case anything happens, and I can draw attention away from you."

"And put yourself in danger?" She scoffed and set down her empty glass, turning toward the thrones. "You'll do no such thing. Nothing is going to happen because *I'm* getting to the bottom of this."

I growled, my bat ears growing. "Willow…"

She didn't hear me as she stormed to the tall, regal seat beside her mother, biding her time while casting narrow glares at the crowned woman.

I rolled my eyes. Why did she always have to make my job difficult?

"—Well, well, well," a pompous voice rang behind me suddenly. "If it isn't the little servant girl playing dress up."

My annoyance bubbled hotter. I flicked the ashen-haired prick and his posse of hecklers a glower. "Be gone, Felix," I muttered. "I'm not in the mood."

Willow's bratty cousin twitched an eye. "You will give me a proper title while addressing royalty."

I gave a haughty laugh. "I believe you mean honorary royalty—"

Slap!

He struck my cheek, pain flaring. Felix's white wolf ears were grown, and they curled back in a livid snarl. "Perhaps I wasn't clear. You *will* address me properly, mutt."

His jeering posse surrounded me suddenly, closing in and making me tighten my wings. Felix ignited his hands with bursts of fire and stepped forward—backing me into the circle.

"You may have been singled out by that mongrel princess," he spat, "but a vermin's opinion carries as much weight as a wayward vagabond in these beautiful, hallowed walls. But at least a *vagabond* would accept they were unworthy to even gaze upon these walls…!"

He sent a scorching ball of fire at my feet, making me leap away in a yelp. It puffed into smoke and left a burnt smudge on the marble floor.

"—that their *mothers* are clumps of mud on our boots—"

He sent another flame hurtling for me, and I quickly evaded, only to have his posse shove me in front of him.

"—and they themselves are the disgusting stains left behind on the rug!"

He sent a third gout, and this time I jumped in the air, spread my wings, and flew over the ring of tormentors.

I landed behind them and dashed off, my lungs closing as my vision blurred with tears.

I could hear their cruel laughter fading behind me.

I wiped my eyes as I soared up to the palace's spired roofs. My messenger, Dusk, soared into view and flew at my side, cawing as if to tell me she could feel my distress. I found the tallest rooftop of the palace and landed with an ungraceful *thump*. Dusk landed beside me, rubbing her feathered head against my side to console me. My wings lowered as I clung to an iron spire, curling into a ball and hugging my knees.

"—Lilli?" My mother called suddenly. She flapped into view and alighted on the roof beside me.

I didn't look at her. I only stared ahead, hugging my knees tighter. The cavern mists were beautiful tonight, the overcast sparkling with low, blue lights that floated and twirled between the tall, rocky pillars that were scattered throughout the caves.

Damn it. I let him get to me again. I was fourteen for Death's sake—I wasn't such a child to cry every time I heard one of the lords or ladies gossip about me, was I?

"What do you want?" I sneered at my mother, wiping my lids raw before she could say anything.

"I heard what Prince Felix said," she murmured, coming to embrace me.

My wings stayed indignantly stiff as hers wrapped around me, providing warmth in the chilled air. I wasn't wearing a cloak. I'd rushed out of the ballroom so suddenly there wasn't time to find one. I'd discarded my white, traditional mask to rub at my eyes, which were now puffy and stinging.

Mother sighed. "It's only words, dear. They don't understand what your father and I have. And regardless of what they say, you know Willow and the twins will always love you for more than just your blood—"

"I didn't ask for consoling," I muttered. "Just leave me be."

Mother exhaled softly. "Lilli..."

"I said leave!" I pushed her back, rising. "You don't know what this is like, Mother! What does a dirt-scrubbing *servant* know of the expectations set on a proper noblewoman—!"

She slapped me, my cheek blooming with pain for a second time tonight. This one stung the worst.

"*Lilli.*" Mother's stern tone made me cringe. "There are more important things than being a 'proper noblewoman'."

I barred my sharpened teeth, angry tears welling. "That's simple for *you* to say," I chewed bitterly. "But it's your fault everyone looks down on me to begin with…!" My face burned, the place she'd hit still stinging as I held a tender, resentful hand to it. "It's because of your stupid… tainted… *peasant* blood…! I wish Father knew better and married a *real* Howless and let you clean away at his floors where you belonged!"

Mother's stunned face hurt far worse than my throbbing cheek.

I leapt off the spire and soared away, not daring to look back.

22

XAVIER

My fingers shook as Alex and I stood in the crowded ballroom, my glass of sparkling cider spilling from my frightened tremors.

There were so many people. So many cameras, so many reporters… I was getting dizzy, my lungs knotting.

Alex clapped a hand on my shoulder. "Breathe. You'll be fine."

"R-r-r… right," I stammered, gulping. "Right. I… I think I just… need some air…"

He nodded and kept a steady hand on my arm as he guided us out to the gardens.

I patted my vest pocket, feeling the solid edges of the long box hidden within: Willow's vines. I blew out a nervous breath, which fogged in front of me with every anxious heave.

"I-I can't…" I wheezed for breath. "I can't do this, Alex. Maybe I can give Willow the vines in private and the reporters can scavenge the aftermath and…"

Alex shook me by the shoulders. "Calm down. Relax. She's the Bloody heiress, so it *has* to be broadcasted—you'd better come to terms with it. She's probably just as nervous about it as you are."

"You're right," I shivered. "You're… you're right… She's Death, for Death's sake, I…" My stomach twisted and gurgled. "Oh, Bloods, I'm going to vomit…"

"Not on my boots, you aren't!" Alex cried.

He pushed me to the hydrangeas nearby. My dinner sloshed into the bushes. By the time I was finished spitting up the last of the bile, I was quaking on all fours.

"I-I-I-I-I can't d-d-do this, Alex…!" I retched again, my nerves squeezing my abused stomach further. I gasped for breath, clutching my head to keep everything from spiraling out of control. "There's—there's so many people in there…! There's so many shifters in Grim—in the *whole Bloody world*…! What if I mess up the ceremony?!"

Alex rubbed his eyes. "How in Death would you mess it up? You give her the vines, she gives you the ring, and you're done."

"What if the vines aren't good enough?! What if I trip and drop them?! What if everyone thinks the vines aren't proper for a princess?! Bloods, I should have stuck with the more traditional ones, what in Bloods was I thinking getting her butterflies—!"

My eye caught a glint from the caverns' ceiling mist suddenly. It was one of the Floating Lights, falling in a flighty spiral. *Bloods, that's the brightest one I've ever seen*, I marveled in wonder. It glittered down like a gorgeous wisp of pure, blue radiance, a swath of mist trailing in its descent as it disappeared beneath the dark canopy of the Weeping Woods in the distance.

"A Fallen Light…" I forced my breath to calm, glancing at Alex in a gulp. "Is… is it true the Fallen Lights bring good luck…?"

Alex shrugged. "I suppose. That's what everyone says, at least."

"Perfect…!" I hurried through the gardens toward the Weeping Woods. "Then I'm getting that Light! One *that* brilliant ought to be double the luck!"

Alex hurried after me. "Wait! We can't just leave…!"

"We won't be long," I insisted, grabbing a lantern that had been hanging on a statue in the gardens. "I need all the luck I can find. Once we have that light, we'll… come right back."

Alex grumbled, grabbing himself a second lantern from a different statue. "Gods damn it… Fine. But if we're not back in time, *I'm* not to blame if Mother Cleanses you afterward."

I led the way through the royal cemetery, ducking under the canal, and peeled back the veiling branches of the misty Weeping Woods in a nervous laugh.

"D-don't worry," I assured with a tight smile, trying to hide the terror from my voice. "It… it won't come to that."

Alex gave a hard sigh, following me into the woods with a mutter, "Why do I not believe you?"

23

KAEL

I stepped up to the towering, iron gates of Grim's royal palace, sucking in the frigid air. The muted sounds of stringed music wavered from inside the palace as well as from the streets.

Grim… My, how long it's been since I've seen home.

Apart from the centuries I spent in that empty prison, it'd been longer yet since I said goodbye to my parents here in the caves. I was so young and naïve back then.

And incredibly, hopelessly stupid.

Hsss!

Something hissed beneath me, and I flicked my gaze down. There was a small, long-snouted serpent hissing by my boot. It flared its purple-and-black spines at me.

"Ah, a little Poisondragon?" I bent to the thing curiously. "Death, it's been some time since I've seen your kind… You and I are now rarities alike, it seems."

The little dragon hissed at me again—and slashed two of its venomous spines over my ankle. The initial cuts stung slightly, but nothing more.

I hummed. "Apologies, small one. I have venom of my own. I'm afraid we're immune to one another."

The Poisondragon cocked its head at me, perplexed. Then it hissed once more and slithered away, hiding behind a thick shrub.

"A wise decision, small one." I smiled thinly after the dragon, then pushed to my feet. "Our kind will survive through hiding, indeed."

I slid a hand through my hair, taking in one last breath of the long-forgotten scents of the caverns… then started toward the palace.

"—Halt!"

A guarding Reaper had apparently approached me from behind. I was too busy reminiscing to notice her, it seemed.

The Reaper threw her scythe in front of me to block the way. "Stay where you are, vagrant," the guard spat. She eyed the thin blade sheathed at my hip. "Have you a permit to wield that? Give me your identification, or off with you!"

"Ah…" I gave a brooding rumble. "It seems I'm not remembered… nor are the crimes against me." I delicately pinched her glowing, crooked blade. "Perhaps I shall amend that tonight."

From my fingers spurted black, jagged veins. They squirmed and oozed over her scythe, stretching and snapping until the weapon was coated in the slime, spreading onto the woman's hands and crawling under her armor.

She screamed as the infection hissed through her bones and devoured her soul, which misted into vapor. She gave a slow, agonizing wail and collapsed to the stone pathway, writhing and foaming at the mouth as her skin melted away until half her skull was visible under her blackened flesh.

She gave one last, sputtering breath before growing still at my feet.

"It seems I am someone your era is no longer familiar with," I hummed dully. "Pity. We used to be well respected Evocators in Grim's fair country. I suppose after we were hunted, the centuries have proven to make our native land forget us as well… But the hunters made one mistake."

I stepped over the woman's disfigured corpse.

"They missed one."

24

XAVIER

"Are you certain we're in the right area?" Alex grumbled.

We searched the misted woods for that Fallen Light for half an hour, but we still hadn't seen even a hint of it in this dense fog. A chilled wind swept past, rustling the willow leaves surrounding us.

"I'm certain," I said, holding my lantern ahead to better see in the mist. The lantern housed an older Fallen Light, one that the palace servants had found and placed in the lanterns around the grounds earlier. The wisp of cold light bounced in the fogged glass, and I rubbed a sleeve over it to clear a path for the light to get through. "It was somewhere over this way, I think."

"You *think*?" Alex scowled. "You didn't drag me all the way out here simply to get lost, Xavier."

"We're not lost," I assured, though I had been doubtful for the last five minutes. I swore we'd seen that same crooked trunk three times now. Best not divulge that to Alex.

Alex took out his silver pocket watch, craning back toward the blackstone palace, whose tall spires stretched behind the woods much farther than I'd expected.

"It's getting late, Xavier," he said. "Lilli wished to meet with me about something, and Mother wanted you in the ballroom at exactly eight-thirty. We need to return now, if you're going to do… er, well…"

I sighed, lowering my lantern. "R-right… you're right. I suppose I can give her one of these older lights…"

"Just give her the vines. Old lights don't have any luck left in them, it'd be pointless. Let's just…" He trailed off, head cocking. "Do you hear something?"

I listened, noticing a faint twinkling in the distance, like wind chimes. "Is that…" I began, frowning at the familiar melody. "The Requiem? From Willow's music-watch?"

—Alex yelped in fright suddenly, dropping his lantern and held up his right hand to gawk at it.

His Crest of black diamonds was shining with a strange light.

One of the diamonds was pointing in the direction of the wind chimes, and they switched when he would change orientation. I saw my own Crest was also glowing, shifting toward the music.

Our Crests only did this around Willow's amulet. And the music playing was the same…

Exchanging a glance, we started toward the sound of the wind chimes, following our gleaming Crests, specks of ash fluttering around us in the mist.

They guided us to the edge of the forest, which ended at the base of a mountainside. We followed the edge of the mountain, led by our glowing crests, and the diamonds gleamed brightest at the mouth of a cave hidden behind a curtain of drooping branches.

We both pulled the branches aside and stepped into the cave.

Stopped.

Before us loomed an enormous, mystifying willow.

Its long, white branches rolled to the grass in a beautiful cascade of leafy hair, barely brushing the trickling surface of a small creek that ran through the mountain's cavern at its thick roots. The glorious tree radiated with a chilled aura the likes of which I'd never had the privilege to behold.

"Alex…" I whispered. "Is… is that…"

Alex hushed, "the Willow of Ashes…?"

There was nothing else it could have been. This was the lost Relic of Death. The holy site of the Seamstress of Soul that was said to connect her holiness to our mortal plane.

The Relic that shouldn't exist.

The willow's crystalline leaves trilled with music when they delicately hit against each other in the cavern winds. The melody, strangely, was always the same.

The same as the Requiem from Willow's amulet.

Alex and I slowly approached the fabled tree, marveling at its pure, unquestionable majesty. We each hovered a hand over its smooth bark. Our Crest of black diamonds gleamed brighter than we'd ever seen.

At last, after fourteen years of bearing these strange Crests… We'd reached our destination.

We touched the tree at the same time.

A wave of power thrummed under our palms, flooding down our arms and vibrating our very souls. I wasn't sure how I knew Alex felt the same, it was simply a feeling—a connection tying us together through the Willow.

"It's… warm," Alex hushed.

"And soft…" I added breathlessly, gently peeling my hand away to stare at my palm. It was covered in white flakes, which began to glow and float off my skin before delicately returning to the tree. "It's ash," I realized aloud, rubbing the flaking bark again. "It's literally *ash*. Just like Willow's hair…"

Alex's brow furrowed. He knocked on the bark lightly. "Yet, it feels like crystal underneath. What exactly is it made of?"

I gave him a flat stare. "It's a holy Relic of Death that isn't supposed to exist, Alex. What does it matter what it's…"

A distant bell gonged from the city miles away. It was so faint, I could barely hear it. I grew my wolf ears to listen closer. Yes, it *was* a bell gonging—from the clocktower of the temple in town.

Alex checked his pocket watch. Flinched. "Bloods… We're going to be late."

"Death." I glanced from the exit of the cave back to the holy Relic, conflicted. I pursed my lips. "Damn it… well, we know where it is now, don't we? We'll come back. With Willow next time."

Alex nodded. "Good idea. I have a feeling she can tell us more about it… and perhaps we'll finally—*finally* learn why we have…"

He lifted his right hand, staring at his Crest of black diamonds. I lifted my left and stared at mine as well.

Willow must know something, I decided, my blood pumping determinedly. *It's exactly like her amulet… there is more she hasn't been telling me.*

Alex and I gave a low, respectful bow to the looming Willow of Ashes, murmuring a soft prayer to the Seamstress…

Then we hurried back toward the palace to find Willow.

25

WILLOW

I sat on my designated throne beside Father and Mother, pretending to watch the guests while sneaking sidelong glares at my mother.

Father was his usual cheery self, but Mother's gaze was still one of panic so intense, I scarcely remembered a time she looked so alarmed.

"So, Mother," I began for the fifth time in the last twenty minutes. "Are you *sure* everything is well…? Absolutely, positively, undeniably well?"

"Fine," she assured and kept her watchful gaze on the crowd of nobles and floating ghosts. "Just fine, dear… Why don't you go and find Xavier, mm? And Alexander and Lilli, while you're at it…"

She wafted a dismissive hand at me.

I growled and slumped in my seat, giving up. "Oh, fine… Bloody cryptic, you are…"

Defeated, I slid off my throne, striding into the crowded ballroom. I didn't know where either of those she'd mentioned were anymore, but they must have been somewhere around here—

A scream split through the room near the entrance.

The music screeched to a halt.

Then, in a fearful ripple, the crowd parted to make way for a lone man.

The newcomer had greasy black hair, cat ears curled tight to his skull, his legs eerily limp as he strode across the marble floor with bare feet. His ripped clothes were splotched with stains. His Grimish-grey skin was covered in grime and sweat. He dragged a thin blade over the marble at his feet, a soft squeal scratching in its wake.

Behind him, an armored guard collapsed with a clatter. His corpse burnt away to reveal bits of skull underneath.

Another guard nearby reached for the intruder—

The greasy man barely tapped the guard's shoulder as a flurry of black, sticky veins squirmed out of his fingertip and crawled into the man's exposed neck. The guard clapped a hand over the spot and screamed in pain, his skin fizzling away in a disgusting hiss.

His corpse fell at the intruder's feet, prompting the crowd to scream and rush away from him, leaving a wide, *wide* gap.

The intruder's yellow eyes glinted as he gazed at my mother and father.

"*Chanerr nohkosch*, your majesties…" he rasped with a bow. "What a lovely celebration… I hope you don't mind if I make my own entertainment?"

No one dared to speak, a crawling silence choking the ballroom.

"My, my," the yellow-eyed man drawled, sounding surprised as he registered my mother's face and waltzed across the ballroom floor where the crowd of guests and I cowered out of his way. "What have we here? Azure hair and eyes? A face that resembles Queen Crysalette of Aspirre?" His smile curdled. "If it isn't little Myra…"

He swung his blade against the marble floor with a *CLANG!*

"All…"

CLANG!

"Grown…"

CLANG!

"… up."

I staggered back—bumping into someone. Bloods, it was Felix. My cousin didn't seem to notice me at all. He was transfixed by the intruder, a pale look of terror cinching his face.

Felix suddenly turned tail and broke into a frenzied run, his boots screeching over the floor as he left me alone in the center of the ballroom.

One of the madman's cat ears swiveled at the noise. Then his yellow eyes snapped to me.

"And what's this?" His grin showed hungry, sharpened teeth. "You had a kit of your own? And with the Death Line, no less…" He chuckled low. "Oh, you'll be perfect to lure Dream out, won't you, mongrel?"

"WILLOW!" My mother roared, leaping from her throne. "FIND XAVIER!"

The man lunged for me with his sword cocked. I yelped in fright, fumbling out of the ballroom as he chased after me—

FWOOOSH!

My father sent an inferno of orange fire between the man and me, blocking his path—and blocking my view. I tried to see over the flames, but the air wavered from the heat, smoke rising as the flames caught onto various drapery that hung from the walls.

"Father…!" I yelled, my grown fox ears folding to my neck. "Mother!"

"Get *back*, cretin!" the voice of Mother Alice barked from the other side of the fire wall. "You'll not lay a hand on this family so long as we remain standing!"

The clamor of battle sounded, and each ring of metal sent another wave of terrified tears down my cheeks.

I evoked my fire Hallows against the wall of flames blocking my way. I strained as a small piece of the fire began to bend to my will, the tiniest slit peeling apart to let me see what was happening.

But when I squinted to look, all I saw was my mother's face staring back at me.

"Go, Willow," Mother urged, her voice trembling. "Find Xavier."

I wailed, "But what about you?"

"We'll be all right," she assured. "This was the only path that could keep the most people safe… Now *find him*!"

She reached through my slit and shoved me back.

I lost control of the fire, and it closed just after she'd pulled her hands in safely, a puff of smoke slithering out from where the slit had been.

I let out a shuddering sob, then turned and ran to find Xavier as Mother had ordered.

26

ALICE

The palace ballroom raged with flames as the thick smoke billowed in the high-arched ceiling.

A wooden beam *cracked* above. The chandelier it held ripped off its mount, hurtling down.

I squinted through the spiced smog, following its trail. Under the chandelier's shadow was a bronze-skinned woman clad in white, her azure locks frazzled over her shoulders in tangled curls.

Myra!

The queen hacked the smog from her lungs, unaware of the danger over her jewel-blue head. She called desperately, "Serdin! Serdin…!"

She fell into a coughing fit.

"Myra, *move!*" I shouted, sprinting to her. My boots skidded at full speed, and I slammed into her, both of us hitting the floor several feet back.

CRASH!

The chandelier shattered, its crystals and glass ornaments bouncing away.

I blew away a strand of my long, grey hair, the locks sprawling over my face and partially blotting my view. *Damn it all, I wish I'd been prepared for this!* I preferred keeping my hair in a braid for these emergencies, but damn me, I was off-duty today. It was festival, for Death's sake! How was I to know my personally selected guards would be cut down like weeds against *one Bloody man?*

My ivory gown was stiff and ripped now, the blasted skirt tangling my legs. Furious, I rolled off Myra and pushed on all fours, coughing. I ripped the skirt with my claws, freeing my legs from the knees up.

I shoved to my feet and growled, "Are you all right, Myra?"

Myra nodded and let me help her up.

Bodies littered the pooling floor around us. They had been noble guests of the ball, servants, guards… their skin had been blackened, cheeks and eyes burnt away and rotted, several bones protruding from their veiny flesh.

That magic he'd used… If I hadn't known any better, I would say he was using Infeciovoking. But that was impossible. Only Serdin's family had that element. Those who once possessed poison Hallows died out centuries ago.

But those veins…

I hovered a hand over the long chain wrapped round my wrist. Two glowing scythe-spheres dangled from either end.

The assailant had vanished along with Serdin somewhere in here. I may not have been dressed appropriately, but I thanked Bloods I never left my scythes at home.

Myra clasped a gloved hand to her mouth. "Alice, have you seen Serdin? I-I lost him when he went after Kael."

"Went after…" I paused, turning on her with a furrowed brow. "That's right… he knew who you were, didn't he? You know who this lunatic is?"

Myra gave a gritty cough. "I… only saw his name in a vision…"

"Alice!" my husband's voice cut through the crackling flames.

"Lucas!" I called, succumbing to a coughing fit, my voice raw. "Lucas, over here…!"

I couldn't find him. He must have been behind the wall of fire.

Suddenly, the wall of flames bowed apart, splitting to form a path. A black-haired man with glinting, sienna-eyes appeared through the gap.

It was Matthew Inion, my squad's master sergeant and Claws of Grim's military. The man was evoking his fire Hallows onto the flames to make an opening, his gloves burnt and singed at the palms and fingers.

Matthew spotted Myra and me, and he twisted back. "They're over here!" Matthew called behind him. "Fangs Alice has the queen secured!"

He kept the fire spread open and stepped aside. My husband stepped through in a rush. The ashen-haired king ran through next, using his own Pyrovoking to push back the fire alongside Matthew.

Daniel was next to follow the king, batting away the smoke with his leathery wings. Behind him hurried a young man—Matthew's son, Matthiel. The teenager pulled his soot-stained collar over his mouth and nose to avoid breathing in the smog.

Their white garbs were flecked with black soot and grey smears of ash. The king's suit was ripped at the shoulders and waist, as if he'd been in battle on the other side of that wall.

Myra and I met them halfway, stepping over bodies.

Serdin pulled Myra in for a relieved embrace, kissing her brow as he took her fingers anxiously. "Are you hurt?" Serdin asked, panting. "Where is Willow?"

Myra was in tears. "I-I told her to find Xavier. I wanted her *out* of here."

The young Matthiel's grown wolf ears folded determinedly, and he straightened with a sense of duty. "I'll find Her Highness and Xavier!"

Claws Matthew glared at his son. "You'll do no such thing, boy. You're to stay here where I can Bloody well see you—"

"I'll not sit still while Her Highness may be hurt!" Matthiel barked, dashing off before his father could snatch his arm. "I'll find Alexander and Lilliana as well!" Matthiel hollered back. "We'll all keep Her Highness safe…!"

The boy disappeared into the corridors, causing his father to chew on a curse.

Daniel glanced about the smoky ballroom, his look worried suddenly. "Lilli… Bloods, where *is* Lilli?"

I tossed my head to the west entrance. "Your wife went to find her before this happened. With any luck, your daughter will be safely off the premises."

Lucas flicked me a concerned glare. "And our boys?"

I shoved down the worried lump in my throat. "I don't know," I growled. "But if they're not here, all the better."

Lucas nodded. "Perhaps it's best if they all stay together, as Matthiel said."

"Agreed," I muttered.

Another support beam *cracked* and splintered to the floor in the back, a puff of embers dusting its wake.

Then a man stepped over the debris.

The flames around him lit his face, his yellow-eyes glinting in the flickering light.

"It's the assassin!" I screamed, ripping off the chain that was wrapped around my wrist. I pressed the sealing runes etched into the two balls on either end of the chain, my scythes melting in my hands and solidifying into their crooked, glowing shapes. "Formation Alpha!"

Lucas and Daniel quickly drew out their staved scythes and took protective stances at the royal couple's left and right flanks. Matthew drew his own staved scythe and slid to my side as the two of us guarded the front of our charges.

Good, I commended the men in silence. *After so long, they still remember their positions from our honorguard years.*

The king had his own scythe form and gripped the long, black-painted staff while keeping his wife behind him—

A new, bat-winged figure dropped from the sky suddenly, landing behind the king and queen with a deathly fierce grip on her dual blades.

"Maria," I exhaled in relief, thankful she had made it back in time.

Maria lifted her scythes over her angular face, her chartreuse eyes fiery. "Apologies for the late arrival."

"Forgiveness granted," I growled, keeping my eyes on the assassin who lingered behind the wall of flames. "Did you find your daughter?"

Maria hesitated. "Lilli is safely off the grounds."

"Good." My wolf ears curled at the assassin. "Our first priority is to move the queen to a safe location. Serdin, if you're so inclined to join the battle, I'm afraid you may be the only match for a poison-spewer—"

"While I'd love to stay and dance with you all," the assassin drawled, shouldering his sword. "I'm afraid I have a curious gem to catch… before she slips through my fingers." He nodded to Myra with a wicked smile. "It was lovely seeing you again, little Myra… I'd say to give my regards to Dream, but I intend to see him myself before the night is over. *Chanerr Vith*."

The assassin leapt over a corpse and disappeared behind a wall of flames.

27

XAVIER

Alex and I trotted through the weeping woods in excited pants, hopping over creeks and weaving around trees as we made our way back toward the palace.

"I can't believe…!" I puffed, "it really exists!"

Alex grinned back. "I… can't believe our marks… led us straight to it!"

"But… But why didn't Willow ever tell us… tell *me*… a-about it? She must have known…"

"We can ask her after we get back—"

Alex dug his heels into the grass suddenly, and I fumbled to a stop beside him.

"What's wrong?" I asked, panting over my knees.

Alex squinted at the sky. "Is that smoke?"

I craned my gaze up—then shot straight up. "What in Bloods?!"

Half the palace's spired rooftops were in flames. It was the west wing; the ballroom.

We doubled our speed and rushed out of the Weeping Woods, following the canal back into the cemetery. The ghosts were in a frenzy here, spouting about an assassin loose in the palace.

"An… an assassin?" I stammered. Dread coiled, and my breath fell out of me. "Willow…!"

I burst through the cemetery, Alex fumbling at my heels as we hurried into the gardens and climbed up the balcony steps, rushing into the ballroom—

I slipped on some sort of puddle and tumbled forward, my chin hitting the marble floor.

Pain numbed my jaw. I groaned and rocked my heavy head down to rest… then my hair soaked into some liquid on the floor. I'd landed in something wet, the warm liquid running down my scalp and cheek now. I sat up in another pained groan.

Then found myself staring at a man's corpse. And I was sitting in his blood.

I jerked back, the dead man's face staring at me. Alex helped me to my wobbling legs, both of us looking around the ballroom with sickened expressions.

Between the roaring fire patches were dozens of bodies. Guards, guests, servants… it was a varied array of corpses. Some were burnt and charred by the fire, others had their skin melted away as if from disease, their cheekbones and bare skulls poking through.

"Wh-wh… What…" My voice shook, wolf ears growing as the wet liquid soaking one side of my hair dribbled down my forehead. "What happened…?"

Alex's own ears grew and folded down. "One assassin did this…?"

Bile threatened to spew up my throat, the stink of death and burning flesh filling my nostrils. I was accustomed to the smell of corpses and aged skeletons, but this…

This was *fresh*.

I thought I'd be ill. Then memory raced back as I realized I'd forgotten who I was looking for.

"Willow…!" I ran back out to the balcony and sped down the steps, calling back to Alex. "I have to find Willow!"

"I'll find Lilli!" Alex called back as he rushed the other way, the two of us splitting apart toward opposite sides of the palace.

28

ALICE

"Stop him!" I hollered, thrusting hand signals after the retreating assassin. "Don't let him near the princess!"

Maria leapt up and soared over the fire after that madman.

"Don't let him touch you, Maria!" I shouted, running to the wall of flames, coughing smoke. I snapped my gaze at the rest of my team. "Daniel, Lucas, keep with Serdin and Myra! Escape the smog! Matthew, with me! Clear us a path!"

Matthew waved his hands at the licking fire, using his Pyrovoking to make the flames pour away like water and creating a passage large enough for us to run through.

We bolted for the exit where the infectious man had left…

I stopped in the hall.

Two figures were slumped on the sticky, marble floor. The first figure was a boy with shaggy, shadow-grey hair. The boy was crouched over the second figure: a limp body splayed on the floor whose skin was rotting away.

The boy was my son, Alexander.

The body was Maria.

Maria's face was blackening. Her skin peeled away in patches, cheekbones poking through and eye sockets sinking horridly. Her chest and back, apparently pierced by a thin sword, leaked with dark ooze.

My son gasped in heaves over her, clutching the woman with shaking arms. Maria whispered something to him with fading breaths. It was so soft, I couldn't hear a word of it.

The marble was streaked in blazing red, as though my son had tried to pull her over the floor. The same color stained his ivory garments.

A hiss came, Maria's half-melted skin simmering as a white mist rose from her, wavering like ethereal dust and evaporated in a hush.

My son ripped a scream.

"A… Alexander…" My voice trembled, gaze falling to Maria's limp form. "Maria…"

A sob broke free, and I lost grip of my chained scythes. The weapons clattering to the floor. I sank to my knees and crouched over Maria. A rolling pain lurched as I scooped the only woman I truly called a friend from my son's arms, lifting her tenderly.

"Go…" I whispered to Alex, my throat tight. "You shouldn't be here."

His mismatched eyes were lined in red, his bloodied hands shaking. "I…" He swallowed hoarsely. "I have to find Lilli… I-I promised her…"

I paused. *Promised?* That must have been her final words to him. My sharpened teeth gritted so hard my gums wailed. But I ignored it, nodding.

"Find your brother as well," I ordered. "The assassin is after Willow. If you find them in time, stay together. Do *not* separate."

He nodded, rubbing his eyes vigorously and coughing from the smoke clinging to his lungs.

I watched my son dart out of sight.

Nira, I prayed to the Seamstress, *please, hear me—keep them safe.*

I looked down at Maria's burnt face. *That mist… it was her soul leaving.* Tears swelled. Maria's beautiful, chartreuse eyes were stale and placid, staring at the hall's arched ceiling emptily.

I held her tighter, her warmth fading. "Oh, Maria…" My throat reverberated, fury heating. "He will pay for this…"

XAVIER

I stumbled through the palace halls, fighting back the vomit climbing my throat with every ripping wheeze.

Fire crackled in growing patches around me. The fire had already reached the east wing? This area wasn't completely charred and blanketed in flames like the ballroom had been, but the smoke was still suffocating. Though there was, I thanked the Seamstress, a lack of bodies here. Whoever this assassin was, he must have hit the west wing first.

My footfalls didn't echo in the hallways tonight, as they usually did. There was too much activity among the servants and wispy ghosts. Most were buzzing about the fire, but few knew the full scope of the horrors found in the ballroom.

The crowd parted for me when I rushed through, their faces riddled with shock when they saw me. I knew why they stared. My pure white, silken doublet was coated in ash and soot, mixed with crimson smears. None of the blood was mine, but it was still terrifying enough to cause a stir.

I raced up two flights of spiraling stairs, heading for Willow's chambers with a thundering pulse pounding my wolf ears.

Please, I begged the Seamstress, blood dripping into my lids and stinging my already misting eyes. *Please, don't let her be…!*

The melted faces of the ballroom flashed to mind. What if I was too late? What if I found her like them…? Bloods, if I had just been there with her instead of running off from my own damned nerves…!

I gritted my sharpened teeth, speeding up.

"Young Howllord!" A voice barked at me when I reached the third floor's corridor.

I was blocked by a cluster of royal guards, their scythes drawn and silver helms shielding their faces.

The captain saluted me with a gauntleted fist to his chest, his eyes alighting with recognition under his visor. But then he frowned. "I don't have to tell you this is an emergency, my lord, so forgive me: which twin are you?"

"Xavier," I puffed, wiping the sweat and ash from my brow. The sleeve came back with red in the mix. "I'm… I'm Her Highness's betrothed. Please, let me through!"

"We've searched her chambers, my lord, she isn't there." His sharpened teeth barred. "We'd hoped she was with you."

She isn't there? My stomach coiled sickly. *What if… what if she'd been one of the corpses we couldn't see past the fires…?* "Tell me you've checked the ballroom?!" I demanded, refusing to believe I'd left her there to die.

"We've checked," he assured. "From what we could glean, Her Highness was absent. The queen informed us she fled to find you, my lord."

I loosened my lungs in slight relief. "Thank the Gods… Where else have you looked?"

"I have Reapers searching the courtyard as we speak." He tossed hand signals to his cluster of soldiers behind him, prompting them to march down the stairs ahead of us. The captain gripped my shoulder and pushed me after them. "We'll find her, make no mistake. Just stay close to us, Howllord, this monster is not to be taken light—*ghk…!*"

There was a small cry of cracking platemail behind me, making me whirl.

Where the captain's lower face was still visible, I saw his jaw contort in pain. Then I found the cause: a thin rapier was sticking through his abdomen, so straight it was almost invisible.

The blade dripped with the man's blood, stinking of oils and iron. It made little sound as it was pulled out.

The captain fell forward, and would have collapsed on me if I hadn't leapt back. I stared at the dead man at my feet.

My gaze didn't linger on the body long. There was a pair of bare feet on the other side of him, soaked in red.

Glancing up, I found myself staring into two yellow orbs glinting in the dim lamplight, the assassin's face cloaked in shadow. From the silence came a scraggly, echoing chuckle.

"You're Her Highness's betrothed, you say?" he rasped, each syllable bouncing off the high arched ceiling. "How very convenient…"

I cursed and darted for the stairs, hearing his heels thump after me from behind. I was nearly at the stairwell—but slipped on a red puddle and fell forward. My head *cracked* against the first step's edge.

Pain stung at my brow—then my hair was yanked up by merciless fingers.

That low, scratching voice growled in my grown wolf ear. "You'll make for fine bait, I should think. Eh, pup?"

I quickly grasped the man's wrist, evoking my soul Hallows to cast a Sensory-Illusion, making him feel a sharp, searing stab along his arm—something I'd felt years ago, when I was pricked by Poisondragon quills along my back.

He screamed and released me, flinging back his hand to look at it in shock. But he soon blinked and clicked his tongue. "Damned Necrovokers and your illusions… A fair trick. But nothing more."

He started for me again, stopping short when the glow from my Death mark faded. My Crest of three black diamonds had returned under my knuckles.

He stared at my Crest with sharp, yellow eyes. "Blood and bones…" he whispered. "You bear the Crest…?"

I jolted down the stairwell.

The assassin hesitated in his chase this time, but I still heard the *tifft, tifft, tifft* of his footfalls echoing above me.

I leapt over the last two steps and skidded onto the first level's floor, breaking into a frenzied sprint outside—

A hand shot out of a tall bush and clapped over my mouth, yanking me into the shrub.

"*Mmm!*" I tried to scream through the hand around my mouth, flailing wildly.

"Hush, Xavier!" A familiar boy's voice whispered in my wolf ear. "It's only me, for Death's sake. Be calm."

It was Matthiel Inion.

I relaxed, but only slightly, prying the boy's hand off my face. "Bloods, Matthiel!" I gave the sienna-eyed boy an annoyed glare. "Don't scare me like that. I thought my heart would pop from fright."

He snorted. "You'll live—"

Footfalls crunched the grass outside our shielding bush.

We froze stiff. Both our grown wolf ears perked straight up. The footsteps outside paused. Our breaths snuffed into terrified silence. We waited there for three horrifying seconds…

Four seconds…

Five seconds…

Six…

Seven…

By the eighth second, the footfalls continued onward, fading until they disappeared entirely and all that remained was the whine of crickets.

We melted in relief inside the bush, and I pushed out a breath. "Thank Bloods…"

Matthiel narrowed his eyes at me. "You're alone? Her Highness didn't find you?"

I shook my head. "I checked her chambers, but she wasn't there. I don't know where she could be."

Matthiel cupped his eyes in a groan. "Well, isn't that just Bloody wonderful—?"

A trilling chirp sounded outside the bush suddenly. It was a familiar, musical chirp, perking our wolf ears eagerly.

"Jewel!" We exclaimed at once, craning our heads out of the bush.

Willow's tiny Songcrow was buzzing at our faces anxiously.

I fumbled out of the bush, Matthiel tripping after me. I panted to Jewel, "Can you take us to Willow?"

Jewel gave a flighty, affirming twitter before speeding off toward the deeper part of the royal gardens.

"Come on!" I hollered to Matthiel, the two of us hustling after the tiny crow.

29

WILLOW

I sat within the grove of dwarfed willow trees and huddled on the bed of Candle Lilies. This was the usual place Xavier and I met in private, perhaps he'd think to come here if Jewel couldn't find him?

The melted faces of the ball's guests were burned in my memory, tears stinging my swollen eyes. I hugged my knees, biting back a sob.

What if Jewel couldn't find him? What if she was caught by that assassin? Bloods, what if Xavier was already dead—

The veiling branches were pulled apart suddenly, making me start.

It was Xavier and Matthiel. Jewel fluttered between them proudly.

"You're all right!" I fumbled to my feet, an undignified sob breaking free. Relief flushed so strong, I could barely breathe as Jewel alighted into my cupped hands. "You're all safe…! Thank the Seamstress, I-I was so worried…!"

"*You* were worried?!" Xavier reeled me in, squeezing me tighter than ever. His voice was strained and shaken. "I had no idea where you were…! I-I thought you… I thought you were…!" He shivered, hugging me stronger for one last, lingering minute, then calmed himself and loosened his grip. "We need to get out of here. Have you seen Lilli and Alex?"

Lilli! Bloods, that's right—she was still missing! And Alex didn't come in with Xavier *or* Matthiel!

My head shook, terror flooding all over again as my throat pushed out a frightened squeal. "N-no…! They're still out there…!"

"It's all right!" Xavier assured quickly. "I'm sure they're fine. We'll just have to find them."

Matthiel peered at Jewel in my hands. "Or have them find us?"

I swallowed and nodded, lifting my little crow. "Jewel? Can you find Lilli and Alex?"

Jewel gave a confirming twitter, then fluttered out of my hands and zoomed away.

LILLI

I wiped my eyes dry as I soared back toward the palace; back to find my mother.

Bloods, why did I say such cruel things…? How could I face her now?

Idiot girl! I pounded my head. Dusk gave a sympathizing caw as she flew beside me. *You're no better than Felix…*

I sucked in a shuddering breath. I had to apologize. But would she even forgive me—?

Something caught my eye up ahead. I spread my wings to make an abrupt stop, flapping in place. A bright, orange glow emanated from the palace grounds in the distance. *What in Death…?*

I soared over the palace walls, Dusk flying like a bolt at my side.

Death's Head, the palace was in *flames!*

I gawked at the horrifying scene as I flew around the perimeter, lowering altitude to avoid the billowing smoke climbing toward the cavern's ceiling. It was so thick, the dark smog swallowed the Floating Lights that dared to drift into its curling snares.

"Lilli…!" A distant voice called my name from below. "Lilli…!"

My gaze snapped down. One of the twins ran through the royal vineyard.

I dove down farther. It was Alexander. When I touched down to meet him—

I reeled back in horror. Alexander's white suit was stained in blood.

"Alex!" I shrieked. "What happened?! Is… is that your blood or—?!"

"Not mine!" He hacked the smoke that clung to the air. Fire blazed from the palace windows, embers and debris flaring in the wind, screams echoing…

I stepped back. "W-what's happening?"

Alex coughed the fumes from his lungs, covering his mouth and nose with a crimson-stained sleeve. "There's an assassin in the palace!"

"An… assassin…?" My breaths turned ragged, trying like Death to process this. "Bloods, *this* must have been why the queen was acting strange…! And Willow's vision…!" I froze. My grown bat ears curled as I growled, "*Where is Willow?*"

"I don't know," Alex panted. "X-Xavier went to find her in her chambers!"

"Come on!"

My arms latched round his waist, startling him.

Alex protested, "W-wait! What are you—*aaahh!*"

I flexed my wings and heaved both of us in the air, soaring toward the castle's east wing.

From this vantage, I could see most of the grounds along with the people running below us. There were so many bodies at the front gates… So many dead… Was this really the work of one man?

Alex squirmed in my arms, not seeming sure what to do except hold onto my neck. His eyes were glued to the ground, either uneasy or fascinated by the view. I blushed, suddenly realizing this was the first embrace I'd ever shared with my fiancé.

—Not the time!

My head shook, keeping focused. We soared over the royal gardens, and I had my sights on Willow's terrace.

But a flighty twitter sounded. Jewel buzzed in front of my face with frantic chirps.

"Jewel!" I gasped. "Can you take us to Willow?"

Jewel chirped twice and fluttered deeper into the gardens.

I raced after her, hauling Alexander with me. Jewel led us to the ground and zoomed into a shielding grove of dwarfed willow trees. When Alex and I touched down and ran in after her, we found Xavier, Matthiel and Willow waiting for us.

"Lilli!" Willow wailed and latched onto me in a shuddering sob. "You're all right!"

"Yes, I'm fine…" I pushed her at arms' length to examine her with a strict eye. "Are you hurt, Willow?"

"N-No." She sniffled and rubbed an arm under her nose. "It-it was horrible, Lilli…! Their souls are gone…! They're *gone*, Lilli—destroyed! He's poisoning everyone…!" Her voice tightened to a whisper, and she began praying breathlessly.

I'd seen as much, given the bodies splayed at the front gates. My own tears threatened to spill, but I swallowed to stay on task. I had a duty to carry out. Holding my breath, I slipped off a bracelet I was wearing and thrust it before Willow's face.

"Willow, it's time," I said, my voice like granite. "I need you to put an illusion into this! Give me your hair and eyes!"

Willow blinked at me. "Wh-what? I already told you—"

"You must!" My tone hardened. "*This* is part of my job as your Aide…! And… as your friend." I shut my eyes and softened my tone. "Please… give me the illusion."

Willow clenched her fists. "No."

Annoyance simmered, and I growled. "For the love of Gods, Willow, it's my job!"

"Job or not! I won't let my sister give her life for my sake—!"

"ENOUGH!" I roared, flapping my wings in a furious gust of wind that sent her tied up hair wafting back, her bell jingling. My tone dripped darkly. "If you do not give me that illusion, Willow, I will find your mother and have *her* give it to me! Then I'll find the assassin myself and make sure he follows me instead! Would you prefer that?! Because Seamstress Cleanse me, I will!"

That shut Willow up, albeit bitterly. Even the three boys went rigid, none daring to test me.

"That's what I thought." I calmed my tone, but only slightly. "Now… my *disguise*, Willow?"

Willow was silent for a long while. She was obviously not happy, her look resentful at me. Her arms shook, gripping the bracelet I'd given her.

Then, shutting her eyes and turning away, her fingers gleamed azure, sealing her Hallows into the bracelet while scratching the proper markings with a claw.

She handed it back to me as I rose, and she growled. "Don't you dare go looking for that murderer, Lilli… Report back to me immediately when this is over."

I nodded, slipping the jewelry on. I watched as my black hair fazed white in a slow, glittering trickle. It did nothing for my wings and *length* of hair, but it would do. Once the illusion was set, I let out a nervous yet resolute breath.

"I will," I said, trying not to quake as I turned to leave.

"Wait a damned minute," Alexander blurted. He grabbed my arm. "You can't just run off alone with a murderer on the loose! That monster just killed your…!" He shut his mouth. For whatever reason, I caught his gaze drifting to the blood staining his suit. His eyes misted, but he shut them and barred his teeth. "I'm coming with you."

Xavier was the one to protest, his voice cracking. "What?! But, Alex—!"

"Xavier, you're not about to leave Willow, are you?" Alex snapped.

His brother faltered. Xavier's breath shuddered, and he laced his fingers through Willow's. "No… not after what I saw in the ballroom."

"And after what *I* saw…" Alex's tone was tight. He glared at me, making my wings stiffen.

What was that look about? What in Bloods did he see…?

"I'm not leaving *you*, Lilli," Alex said. "I have a promise to keep. To your mother."

My brow furrowed. "What in Nirus did you promise to my—?"

"It doesn't matter!" Alex interrupted, "Come on, Lilli! We shouldn't stay here!"

He started to lead the way out of the veiling branches of the dwarfed willow trees.

"Alex, wait!" Xavier snatched his brother's collar, pulling him back. He clasped hands with Alex, reeling him in for a tight embrace. "Find us after this is over." Xavier said. "And for Death's sake, be safe."

"And you as well," Alex replied, squeezing him. "Born together."

"Die together," Xavier finished, his voice stern. "*Only* together. Don't you dare break that."

"I won't," Alex hushed. They each drew in hesitant breaths… then peeled away, Alex following at my side while Xavier fled with Willow and Matthiel.

KAEL

"Surely, this is a mistake…?" I rumbled from my perch atop an autumn-leaved tree.

I watched as the teens split into groups and ran in opposing directions through the royal gardens. One party consisted of two members, a boy and a girl, but I couldn't glean the boy's face. It was blocked by the white-haired girl running at his side.

The second party had three members, this time with two boys and one girl. This girl's white hair was far, far longer than the other Howless, and a bell tinkled from the tied-up strands as she suddenly shifted her hair color into a charcoal grey hue with illusion Hallows.

The Hallows that only the granddaughter of Dream would possess. And one of the boys with her was the same, odd-eyed young man that had the Crest on his left hand.

The mark of the Shadowblood.

"He is far younger than I was told…" I murmured, rubbing my stubbled chin. "Dream's Champion was said to be a man. Not a boy. Was I freed earlier than Dream's prediction…?"

I supposed these were meaningless questions. If the world was to be safeguarded, the boy had to die. No matter how young he may have been.

Troubling, I brooded. *But it cannot be helped.*

I climbed down from my perch and hopped onto the grass… Landing with a *thmp* right before the disguised princess and her teenaged guards. They drew back in a start as I loomed over them.

"Your Highness," I growled—then snapped my gaze at the heterochromic boy with a twisted glower. "And if it isn't Dream's fabled champion... Oh, but we've all been waiting a long, *long* time for your coming."

The third boy with sienna eyes shoved in front of the princess and ignited his hand in a burst of fire, throwing it at my feet. I was forced to step back as the trio fled.

My lips tugged into a snarl. "And thus, the hunt begins, Champion of Dream..."

30

XAVIER

Willow, Matthiel and I raced through the gardens and fumbled into the cemetery, climbing under the canal and sprinting into the bustling city.

The assassin pursued no matter where we went. We pushed through the crowd of people in the markets, we turned corner after corner, we ducked around hover-coaches and numerous porters… yet he always appeared behind us. As if we hadn't gained *any* distance.

We turned one more corner, looking back as we ran. The man had at last disappeared into the crowd—

My nose slammed right into him. Somehow, he'd slipped in front of us, and the collision knocked me on my back.

His yellow eyes glinted as he towered over me. I shuffled back until I hit Willow's legs.

"This game has been amusing, children," the assassin rumbled. He reached for me, his hand festering with black, jagged veins. "But it's time to come with me—*AAARGH!*"

Matthiel leapt in front of us and threw a gout of fire over the man's hands. The assassin was forced back, dunking his hands into a nearby fountain to douse the flames as we made a run for it—

"*You infuriating whelp…!*" The man roared at Matthiel. The water around his hands suddenly bled black, poison bubbling in the fountain's pool. The assassin smacked the infected water and sent a blackened splash flying toward Matthiel.

Matthiel shuffled back to evade—but he tripped over a merchant's wagon of flour and *puffed* into the powdered sacks, a white smoke hazing around him as he hacked and coughed.

With Matthiel fumbling to get out of the wagon, the assassin stalked toward Willow and me instead.

Willow grabbed my hand and yanked me along. "Come on!"

I hesitated, my legs stiff as I looked from the assassin to Matthiel, who was still struggling in the wreckage of the wagon.

"But—Matthiel…!" I sputtered.

"He's not after Matthiel!" Willow barked and pulled me into a run. "He's after *us*! The best way to help Matthiel is to lead this lunatic away from him! Now come on!"

I finally complied and sprinted beside her. I craned my gaze back. Willow was right. The man ran after us, not even looking back at Matthiel.

We hustled as fast as our legs could manage, but he was still gaining on us. We hung a sharp left around a corner building, the air thickening with warm, sulfur-scented steam.

We're nearing the geyser fields, I realized, my nose crinkling at the foul-smelling steam.

An idea struck me. I whipped my gaze around, looking for a particular building I knew should be located near the geyser fields.

There, atop jagged hills with a long flight of stone stairs leading up to it, was a high-arching building lit with many cool lamps and pluming with the thickest sulfuric steam found in the geyser fields.

It was a Surfacing Port. A geyser station that transported passengers to the surface lands.

"Willow!" I shouted, snagging Willow's wrist and tugging her up the stone stairs toward the station. "We can go to the surface…! He won't follow us there!"

"Are you sure?" Willow's azure eyes were wide with skepticism.

"I'm not sure of anything right now!" I yelled, hurtling up the stone steps in a winded pant. "But it's better than running in circles!"

She didn't protest, nodding her agreement as we reached the top of the steps and barreled into the Surfacing Port's wide entrance.

We pushed through the crowd of shifters in the station, startling many of them and earning ourselves a number of craning gazes.

We ran into the first surfacing pod available. It was a round, metal vehicle that waited above one of the bubbling geyser pools lined throughout the platform. Judging by the ever-growing size of *this* pool's bubbles, this pod was about to ascend any moment.

Willow and I darted past the steward who was boarding passengers and leapt inside the pod, ignoring the steward's protesting shouts as we found an empty compartment room and hauled the metal door shut.

Screams ripped through the pod behind the door. The frightened voices were muffled, but every whimpering plea was crystal clear in my grown wolf ears right before each dying shriek curdled and dimmed.

Chungh!

Our door gave a sharp clang suddenly. I yelped and fell back into Willow.

Chungh! Chungh! Ratta-ta, ratta-ta, ratta-ta…

The assassin was trying to break down the door, the window's shutters rattling wildly with each heavy hit.

Chungh! Chungh-Klang!

Willow cupped a hand to her mouth. "They're dead…" She sank to her knees. "They're all dead. Aren't they?"

Tears stung my vision. I couldn't bring myself to answer.

Hssssssss…!

The geyser beneath us hissed and bubbled suddenly.

From the compartment's circular window, a furious stream of boiling water rushed upward, bubbles rolling over the glass. The Surfacing Pod rumbled as it lifted off its suspended platform. Then it began to rise along with the stream of water.

The sudden lurch of g-forces pulled at my stomach—and it must have pulled at Willow's as well because she squeezed my ribs in fright.

Death, that's right. We're going to the Bloody surface. With everything that happened, I nearly forgot her fear of heights. Neither of us had ever been as high as the damned surface. This must have sent her further over the edge than she'd already been. *Damn it, I shouldn't have brought her here... idiot. I'm a Gods damned idiot.*

I held her close, but knew it would never be enough to make up for my stupidity. We were trapped in here. Our deaths waited on the other side of this door.

I'd killed us both.

The deafening clatter of the assassin's pounding rang from the door as we ascended toward the surface.

31

LILLI

When Alex and I split from the group, the two of us hurried in the opposite direction.

We wove our way through the gardens, past the orchards and into the cemetery, ducking into the canal that would lead us into town—

We stopped, our ankles splashing to a halt in the canal's waters.

Before us stood a middle aged, black-haired man with yellow eyes. It was as if he'd been waiting for us.

"Your Highness Death?" the man took another step toward us, his gaze set on me and my falsely white hair.

"Death!" Alex cursed and snatched my hand, tugging me across the other side of the canal as we hurried into the city. "Keep your wings folded!" Alex warned as we ran, that yellow-eyed man chasing after us. I could only assume *he* was the assassin, given Alexander's reaction. "Your 'illusion' plan will crumble if he sees your wings!"

Nodding, I let him lead me into town as we wound through bustling streets, that man close on our trail. We had him chase us for what seemed like an hour, biding time for Xavier and Willow to escape—

The man slid in front of us from around a corner building, catching us off-guard.

"Please!" the yellow-eyed man panted. "I-I don't mean any harm! Seriously! Look, it's not safe here…!" The creases at his brow crinkled. "Wait… The Death Princess doesn't have wings."

My bat ears curled, and I discarded the bracelet in a huff. No use for it now that we were found out. I took a proud stance in front of Alex, plucking my scythe-spheres from my necklace and had my scythes materialize.

"You'd better grow accustomed to disappointment, *assassin*," I sneered. "The real heiress has already fled to safety."

"Gods damn it…!" The man let out a furious scream, ruffling his black hair. "Great! Just great! Now *he's* probably already found her…! ARGH!" The man rushed out of the street, disappearing into the city as the fires blazed from the palace in the distance.

Panicked, Alex and I sprinted after the man.

"H-hey!" I shouted. "Get back here…!"

WILLOW

Chungh!

The compartment's metal door continued to tremble.

Chungh—klung!

The banging intensified, rattling the window's shutters.

"Death," Xavier cursed as he held me tighter. His grown wolf ears dropped to his neck. Then he pulled away from me and searched this Surfacing Pod's dim room. "There has to be some way…"

He rummaged through drawers, peered under seats, upturned cushions and reached over empty luggage racks with impressive haste. After nearly an hour, he must have done the routine over a hundred times, the door still clanging away to the point of white-noise.

Why did he bother looking anymore? There was nothing here that could help. There was no escape.

The banging continued at the door, ruthless and angered.

Oh, Death's Head! I gave in and helped Xavier tear apart the compartment. *We've no choice left, have we?*

Stumbling to the window opposite the door, I rubbed my sleeve over the fogged glass and cleared a spot. There was nothing but bubbles outside, surging within the scalding liquid as our Surfacing Pod was lifted by the geyser. Our speed had declined, as far as I could tell, the weight pulling my stomach lessening a small amount.

"We haven't reached the surface yet." I panted, jolting when another metallic *clang* bellowed from the door. "How much longer?!"

"I-I think the geyser erupted an hour ago." Xavier joined me at the window, dabbing his sweaty neck. "It can't be much longer. I'm more worried about how we plan to get past him once we reach the surface."

I sank to the floor, shivering despite the sweltering heat. "Bloods, we've trapped ourselves like feral mice. We're going to die in here."

Xavier lightly knocked on the window, testing it. "Maybe not… There's another way out."

The pod rumbled and slowed, and I heard the hiss of water fade as bubbles fled from the window, leaving naught but a streaky haze on the glass.

Crash!

The shutters at the door burst apart, glass shattering underneath. The assassin's pale arm reached through the small window and groped for the latch.

"Death!" Xavier pounded our opposite window, bloodying his knuckles. He hadn't even made a hairline fracture in the glass.

The assassin's hand wriggled the door handle, his claws scraping the metal. I panicked and evoked my fire Hallows and threw a blast of orange flame at his fingers, making him roar in pain and retract his arm from the door window. That bought us some time, but there was no telling for how long.

Our pod came to a stop. The hiss of hydraulics whistled outside. The compartment shook as the ride stabilized.

Sorrowed Death, we've reached the surface!

Xavier kept pounding at our window. This glass was thicker than the one that monster had broken at the door. Xavier would never shatter it in time, not with his knuckles. What he needed was a tool.

My eyes darted round the pod, looking for something—any-thing—that would help. I spotted a lantern bolted to the wall. I rushed over and seized the lantern by its metal bracket, then evoked my fire Hallows. Flames burst from my palms and licked over the bracket, heating the iron until it blushed a brittle red under my fingers. The metal gave little resistance as I ripped it off the wall.

"Move!" I ordered Xavier.

He saw me brandishing the lamp with a wild glare and promptly stumbled out of my way.

I *smashed* the window with the heavy lantern.

My boots crunched down the jagged edges before I pulled Xavier by the sleeve. "Come on!"

I climbed out first, wincing while sliding down the slippery, hot wall of the metal Surfacing Pod. The bulbous curvature served as a slide and guided me down.

But the slope disappeared from under me. Suddenly I was hurtling for the empty, dark chasm that led back to Grim's geyser pools.

I shrieked—

Xavier caught me by the wrist, my shoulder slamming into the pod. My disguised grey hair fanned into view, the bell jingling in a frenzy. I craned my gaze up, seeing Xavier was gripping the window's open frame with one hand while his other hand kept me dangling.

Blood seeped between his fingers the longer he held onto that broken window frame. Steam sizzled under his palm. It smelled of burnt flesh and sulfur. Xavier scowled fiercely, determined to keep me lifted. His face was red from exertion and the blood of that *demon's* past victims.

Xavier managed to push out a breath and rasped, "The beam!"

I found the support beam he meant. It was part of the elaborate mechanisms that locked the Surfacing Pod in place while it waited for the geyser's next eruption.

Xavier swung me like a pendulum, gaining momentum, then released me.

I screamed while grappling the slippery beam as best I could. My boot slipped, but I dug my claws in the metal and steadied my quivering arms. The chasm spun beneath me.

Merciful Nira! How far up were we? I'd never live through a fall like that.

Xavier let out a curse above me. He stared in horror through the pod's open window.

—then a violent hand reached through the broken frame and swiped for Xavier.

Xavier ducked, swinging himself like he'd done with me, and leapt for the beam. He landed gut-first and gagged as if he'd vomit, but swallowed and shouted, "Go!"

My frozen limbs burst alive, crawling toward the platform.

There were shifters packed in the station, though they didn't seem hurried to catch their pods. They were afraid. Shouts and cries echoed in the misty station. It sounded like Reapers were rushing out with patrons and stewards. Had the pilot alerted them before we arrived? Better still, was the pilot alive?

A team of Reapers waited at the edge of the platform, their scythes in hand and at the ready. The soldiers spotted us crawling along the beam and gaped. They swiftly put away their weapons to reach for us.

Thank the Seamstress!

I reached a shivering hand out. A Reaper snatched my fingers, pulling me onto the platform. Now safely on solid ground, I twisted back to find Xavier. He was still stuck on the support beam. He crawled closer—but slipped and nearly fell. Two Reapers caught him and hauled him onto the platform beside me.

"Gods, they're covered in blood," a brown-haired man murmured.

I stared at his brown hair in a daze. *Colored hair…* He was Landish. Most everyone here was. Their skin tones were various degrees of bronze and brown; their hair different shades of copper, burgundy, blond and brunet. We really were on the surface. I knew that had been obvious from our hour-long travel, but the true gravity of it had my knees shaking. We were on the Bloody *surface.* Our home was so, so far beneath us…

The Landish man tapped a finger to the communicator hooked to his ear. "Search the pod! See if anyone else survived! And for Land's sake, if you find the hijacker, kill him on sight—"

"The pilot lives!" a voice cried from the pod. It had been another Reaper. He'd apparently ventured inside to investigate before the order was given.

The Reaper lugged a limp man onto the platform. The victim's tangled black hair tumbled from under a grey, uniformed hat that indeed marked him as the pilot.

The Reaper beside us hollered back, "Any sign of the hostile?"

"He's vanished!" The Reaper dragged the unconscious pilot toward us. "Have everyone search the station before he escapes!"

"Damn it all… keep an eye on these Grimlings and wait for the Medics! We can't afford to lose the fugitive!"

I winced when Xavier squeezed my arm with claws fingers. His mismatched, blue-and-white glare was keen on the new Reaper heading for us.

"It's him." Xavier's wolf ears curled, and he whipped his gaze at the knights protecting us. "That isn't a Reaper! It's *him*—!"

The fraud dropped the pilot and shot a black-veined hand at us.

Xavier yanked me out of the way, his shoes shrieking over the tiled floor.

The assassin redirected his infected hand to the Reapers surrounding him—dropping them like flies. Then he shouted orders at the crowd, telling them to stop us, that we were witnesses, that we needed protection.

Bastard! The oblivious Reapers were responding favorably, and we now had to dodge and shove our way through the groping mass.

Our boots screeched when we veered left and rushed outside.

—*HSSSSSSSHHHHHH!*

The moment we left the station, we were blasted with a wall of pouring water.

"What in Bloods…?" Xavier lifted a hand to shield his eyes from the flood. "What is this? A… a leak in the ceiling?"

My disguised, grey hair was soaked through in seconds, and I hollered over the torrential shower. "We're on the surface now! They don't have a ceiling, remember?! I think this is what they call 'rain'—!"

A bright string of light shot from the clouds and a deafening roar shook the canyons.

I wasn't the only one to shriek.

Xavier stumbled to his rear as the rocky terrain bloomed with light. It only lasted a brief, flickering moment before it dimmed again.

I helped Xavier to his feet and hollered over the hissing water. "What was that?!"

"I-I-I don't know!" He shivered, his fingers almost cracking mine in a Deathly fearsome grip. Bloods, this 'rain' was relentless.

Something caught my eye in the distance. A silhouette was moving fast toward us from the radiant station. *Death!*

I jerked Xavier along. "We have to keep moving!"

He stumbled behind me, keeping our fingers latched.

I took us off the lit trail. If we wished to lose that monster, we wouldn't do it by taking the predicted paths. The further we moved from the station, the darker the canyons grew. The only lights we had were those terrifying flashes that cracked through the clouds, but on we trudged through the shower—

My foot suddenly caught air, the breath hurtling out of me when I dipped at the canyon's ledge. A new bolt of light sparked alive to show a sloshing bed of water beneath me.

My foot slipped on the edge. Xavier reeled me in before I fell, bits of rock crumbling under my boots.

"You've ventured far enough," crunched a voice behind us.

The assassin's black hair was stuck to his bristled face, the strands drenched from the pouring water. His honey eyes burned in the new burst of light.

Xavier raised a hand to the beast in warning. "Stay back…!"

The man's chuckle lilted. "Your illusions won't work again, corpse-raiser. I know your tricks."

I bellowed from behind Xavier, "*My* tricks leave a mark!"

Sucking in a breath, I evoked my fire Hallows as a bright glow came from the Death mark at my chest…

But the moment the smallest flame puffed from my palms, it was doused by the pouring water. *Damn it all!*

The monster laughed. "Welcome to the surface, my little heiress… The rain is lovely this evening, don't you think?"

I chewed on a string of obscenities. Not only was fire useless, but there wasn't a need for my illusion anymore. He must have guessed who I was long before we stowed away to the surface. I slid off my enchanted earcuff, watching in a blinding flash of light as my grey hair bled white. I tossed the jewelry aside.

"I still have one element I'm sure you're familiar with," I shouted and evoked my infection Hallows next, my hands spewing small, black veins as I stepped in front of Xavier.

My throat blistered, breaths growing ragged. *Bloods…* My energy was quickly draining. The longer I pushed this element out, the sooner I risked collapsing. *Damn my pathetic stamina… I need a backup plan.*

I reached for the glittering hairstick speared through my bundled locks. My glowing scythe materialized in my poisonous fingers, the blade and staff soaking in the infection magic until the weapon oozed black.

The man scoffed. "You realize your poisons will do nothing to me?"

My throat clicked. "Perhaps. But even serpents grow ill when injected with venom. And I guarantee my scythe will leave a *mark*."

I rushed for him, slashing my blade with a guttural roar.

He deflected with his thin sword, our poisons slurping together for a brief second before we split the blades apart.

The sky exploded again, and I struck relentlessly, sweeping and slicing and swinging and parrying.

I sliced his shoulder once, nicked his side, and almost split his throat until he ducked away milliseconds before I made purchase.

We were both panting for breath soon enough, keeping our weapons raised and our glares fixed on each other.

We were getting nowhere. He'd failed to land a hit on me yet, but with my weak Hallows, I didn't have the same poison resistance as him. It would only take one strike, and that would be it for me.

I flicked my gaze over my shoulder. Xavier was still behind me by the edge of the cliff, staring at me helplessly. He didn't have any weapons. Nor did he have Hallows that could help in this situation. And *my* Hallows was draining quickly.

I wheezed for breath, my vision spotting. My infectious veins began to drain away from my scythe.

The assassin gave a gravely rumble, "Interesting… the mutt hasn't much stamina, does she?"

"I have plenty of stamina, beast," I spat. "And I… I have other elements you may not be as familiar with…!"

The assassin didn't seem fazed, his tone dull. "I'm familiar with all of Aspirre's Hallows, dear child… Far more intimately than I wish to be." He sighed, shouldering his sword. "Dream's granddaughter… You have his eyes, indeed. To be kin of that coward… what I wouldn't give to have my hands around his scrawny neck…!"

His cat ears curled, but he shut his eyes and swept his blade to the side calmly. "All in due time… With his prized treasure here, he will meet his retribution." He chuckled, looking at Xavier. "Centuries he's been patient. It seems the right era has come at last… Only for the lad to come running before my very feet." His laughter twisted.

He's… after Xavier? I craned back to Xavier, puzzled. Xavier shook his head at me, equally confused.

"I don't know what you want with him," I growled, thickening the poisonous veins around my scythe once more. Each vein that poured out of me stretched with intense pain, my soul feeling ripe to snap. But I ground my teeth and took a defiant step forward, wheezing. "But you'll… not lay… a claw on him—!"

A sharp *crack* sounded under Xavier and me.

The ledge broke beneath our feet, and my stomach lurched as we tumbled downward.

I hit something rocky and solid, my whole body numb with pain. I gave a strained breath, but the sound of the hissing water fizzled into nothingness as my world was swallowed in darkness.

A spark of light shot above, jostling me awake.

Everything ached.

My vision blinked red and yellow, ears pounding hot. I reached a hand to my brow, and my fingers came back bloody. *What happened?*

This damned water was still pouring everywhere, but the bolts of light had quelled for now, leaving darkness.

I heaved up to sit, bleary. "Xavier…?"

I only heard the hissing shower in reply.

"Xavier?" I tried again, louder, my throat splintered. "Are you there?"

The lights returned in a roar, frightening the dark off the terrain—and glinting off the yellow eyes of the assassin looming above me.

I tried to yell, but the man clamped a hand over my mouth and shoved me down.

A sudden gust of static pricked my lips and spread over my muscles like a crippling wave of needles.

I dropped in an instant, joints locked and throat squeezed shut by its own volition. My lips shaped the curses and grunts I longed to spit, but all that came were quiet breaths.

Another flash bloomed, and he reached for me, a cruel grin tugging his lips.

"—Willow!" Xavier's voice tore through the chatter of water suddenly.

The man's hand retracted. He pivoted, walking toward where Xavier had called.

Death!

In a new flicker of light, I saw Xavier lying against a jagged rock some yards to my right.

"Willow?!" He called for me again—but was cut off when the man grabbed his throat and lifted him off the rock.

I tried to scream, tried to warn him, but my vocal cords were numb. *What has he done to me? Was this… some sort of paralysis?*

A new flash came. Xavier was wailing in pain, black veins spreading from the assassin's hands and pulsing under his victim's skin, leaking into his eyes until…

Until Xavier fell limp in the man's hold. He ceased his struggling. And his mismatched eyes grew dull.

The last flash of light was a quiet one. As was Xavier's fall as the assassin loosened his fingers from Xavier's throat.

And sent him spiraling to the crashing waves below.

LILLI

"AAAAAAAHH…!" Alexander suddenly doubled over, falling to his knees in the city streets of Grim. He clutched his head as if in agony.

"Alex?!" I scrambled beside him, holding a cautious hand to his back and sweeping one of my wings over him. He was breathing hard, gasping for air.

"Alex, what's wrong?!" I tried to find any sign of a wound, but he was already covered in so much blood. I couldn't tell if any of it was his.

"Zzz… X-Xavier…!" he gasped, tears streaming. He was choking in pained hiccups, his hands balled over the rough ground. *"No! Don't… Please…!"* He screamed. "Xav…!"

The light faded from his eyes and he collapsed to his side. I quickly pulled him up to my lap, screaming. *"Alex!"*

He didn't wake.

I shook harder. "Alex…!"

He still didn't wake.

Footfalls trotted behind me, and my head snapped up. Matthiel had come panting up to me, the Howllord covered from head to foot in flour.

"What happened?" Matthiel questioned as he helped me lift Alex by his arms. "Did the assassin touch him with his poison?"

"I-I-I don't know," I stammered, heaving Alex's unconscious body upright until his legs dangled over the cobblestones. Alex's head rolled back and flopped onto my shoulder. I felt his breath on my neck.

I murmured shakily, "He's still breathing, so he's alive… but we need to take him to the infirmary."

Matthiel nodded. Then he glanced over his shoulder in concern. "What of the assassin?"

I shook my head. "We can regroup after Alex is seen to."

"Right," Matthiel agreed. "I just hope Xavier and Her Highness had enough time to escape."

I sighed, hefting my half of Alexander. "I hope so, too."

"—Howless Lilliana!" a man's voice shouted as he shoved through the crowd to meet with us. It was Matthiel's sienna-eyed father, Matthew Inion. His wolf ears were grown as he panted over his knees, his scythe clutched in one hand and his gaze focused solely on me.

Matthiel frowned. "Father? How are the king and queen?"

"They're safe, thank Death," Matthew puffed. Then he shook his head. "But, Lilliana… your mother…"

My wings went stiff. I didn't like that tone. "Wh… what about my mother?"

He shut his eyes, his wolf ears folding to his neck. Then he hung his head.

32

WILLOW

"X-Xavier…" I sputtered, my numb jaw prickling as I finally regained some motion in my muscles. I could barely feel my arms, but willed them to crawl over the slippery rock toward the assassin by the cliff.

Toward the monster who'd sent Xavier to his death.

"You…" I seethed and dragged myself forward, tears washed away from the relentless rain. "You…! Damned…! *DEMON*…!"

I'd barely moved a few feet over the rock, but my voice caught the assassin's attention. One of his cat ears flicked to me.

"Ah, Your Highness Death." He stepped toward me. "I'd nearly forgotten you. Now, what say you to summoning your dearest grandfather, hm? My compatriots and I would be most appreciative…"

"—Your Highness…!" a woman's voice called suddenly from the skies. "Can you hear me…?!"

A winged figure cloaked in white flew above us. Her glowing scythe streaked through the darkness like a beacon cutting through the storm.

I didn't recognize her. But a roar of shouts and commands buzzed above us on the main plateau we'd fallen from. They sounded like other Reapers—all shouting my name. The Reapers from the Surfacing Port must have heard about the assassin from the Death Palace and put two-and-two together when Xavier and I fled from there. Now it sounded like several squads were up there searching for me.

The first winged woman who'd called me flew right above the assassin. She gasped when I limply pushed to my hands and knees in a heavy pant.

"Your Highness!" She shouted, giving a sharp whistle to alert the other Reapers. "She's over here! And the assassin is with her!"

Angered cries sounded from the plateau above us.

The assassin gritted his teeth, his cat ears curling back. He seemed loathe to leave, but being surrounded, he must have realized his situation was too bleak to stay. With a final sneer, he ducked into the rocky shadows of the canyons and disappeared.

"Your Highness…!" the winged woman touched down beside me and put away her scythe. She scooped me in her arms and flapped me back over the plateau. She was taking me back to the Surfacing Port. "Bloods, we need to return you to Grim immediately…!"

"N… no…" My voice was still strained, the assassin's infection magic still numbing my muscles a great deal. "You have to… to find Xavier…" I weakly flailed an arm toward the cliff. "Please…"

The woman glanced in that direction with a knitted brow. "The boy that was with you?"

"He… h-he was thrown off…" Tears spilled, pain twisting to remember the stale look in his mismatched eyes. "Please… Please find him…"

She held me tighter and hushed. "I'll have every Reaper search down there, Highness… I promise. We'll find him. Now rest. Let us worry over him."

I watched as the cliff drifted farther out of view.

Farther away from Xavier.

ALEXANDER

Where… am I…?

Xavier's voice echoed in my thoughts like a cloud of mist, stirring me awake. My eyes peeled open. I squinted under the harsh light.

It's so… dark…

"Are you blind, Xavier…?" I groaned and sat up, rubbing my sore eyes. "It's bright as Death in…"

Wait. Where was I?

It looked like the palace infirmary. I sat on a patient bed with fluid-tubes and wires strapped all over me. The hum of the machines filled the silence while the heart monitor bleeped along with my pulse.

I looked around for Xavier, but didn't find him. Apparently, I was alone in this room. That was odd, considering how clear his voice had been a moment ago. I'd assumed he was right next to me. Had I imagined it?

The door squeaked open. Lilli walked in carrying a tray of food—but she stopped when she saw me.

"Alex!" She dropped the tray in a noisy clatter and rushed to my bedside, tears spilling down her face. "You're awake…! Bloods, we were so worried…!"

"—he's finally awake?" Matthiel piped behind her as his head popped into view beneath the doorframe. "It's about Bloody time!"

When Matthiel filed in to stand on the other side of my patient bed, I gave them both puzzled looks. "How long was I asleep?" I asked.

Lilli answered that. "It's been three days, Alex. We still don't know what happened. You suddenly collapsed."

"But you didn't have a single scratch on you," Matthiel added with a disbelieving shake of his head. "What happened?"

"I…" My head throbbed as I tried to remember, and I clutched my temple tenderly. "I thought… I thought I *felt* something. Something with Xavier…" I looked around the infirmary room. "Where *is* Xavier?"

They both fell quiet.

"Well…" Matthiel pursed his lips. "There's… something you should know."

Nausea simmered. "Where is he?"

Silence.

"Where is he…?" I asked again, my breath ripping sorely.

Neither one deigned to answer. Again.

Panic festered, and I snarled, "Where is my brother?"

Lilli's wings bowed low. Then she whispered so softly, I could barely hear her. "He's… gone, Alex."

My wolf ears grew. "What do you mean?"

"Xavier didn't make it," Matthiel said, wiping his welling eyes. "Her Highness was brought back safely, but Xavier…"

"Willow told me what happened," Lilli added sheepishly. "She'd been found on the surface by other Reapers, but Xavier was… I… I'm so sorry, Alex. Xavier's—"

"No, he isn't." I tore out the tubes and wires stuck to me and slid out of bed—nearly toppling before Lilli caught me.

"You need to rest, Alex!" Lilli insisted as she kept me upright. "There's time for—"

"We should be looking for him!" I snapped, wobbling out to the halls and using the wall for support. "We should be up there searching! We should be—!"

"Accepting when our loved ones are gone!" Lilli barked, startling me. I twisted back and winced. Her narrow face was dripping with tears. "You aren't the only one who's lost someone from that monster, Alex…! My *mother* was…!" Her lips twitched and trembled, and she shoved past me and disappeared in a strained sob.

That's right… I flopped against the wall hollowly. Mother Maria's dissolved corpse flashed back to memory. Her blood had soaked my arms. It had pooled on the floor around me. Her face had been burning away, her flesh melting off her bones and…

My stomach heaved with sour bile, and I dropped on all fours— vomited there in the hallway.

Matthiel rushed out and helped me back to my bed, chiding me for leaving at all, but I was barely listening. I just wanted to sink into the thin, uncomfortable mattress and vanish entirely.

Vanish like my brother.

Tears hit, my lungs strangling as I curled to my side and squeezed out a pained, agonizing sob.

33

LILLI

I waited patiently in the royal cemetery beside my mother's grave, waiting for Xavier's memorial service to end.

My messenger crow, Dusk, was perched on her gravestone alongside my mother's messenger. Twilight had never been the same since Mother's death. The crow's head seemed to weigh as heavy as the tolling bell ringing from the Harmonist Temple in the distance.

It had been a month since my mother's funeral pyre, and a month since Xavier disappeared. They searched the surface canyons endlessly all month, but after what Willow saw… the Death King decided to face the gruesome facts. Xavier's soul was destroyed. Today, he was officially declared deceased.

I glanced up at the palace's spired rooftops. Willow's terrace was in sight, her curtains drawn. She'd hardly left her chambers since she was brought back to Grim. I'd been delivering her meals on occasion, but each time, she hardly spoke to me. She hardly spoke to anyone these days. She was more like a doll, less lively than the ghosts who tried to come in to cheer her. She haunted her own chambers with greater skill than the specters ever could.

I sighed and lowered my gaze to those attending Xavier's memorial. The Devouhs were speaking with my father and Their Majesties. Their tones were so soft, I could only hear them through my grown bat ears.

I found Alexander looming in front of Xavier's memorial. He was staring at his reflection in the polished blackstone like a soulless ghoul.

I pursed my lips, striding up to him.

"I'm sorry," I whispered, staring at the stone as I came to stand beside Alexander. "If there's anything I can do…"

Alexander declined a response.

The silence grew sweltering. I hurried to change the subject. "I… I hear you and your parents are sailing back to the other continent today…?"

Again, no reply. I was only met with the cutting wind rolling by, dragging our hair off to the side.

Hesitant, I reached for his hand. Snagged his fingers. "I'll be here… when you come back. You'll always have family here."

When I was met with silence for the third time, I sighed, releasing his hand—

He squeezed my fingers, not letting me go. His eyes never lifted from the memorial stone, but he kept hold of my hand for a long, quiet moment. Then released me, and returned to his empty stare at the memorial.

My lips tugged with a pained smile. Then I strode out of the cemetery, leaving him with his family.

WILLOW

SIX YEARS AFTER

The temple's choir sang solemnly in this holy house of the Seamstress, cool light spilling inside from the beautiful stain-glass windows.

My gaze swept over the pews of tearful attendees. They were all dressed in mourning white garb, like myself. I also spotted several ghosts sitting among the crowd. Those were the deceased knights and fellow teachers who had known the deceased man in front of me, come to pay their respects.

Beneath me lay the open casket of the late Sir Gale. The antlered senior had passed two days prior, the elderly man's life having expired quietly in the night.

Seeing my old instructor's peaceful face brought a rolling sorrow through me.

I gripped the pure, Crystal scythe with gloved hands. This wasn't a scythe made for demon slaying. It was specialized for Reaping Ceremonies such as this, and couldn't be touched by bare skin where fresh blood pumped. The weapon radiated with a bright, bluish light from staff to blade, its haunting gleam spilling through my dressed fingers.

My crowned father stood beside me on the elevated stage of the temple. Everyone waited for me to begin the ceremony.

"Willow?" My father whispered. He flicked me a concerned, colorless gaze as the choir continued their prayer. "Will you be all right?"

I nodded, drawing in a breath as I stood taller and addressed the awaiting attendees.

"Friends," I announced softly, "Family… those of the temple. We are gathered here to celebrate the life of Sir William Valvadier Gale. Beloved knight, lord, and teacher to all who knew him, including myself. Sir Gale was a gallant Reaper during his time of service. As a teacher, he always encouraged his students to grow at their own pace, no matter what challenges they faced. I speak from experience when I say his philosophy was met with much success… and he has earned the love and admiration of those whose lives he has blessed. I am deeply honored to guide him to his Afterlife, and begin his next adventure. In the words of the Seamstress of Souls, 'With Death Comes Rebirth'… *Mu necros neschali yettek.*"

The temple echoed with the mimicking voices of the attendees, *"Mu necros neschali yettek."*

I raised the Crystal scythe over my head, held in a breath, then gently brought the crooked blade over his heart. The Crystal blade tore his suit, but fizzled like mist into his chest, his skin unmarred. A soft *snap* sounded, my scythe thrumming as it severed the antlered man's NecroSeam that tethered his soul to his vessel.

I rested the scythe over my shoulder while watching Sir Gale's pale soul rise from his body. The new ghost floated upright to his feet, now standing before my father and me with a dazed expression. He was likely trying to gain his bearings.

The attendees who didn't have soul-sight donned white masks, which were enchanted to allow them to view the departed's soul just as easily as I could.

"*Chanerr*, Sir Gale," I said to my dear instructor, curtsying respectfully. "With great honor, I welcome you to your Afterlife."

Sir Gale's wispy gaze seemed to solidify on my face, understanding. He gave me a pale smile, chuckling as he bowed. "The honor is mine, Your Highness."

A jab of sorrow hit me all at once, and my eyes stung. I rushed to him and squeezed his misty soul with a heartfelt embrace. Sir Gale was startled by the sudden action, but soon gave a sigh and returned the hug, his arms rippling like cool water over my back.

The ghosts in the pews suddenly erupted into jovial cheers, floating up to the stage and grabbing Sir Gale's soul to pull him onto the main floor before the pews.

I wiped away one last tear as I announced, "This concludes the Reaping Ceremony. Thank you all for coming—now is a time to celebrate with the departed. Please, enjoy the festivities."

The awaiting orchestra in the corner started up a more cheerful melody, the ghosts goading Sir Gale to dance with them. I even saw my bat-winged Aide, Lilli, ask for a dance with our old teacher.

I blew out a breath, hanging up the Crystal scythe on its mount behind me. Now that the spotlight was no longer on me, I stepped off the stage alongside my father. We found a refreshment table off to the side and each took a glass of champagne.

Father lifted his glass to me in offering. "Well done, Willow. It was a lovely ceremony."

I smiled, clinking my glass against his. "Thank you, Father. I'm glad I was old enough now to be his guide." I sighed and sipped my champagne, the bubbles fizzing against my tongue playfully.

Father hadn't sipped from his yet, his white eyes growing pensive as he watched Sir Gale's dancing ghost in the crowd. Father murmured absently. "Yes… you're nearly nineteen, now, aren't you?"

I hummed in agreement. "One month left, for that."

"And another year before you're of age for… other things…" He brooded, seeming lost in thought.

I frowned. "Father?"

He didn't seem to hear me. His eyes flicked behind me. Then something caught his eye and he jolted, gulping his champagne in one swig before clacking the empty glass on the table and coughing into a fist. "Ah—ah, Howllord…! There you are."

Puzzled, I twisted behind me.

Matthiel Inion was there.

Now a young lord of twenty, Matthiel was far taller than I. His black hair was silky and combed back in a formal fashion, his sienna eyes as striking as ever. Perched on his shoulder was his messenger raven, Paschal, who had come to him some years back.

My little Jewel fluttered from a lamp and alighted on my own shoulder, twittering in greeting to Paschal, who croaked in reply.

"That was beautiful, your grace," Matthiel praised, taking my hand. He kissed my fingers tenderly, keeping hold of them as he flashed me a dazzling smile. "I'm glad Sir Gale was given such a lovely ceremony. He deserves it, after all he's done for us."

"Yes… He certainly does." I gently slipped my fingers out of his hold, my nerves getting the best of me.

Matthiel and I had been courting in past years, yet it was still hard to… accept. My father had encouraged me to move on after what happened. He thought I could find solace with the Howllord, someday. Perhaps he was right. But it seemed that wouldn't be today.

Matthiel's face pulled slightly at my retraction. He knew the reason. But he didn't protest, as always, and balled his now empty hand, gesturing toward the temple doors instead.

"Would you care for a walk, your grace?" Matthiel asked, his smile still shining. "Perhaps you could use a short reprieve from your duties?"

I hummed. "I suppose. A walk sounds lovely."

I followed at his side out of the temple, leaving the celebrating crowd to their festivities. Oddly, I spotted Father craning his head toward us as we left, looking anxious.

I cast Father a suspicious gaze. His head snapped away and he chugged another glass of champagne.

What's pulling at him now? I wondered, letting the tall doors creak closed behind me.

Once we were outside and strolling the gardens of the temple, Matthiel cleared his throat.

"Princess," he began. His arms folded behind his back in a stately posture. "There's something I… wished to speak with you about. If you'll allow?"

My brow knitted. "I suppose. Is it something to do with my father's behavior?"

He loosened his collar-string, slowing one step behind me and falling out of view. "Admittedly, yes… I spoke with him earlier. I was granted his approval, but…" I heard him exhale a shuddering breath behind me. "It is pending… your own approval."

Now I was even more puzzled, turning to him. "What needs my…?" I stopped.

Matthiel had knelt to the grass. He was holding open a long, velvet box. Inside the box were two glittering, silver chains with prancing foxes and wolves, white diamonds sparkling from them. At the end of both chains were bejeweled hairclips, and encased between them was a large diamond centerpiece.

They were engagement-vines.

"Your grace," Matthiel hushed. His hands shook as he kept the vines presented. "W-Willow… I know I'm not… him…" Matthiel's voice pinched. "And-and I know you'd rather it not be me…"

My tone hardened. "Matthiel—"

"I'm not asking for the same love you gave him," he blurted. "I know you can't change how the Seamstress wills you to feel… And that you'll find him again in the next life, far happier with him than you ever could with me." He lowered the vines over his lap. "But please. Don't chase after the next life at the expense of *this* life. If you must wait, could it not be with company…?" His black wolf ears were now fully grown and folded down. "Company whose love is already yours…?"

I stared at the vines as if they were serpents. My legs numbed. Then, silently, I sank to the grass with him.

"I…" My tone had lost all emotion. The one speaking for me was the Heiress of Grim—whose duty was to her people. So long as she kept her responsibilities, she no longer cared who stood at her side during them.

I took the vines from Matthiel with gentle fingers. "I… accept."

After retiring to my chambers for the night, I stared at my reflection in my vanity mirror. My new vines sparkled beautifully from either side of my head.

In a sigh, I unclipped the vines and replaced them in their velvet box. I pulled open a drawer on the vanity to put them away.

But there was a different box in the drawer. It was another velvet case, similar to the one Matthiel had given me.

My eyes lingered on the older box. I picked it up, opening the case. It revealed another set of silver vines.

These were the ones Xavier meant to give me.

The vines had fallen out of his pocket in his rush to find me back then. After he disappeared, they were found in the palace gardens. I still kept them along with the smaller, square box with the ring I had planned to give him that same night.

The older vines were designed with silver butterflies, speckled with tiny jewels of diamonds and azure. The vines Matthiel gave me today had more jewels than these. The newer ones shone with marvelous splendor, having been polished recently... and yet these tarnished vines seemed to gleam with more brilliance.

I could be content with Matthiel, I assured. *He'd provide me a family, produce a healthy heir for the throne...*

I closed the case, putting the old vines away.

A knock came at my door.

"Willow?" My father's muffled voice called from the other side.

I called out, "I'm here, Father. You may enter."

The door creaked open, and my father's smiling figure stood under the frame.

"Willow," Father chimed brightly. "I've just heard the news! Your mother and I are so proud...!"

"Thank you, Father," I said, my tone apathetic as I rose to meet him.

He gave me a tight hug, and I returned one, though it was half-hearted. He certainly noticed, but raised no comment as he awkwardly released me and stepped back with a cough.

"Er, *Khm-hmm*! Well..." He folded his arms behind his back. "I'm glad to see you'll have some company in our absence, at least."

I paused, my head cocking. "Absence?"

"We've been called to council with the Sky King," he explained.

That was enough to resurrect my attention. "The Sky King? In the Sky *realm*…? On the floating islands?"

He nodded grimly. "Yes. Your mother and I are expected to be in Culatia by next week. We're leaving tonight."

"But… why?" I questioned. "Most council meetings with the other Relicbloods are done through communicators, aren't they?"

"They are," Father agreed, sounding annoyed. "But it seems Rojired has a need for us *physically*. He refuses to tell us more until we arrive." He pulled at his knuckles anxiously. "I know it's last minute, but… do you think you'll be all right on your own? I've asked Daniel to take care of any royal duties in my place, so you could rest after this morning's ceremony."

I nodded, my hum absent. "Yes… thank you. I think a rest is needed."

He smiled and put a hand on my shoulder, chuckling. "Indeed. We're proud of you, Willow. You've made a mature decision today, with Matthiel. Though, perhaps…" His eyes saddened, and he flicked the silver bell that tied my hair together. The sound of it startled me. I forgot I was still wearing it.

Father untied the ribbon, letting my long hair tumble to the floor. He held the ribbon and bell out for me to take. "Perhaps it's time to forget and move on now…?"

I stared at the bell, nausea rising. I steadied my fingers as I took the jingling ornament. "Yes… Perhaps it is. Enjoy your trip, Father…"

He nodded and left, closing my doors with a soft click.

I sat back down in silence. Then laid the bell and ribbon on my vanity beside my new engagement-vines. I gave a heavy, exhausted sigh.

"—Willow."

I yelped in fright.

A boy stood before me now, no older than me by the look of him. His curling azure hair framed his round face, ice-blue eyes curious as he stared at a tapestry hanging on the wall. He wore an orange robe, the hood folded over his shoulders. Atop his head was a white-gold crown with a fox etched at the center and small, round bells jingling from the rim. A crowned Dream mark peeked through his curling bangs at the center of his forehead.

"Grandfather?" I rose, startled. "What are you… hang on, why are you in Grim? I thought you'd be in the Ocean realm for their annual festival?"

"Normally, yes," the young man hummed, still studying the tapestry as if trying to understand its confusing concept. I wasn't sure what he found so interesting. It was just patterned with an uninspiring motif of crows, wolves and skulls. "But there were a few… concerns I had to see to."

"Concerns?" I asked. "Such as…?"

He looked at me for the first time since he'd suddenly appeared, his expression unreadable. "Such as the Death Princess running away to the surface."

For a moment, I wasn't sure I'd heard him right. I opened my mouth, shut it. Started again. "I'm not running away to the surface."

"I know," Grandfather said. "That's precisely what I intend to fix."

I massaged my temple. "I don't understand…"

He turned to a painting on the wall and observed it like a curious child, scratching at the silver frame. "I Saw in the Orbs that you've recently been engaged? To the Inion boy?"

"I… have." I raised an eyebrow. "Why?"

"Just making sure I wasn't confusing your present with your future. Well—" His head cocked at the painting. "What little future you have left."

I stared at him, silence filling the air between us. "Ex… Excuse me?"

"Oh, sorry. Am I'm not being clear?" He turned away from the painting to face me again, his azure gaze a blank slate. "You're going to die soon. The Orbs have shown me your future—what little time is left. You have but two options before you: either stay here and be killed before you can so much as plan your wedding—"

"Who's going to kill me?" I blurted.

"Your cousin, obviously," he shrugged. "He plans to challenge you for the throne, by invoking Death's Duel. The conspiring little bug that he is, is it so surprising?"

"Felix...?" I held a terrified hand to my neck. "But I... When? How long do I..."

Grandfather held up a pausing hand. "You haven't heard the second option yet."

"Do I even have one? I-I had a feeling the Duel was coming, and I..." I swallowed, calming in a deep breath and stood taller, despite my quivering bones. "I will carry out what is demanded of me... I've trained for this. Cowering now would be—"

"An excellent idea."

I glared at him, correcting, "A *stupid* idea. I'll not die only to be remembered as a sniveling child."

"Well, if you insist on fighting, then by all means... I just thought you should know it could be delayed. You'd have more time to train. And anyway, your first betrothed may need rescuing soon, if the Orbs tell true."

My thoughts fumbled to a halt. "My... first betrothed...?"

"Not the Inion boy," he clarified.

"Are you saying... Xavier is...?"

"Alive?" He rolled back a shoulder in a casual shrug. "Yes."

For the slightest second, somewhere in my shriveled pit of a soul, an old flame I'd snuffed out suddenly sparked alive. I'd nearly forgotten the taste of its reviving heat. The burn was so foreign now, I thought my flesh would melt onto the carpet.

My voice was a trembling hush. "How could you possibly know...?"

"Well, truthfully," he began, rubbing his neck. "Perhaps I've waited too long to show you this, but you've left me little choice now, haven't you?"

He reached into his robe's sleeves, pulling out a small, spherical compartment with a mirrored surface. He pinched the lid with a finger and slid it open. Inside was a ball of light, which began to float upward like a dazzling bubble. Entranced, I reached for the light. Once my fingers came in contact, the light zipped forward and shot to my forehead.

Then I saw it.

It was a memory. The point of view showed the palace orchards, years ago during autumn. A younger version of myself sat behind the memory's owner. The younger me leaned against his back, eating apples. When the short scene finished, I was forced back to the present, in my own point of view.

"This…" I watched the ball of light float back into the sphere Grandfather held. "This can't… But how…"

Dream snapped the sphere shut, looking at me with that blank stare of his. "Don't be willfully blind, child, you know exactly what you saw. And you equally know what it means. Xavier's soul was *not* destroyed, otherwise this memory wouldn't exist. He survived somehow. And it seems he's lost his memories."

I grew sick, tears brimming as that meager flame inside me grew into a roaring inferno. "He's alive…?"

Grandfather placed the mirrored sphere in my hand, curling my fingers around it.

"Yes," Grandfather affirmed, a small grin cracking his face. "Xavier is alive. But I don't know exactly where. I've only narrowed it down to the nation he *will* be in. But now you have two reasons to leave this place. The first is to find Xavier, a task I've had little luck with myself. Perhaps you'll be more fortunate than I." He raised two fingers. "The second is to get away from that monster of a cousin you have. But finding Xavier is most imperative. The Orbs tell me death awaits him in Everland, and I don't mean you, dear. Help him. Give him this memory, and reunite him with Alexander. It will be safest with those twins. Stay with them, and do not return until they're both ready to meet their fate."

He was talking so fast, I wasn't sure what to ask first. My mind only landed on the last statement. "Wh… what fate?"

His grip tightened over my fingers. "Promise me you won't return until they're ready. It's not safe here. If your cousin doesn't kill you, then another will later. Everything is about to change, Willow, and no one is prepared for it without those twins. Find Xavier, and reunite him with his brother. With one missing, there will be nothing left for us."

He disappeared in a blinding light, vanishing into thin air in a quiet rush of wind.

I was left alone in my room, still holding the mirrored sphere.

Find Xavier.

The mission pounded my thoughts like a chisel on stone.

Find Xavier…!

This was now the only demand strangling my swirling mind. With a quick inhale, I came to my senses and hurried to gather my things, heart racing furiously as I left, Jewel fluttering after me.

I will bring you home…!

The adventure continues in the
Necroseam Chronicles series

Read on for a sneak peak of book one:

WILLOW OF ASHES

NECROSEAM CHRONICLES | BOOK ONE

1

ALEXANDER

My placid reflection stared back at me from the polished, black-stone memorial they'd erected for my brother.

Xavier Madison Devouh, it read on the reflective surface, *Devoted son and brother. May the Seamstress guide his soul to a richer life full of peace and prosperity.*

I absently dragged my fingers over the carved letters.

My reflection showed an adolescent, pale face, my shadowy grey bangs tossed about my brow carelessly by the cavern winds. A satin doublet was fastened up to my neck with elegant, silver buttons, gold trim embroidered with intricate patterns along the hem and neckline. A burgundy cloak was clasped at my chest, the cowl collapsed over my shoulders.

My heterochromic eyes were reversed in the reflection. The one, sapphire eye was on the left of my face; the colorless, white eye on the right.

It isn't my face, is it? With the placement of the mismatched eyes, it was *he* who stood there. As though he hadn't vanished; as though the world hadn't shifted and died along with him.

"*… can't…*" his voice whispered in my thoughts, a high-pitched ring whining in my eardrums. "*Please…*"

I knuckled my throbbing skull, banishing the phantom voice. It had begun after he'd disappeared from that cliff on the surface. The voice began as a slight annoyance here and there, yet now it chewed at my thoughts incessantly.

I sucked in a long, shivering breath, then blew it out in a stream of cold fog. My wolf ears grew, draping solemnly to the sides of my neck as a sickness squeezed my chest.

"Alexander?" A soft voice hushed behind me.

I turned, one of my wolf ears swiveling when a woman stepped beside me.

She was a towering figure, wrapped in a fur cloak that hid her alabaster gown and thick coat. Delicate chains were clipped to her hair on both sides, glistening like silken strings that hung from her forehead in a 'V' shape, a diamond droplet glinting at the center. Her grey hair was braided and draped over one shoulder, precious gemstones frosting the strands.

She had wolf ears as well, though hers were naturally showing, unlike mine. My ears only grew in times of stress or sorrow, as most mammals were wont to do. In addition, she had a wavering tail curling round her skirts, which I didn't have with or without stress.

A tiny black bird, which I knew was named Ethil, gripped the woman's gloved finger, and she laid her other hand on my shoulder. "The memorial service ended hours ago," she murmured, her cloudy, blue eyes bloodshot. "Come… it's time we took our leave."

I turned back to my reflection in the blackstone memorial, stealing a final glance at my face.

A final glance at my brother.

"He is gone, Alex." My mother's boney fingers tightened on my shoulder. "Please."

"He wouldn't break his promise." I croaked. The face on the stone leaked with tears. "We promised to die together. Just as we'd come into this life, we were to *leave* it together. He wouldn't break it."

"*Break…*" his voice hushed in my thoughts. "*Promise… we… promised…*"

Mother's grip faltered, removing her hand. "Come… The ship departs soon. Your father is waiting."

Her footfalls clicked down the marble steps, crossing the yard toward the cemetery's exit. Wispy specters and ghosts floated between the tombstones, whispering prayers and murmuring the absurdity of how many new stones had been erected.

Many were lost in the fire last month. Many more were lost to the assassin. Even their ghosts had been destroyed from within their vessels—all the work of one, lone man.

I followed alongside Mother in silence, my soul stretching thinner as we walked away from my brother's blackstone slab.

When we rounded the palace's east wing, I looked to the terrace on the third floor. The latticed doors were shut, thick curtains drawn to hide the Death Princess's chambers within.

Willow had yet to leave her room since the incident. I'd heard she'd been found and rescued from the surface canyons, the assassin chased off. She'd returned to the caverns safely, yet the moment she'd come back, she shut herself in her chambers. She hadn't even come out for combat training all month. She *never* missed training, not in the last four years. Now, only a few servants saw her at all when they brought the heiress her meals.

She didn't come to the memorial today. I couldn't say I blamed her.

Mother and I crossed to the palace courtyard and climbed into the awaiting hover-coach, the silver buggy floating over the grey-stoned pathway as its exposed gears clattered, and the stabilizing hydraulics hissed with steam. The two horses harnessed to the front were whipped into motion, the coach lurching forward and gliding smoothly out of the palace grounds.

The cityscape ahead was lined with sharp spires and gothic buildings, wedged between rocky pillars that stretched from the cavern floor all the way to the ceiling, which was hidden in misty formations that trailed with gleaming, floating lights. The lights wafted in and out of the overcast, the ethereal orbs drifting calmly as they illuminated the caverns with a pale, grey filter.

We arrived at the harbor, merchants and sailors bustling along the vibrating boardwalks. I climbed out of the coach behind Mother, stepping aside as a scaled man with webbed ears stalked past me carrying two heavy crates of fish, then followed Mother to the pier.

Grim's seas were a vast series of wide rivers within the caverns, the lapping water split into branching straits by pillars and rock formations littered along the wide horizon. A thick fog clung to the hidden water's surface, the smoky, grey cloak twisting and licking like a living creature all its own.

I followed Mother along the pier and climbed up the ramp to board our awaiting ship.

The vessel bobbed in the rippling water, the cutting winds beating at the half-mast sails as the hired crew members pulled them down. A raven was perched on the crow's nest, its gaze sharp and inspecting as it cocked its head at me. It was my father's raven, Barrach, watching us to be sure we were all accounted for, and to alert us should any danger arise.

The crew cast us off, and we departed, Low Rastiria's harbor drifting farther and farther away.

"It will take nearly a month to arrive at the other Undercontinent," Mother said. "I suggest we all take this time to... to heal."

I grumbled. "Why are we returning to Low Everland so soon? I thought this was to be our permanent home."

She knelt to me. "It's only temporary, Alex. Your grandfather took over the role of the Death King's Eyes for these four years, and he's at his wits end. Your father is only returning to the post to interview new candidates. Once we're finished, and the role is filled, we'll return here."

"And return to the search?" My voice was tight with anger.

Mother paused. "They *are* still searching on the surface, Alex. They will keep searching, so we can give him a proper burial with a true funeral and—"

"He isn't dead!" I shouted. "He's still up there! He's alive! I... I hear him. It's growing clearer by the day, Mother, I can *hear* him...!" My vision blurred, eyes stinging.

Her own eyes misted and she pulled me in for an embrace, her fur cloak soft against my wet cheeks. "Oh, Alex..." She drew me at arm's length and cupped my face. "I do wish you were right."

She rose and strode into the cabin, delicately dabbing her eyes.

He's alive, damn it. I furiously rubbed my face dry. If they kept looking, they would find him and see.

"*…so much water…*" His voice hissed in my thoughts again, ringing in a shrill whine. "*I… can't breathe…*"

I hit my knuckles against the post, causing the raven at the crow's nest to croak at me angrily.

"Where are you?!" I hollered at the cavern's misted ceiling. The Floating Lights gently twirled and swam within the formations. "Why can I hear you…?"

I sank to my knees and curled against the post, shivering.

The nearby crew members had turned at my outburst, whispering that I'd gone mad.

Perhaps I am mad, I considered, hitting my head against the post like a miserable, hollow shell. *Was it him? Or was it merely my memory of him…?*

Heavy footfalls clunked toward me, and I craned my gaze up.

My father's vassal, Nathaniel, loomed over me, his burly arms set at his sides, his bear-ears perked in my direction from under his raggedy, black hair.

"Ye all right, lad?" Nathaniel asked, cocking a thick eyebrow. He wore a narrow hat with a long plume wavering at one side, and his coat was a stiff, indigo captain's uniform. Nathaniel scratched his scruffy beard and muttered. "Yer scarin' me crew, shoutin' at clouds like that…"

I hung my head. "I'm sorry, Nathaniel… I'll—"

A ghost suddenly phased through the post over my head, the pale specter's feathered hair curling at his cheeks. "Oh, leave the young sir alone, Nathaniel!" the ghost, who was my mother's vassal, Aiden, chided the bear-shifter. "He's lost his twin, is this not punishment enough?"

Nathaniel's ears curled. "Aw, I Bloody know what the lad's goin' through! I was only sayin' nothing's gonna come out 'o—"

"Why don't we see what comes out of *you* when I shove an arrow through your throat and…!"

They kept to their blathering, and I sighed and crawled under them, walking to the ship's ledge.

I folded my arms over the rail, hearing the water lapping under the churning mists, the fog hiding the waves.

"Xavier?" I whispered, staring at the swirling, grey veil. "If I can hear you, can you hear me? Can you tell me where you are?"

"*It's... dark,*" his voice hushed in my thoughts. "*So dark...*"

"How can we find you? What can you see?"

"*Nothing.*" The voice dimmed. "*There is... nothing...*"

"We'll find you," I said, my teeth sharpening, claws growing long and scraping the wooden rail. "I don't care what they say, *I* will find you and bring you home."

"*Home...*" The voice was so soft I almost couldn't hear it. "*Home...*"

My hands balled, and I struck the rail... Then a shadow caught my eye from the mists below.

Within the light grey veil, dark splotches formed. A splintered mast of a ship peeked through the fog, its sails shredded and torn, beating in the cavern winds.

I twisted back to the arguing captain and ghost. "Nathaniel!" I called, getting the captain's attention. "Nathaniel, there's a wreckage here!"

Nathaniel and Aiden stopped their bickering, then came to meet me at the rail. Nathaniel produced a copper spyglass from his coat pocket and held it to his eye.

"The lad be right," he rumbled, sounding troubled. "Aye, I reckon that be the vessel what went missin' these last few days..."

He collapsed the spyglass with a *clack, clack, clack* and shoved it to my chest. "Lad, keep an eye on the mists down there. I'll tell the boys to fetch the dinghies."

I swallowed. "W-wait. How many days has the ship been missing?"

Nathaniel adjusted his plumed hat in a growl. "Three."

The warmth flushed from my cheeks. "Then... then wouldn't they be Changed—?"

"We'll take a look 'n see, lad," he said, tromping off to shout at his men.

I unfolded the spyglass, the lens quivering in my fingers. All I could see was fog. Fog and tall stalagmites, the rocky pillars sprouting from the water and stretching to the ceiling...

I focused on the wreckage's broken mast, seeing its tattered sails in greater detail through the lens. There were no bloodstains on that piece of the vessel. Perhaps the crew survived—

Skririririririri!

I ducked at the hideous shriek that split the fog, its high-pitched echo bouncing off the cavern's pillars, then dying into silence.

The raven at the crow's nest began to croak and caw ceaselessly, sounding the alarm.

The crew scrambled over the deck, Nathaniel shouting orders to take up arms.

Death! I sank to my knees and lifted the spyglass again, sweeping the lens over the fog. Shadows shifted behind the veil. They were creeping toward us, their hisses and bleats trumpeting louder as they neared.

I kept the lens focused on them, licking my lips and calling back, "Nathaniel, they're over here—!"

Skririririiii!

A dripping, skeletal creature leapt from the water and hooked its claws into my shoulder, *yanking* me overboard and dragging me into the water with a cold *splash!*

My pained curses bubbled in the dark waters, my shoulder burning as the creature still had me hooked, and it dragged me farther into the water's depths toward the shrouded floor—

My head hit a stalagmite. The creature's claws ripped out, and the cold water vanished from my skin as blackness swallowed me.

XAVIER

A freezing chill crashed over my skin.

I gasped, but sucked in water. I was drowning, my shoulder burning from puncture wounds.

Panicked, I found the brightness of the surface above, and swam upward. The water peeled away from my face and I wheezed in a reviving breath, coughing and spitting up the water.

Where am I?

I shivered in the freezing water, my burgundy cloak heavy around my shoulders. I unfastened it in case it threatened to drag me back into the water.

There was nothing but grey here. Churning mist draped the water everywhere I turned. I couldn't even see above it.

My wolf ears were already grown, fright shaking my soul as I trembled in the water. "H… hello?!" I cried, coughing. "Is anyone there?!"

My wolf ears picked up shouting within the mist. The voices were nearby.

"Help!" I called, swimming toward the voices, my shoulder hot with pain. "P-please…! I need help!"

A splash came behind me.

I whirled, but saw nothing. "H… hello—*Aaah*!"

Claws dug into my back, hooking me, and I screamed as I was dragged backward—

An arrow shot at the beast, the crystal tip plunging into its skull with an ear-splitting *crack*! The blow was so powerful, a spiral of wind rushed after it and cleared the mist in a wide circle around me.

The creature screamed in pain and released me, squirming into the water out of sight. Now that the mists had cleared, I saw a winged man flying above, a second arrow nocked along his bowstring.

"Young sir!" the bird-shifter called. He put away his bow and arrow and soared down to me, grasping my outstretched hand to pull me out of the water. "the Archer be praised, you're alive! Don't worry, your mother has exterminated the rest of them, all that's left was the one who'd dragged you under."

I blinked at the winged man, baffled. "My… mother?"

He flew us onto a ship's deck, and I fell over my knees and hacked the water from my lungs, quivering at the pain in my shoulder and back.

A wide circle had formed around me, and I heard a woman barking orders.

"Make way!" she commanded. "Make way, that is my son…! Alexander! Alexander, are you hurt?!"

The woman came hustling toward me, clad in a fur cloak and her braided hair tussled and frazzled around the twinkling gemstones pinned in the strands. She crouched and held a tender, gloved hand to my shoulder wound. "Bloods be good, you'll need medical attention… I'm glad I resurrected Aiden in time to find you." She turned to the winged man who'd flown me here. "Aiden, tell the ship nurse to treat Alexander immediately—"

"No," I said, panting over the floorboards. "I… I'm not Alex…"

But why do I know that name? The thought stabbed my brain, and I clutched my throbbing head. *I knew someone with that name… yes, I knew them well… but how?*

I shook my head. I had other priorities to see to. "Was another found?" I asked the woman. Death, but she looked familiar. I coughed. "Other than me? A girl, with white hair. She… she was with me— had you found her as well? Please, there is a man after us, I don't… I don't know what's happened to…"

My temples swelled, and I grunted, head shaking desperately.

The woman's breath died on her tongue. She squeezed my good shoulder and lifted my chin to face her, staring at my eyes. "Seamstress Cleanse me," she whispered, tears welling. "Xavier…?"

"Yes…" I said slowly, the name familiar. "Yes, that's right. That's my name… but I must find my friend." Her name returned in a blink. "I must find Willow."

"Oh, Nira be blessed…!" She took my hand eagerly and dragged me toward the cabin. "Lucas! Lucas, come look, we've found…!"

"Where am I…?" A voice trilled in my thoughts, a whining ring hitting my eardrums.

I screeched to a stop. The woman's grip pulled from my fingers.

"Who… who'd said that?" I asked, a chill prickling the hairs on my neck.

"Xavier?" the voice called, shaking. *"Xavier, can you hear me?"*

I knew that voice… it was… "Alex?" I whispered, remembering the name of my brother.

"*Yes!*" He laughed, though stil sounded shaken. "*Where are you? It's so dark here… There's n-nothing. But I can see the ship. I can see Mother. Where are you?*"

"I… don't know," I admitted, gazing at the woman who now stared at me in shock. "Mother…" I said. "Yes, that's right. That's who you are—"

Her face suddenly shrank away, the world sucked into a funnel as I was thrown backward.

The world I'd seen had been condensed into a single, circular window, which hung suspended in an empty, black void I now floated in. All traces of pain had vanished, along with the chilled water soaking my garments and hair.

I stared at my hands, at my feet. I radiated with a soft light.

In the window, the woman leapt back. "Death's Head!" she shouted, her voice crystal clear and echoing all around this void. "Alexander…?"

The window streaked left and right, blinking. "What in Death…?" Alex's voice hissed. Hands appeared in the window, palms turning in examination. "What was that place? Xavier…? Can you hear me?"

I reached a hand at the window. It was like touching water, the images rippling under my fingers. I pushed on it, pulling myself through—

The void was sucked away behind me, and I collapsed into the outside world, cold and bleeding as the pain burned at my shoulder and back.

Screams echoed from my head.

"Alex?" I panted, searching the deck for him, but couldn't find him. My breaths grew ragged, the screams worsening. "Alex! Stop it, stop screaming…!"

I clutched my wolf ears, but it did nothing to blot out his frightened cries. I pushed on my skull desperately, staring at Mother. "Wh… what's happening…?"

Mother's grey face had drained white, whispering, "Great Mother below."

Author's Note

Dear Readers,

Thank you so much for reading *Princess of Grim*! If you liked it, I would be extremely grateful if you tell others what you think by writing an honest review. It doesn't have to be long… a few words, or even just a rating would be much appreciated. Reviews are vital to an author's career and helps us not only sell books, but provides valuable feedback. Check out my review page at www.necroseam.com/reviews.

If you would you like to find out more about the NecroSeam Chronicles universe, including world notes, deleted scenes, character artwork, and even recorded songs from the books, check out my website at www.necroseam.com!

And while you are there, feel free to sign up for my newsletter to receive announcements on new releases, upcoming conventions I'll be attending, and special promotions!

You can also follow me on my social media accounts below:

Twitter: @AizelleRaine
www.Facebook.com/officialEllieRaine

Thank you again!

Ellie Raine

About the Author

Award-winning and best-seller fantasy author, Ellie Raine, is a voracious BookWyrm when it comes to epic adventures, detailed world-building, and thrilling battles. She grew up in the suburbs of Atlanta, Georgia, where her family raised her right with a healthy upbringing surrounded by fantasy books, comics, and video games. Her award-winning Adventure Fantasy series, *the NecroSeam Chronicles*, was inspired by her favorite fable: The Grim Reaper. It was originally intended to be a video game, but she found the book adaptation to be far more fulfilling and exciting. Her first book in the series, *Willow of Ashes*, has won multiple awards in 2019, including first place in Fantasy for the Writers' Digest Self-Published Ebook Awards. Her other works include a supernatural detective noir, *Nightingale*, published with Pro Se Productions in 2018. Ellie Raine is currently working on several other fantastical projects and only emerges from the depths of her daring tales when she is summoned by her loving king and their darling daughter: the Dragon Princess Felicity.

You can find out more about Ellie Raine and her books at: https://www.EllieRaine.com, and learn more about the NecroSeam Chronicles and its vivid world by visiting https://www.NecroSeam.com!